the magic

of

missing you

DIDI COOPER

outskirts
press

Outskirts Press, Inc.
http://www.outskirtspress.com

ISBN: 978-1-9772-3282-3

Cover Image by Todd Sudora

Outskirts Press and the "OP" logo are trademarks belonging to Outskirts Press, Inc.

PRINTED IN THE UNITED STATES OF AMERICA

For my husband, Todd
My real magic

Prologue
1971

As a little boy Jack Murphy was a quiet child with tousled sandy colored hair and expressive green eyes that spoke volumes when he remained silent. His nose always in a book, reading a map, or drawing detailed pictures of nature, the ocean, or his favorite animals; Jack kept to himself. Although perpetually preoccupied, his parents didn't worry about him getting into trouble because their boy was kind and mindful of his manners, even as he grew to be a teenager. A good student, an avid boy scout, and a capable outdoorsman, Jack never told a soul he suspected he was different. Others didn't know there were times when gentle winds coming from the ocean would whisper words of encouragement in his ear. And there were occasions when squirrels, chipmunks, and birds that frolicked in his back yard told him stories that kept him content and occupied for hours on end. At first, Jack assumed everyone had such experiences. He supposed anyone could stop the rain from falling with just one wish. That almost anyone could hear the babbling conversations of the fish swimming beneath the ocean's currents. Growing up on the coast of Maine, surrounded by nature and the salty sea, it wasn't until the age of eleven that Jack realized he might be different.

His mother would scold him for telling far-fetched "stories" and remind him to tell the truth, or to stop playing make believe because he was growing too old. Jack's father seemed more accepting of his boy's active imagination and would quietly add words of encouragement to his son. "It's okay to believe in magic, Jack," he would say when Jack's mother would leave the room. But his mother's approval was important to him. And as he grew older, he realized it wasn't only his mother who didn't believe in magic. It was virtually everyone else, too. His teachers, his friends on the playground, his older sister. And as he grew from a boy into a young man, he was mocked, ridiculed, and desperately lonely.

One afternoon, a day before his fifteenth birthday, just ahead of a storm about to roll in, Jack looked up at the frantic clouds chasing one another through the graying sky, whispering warnings to the local wildlife of the impending storm. Rarely angry, Jack looked to the sky, and shouted, "Stop. Please, stop. I don't want to be different. I want to be like everyone else. I want to be normal."

Without warning, the skies immediately brightened, the sun's rays began to fight their way through a dense mist, and a woman, seemingly out of nowhere, stepped out from behind the large chestnut tree in his yard. She was an old woman, possibly as old as the looming, crooked chestnut tree she stood before. Though unfamiliar to Jack, he stood in awe of her gentle and loving voice. "Jack, are you sure? You have so many gifts. So much magic within." Her long green coat began to blow in the wind as she placed both hands on her heart, as she continued, "Jack, this town, this land, and this sea are enchanted." She extended her arms, honoring the earthly wisdom she believed so dearly in. "My name is Julia. I've known you from the day your soul was created. The magic vibrates though the earth beneath us. Do you feel it? You are special, Jack. You are gifted with abilities few have." She tried to continue, but Jack interrupted her.

Solemnly, he implored, "I didn't ask for this." Jack's eyes began to water. "Can you help me?"

"Are you sure, my friend? Because once I take this from you, it cannot be returned. It cannot be undone. And after this moment, you will remember nothing about your magic. For the rest of your life."

"Yes, please, I am sure," he begged with teenage desperation.

Suddenly, she raised both arms to the tumultuous skies, the sun's kindness and warmth grew stronger and Jack watched a stranger named Julia, speak silently to the sky. When she disappeared behind the mist, the wrathful skies cleared, the sun began to shine, and Jack Murphy's wish was granted. Forever.

One
2017

J ack Murphy never considered taking his own life, but silently wondered if the world could have done just as well without him. On a foggy morning on the southern coast of Maine, he stood at the edge of an angry ocean, just ahead of an early spring storm and wondered what his life had become. The biting cold mist carried by fierce winds blowing off the Atlantic reminded him he was in fact alive, although he wasn't sure why his life was spared. In a different world, or with the slightest tilt in the earth's axis, everything might have been different.

She was his one true love and the person he planned to spend his days and nights with. It almost happened that way. He imagined them best friends and lovers, having built a loud, rollicking family together, and strolling the empty beach hand in hand, ahead of storms, once the kids were grown. She was the one person who would have made him a better version of himself, he thought. A happier version, at the very least. Instead, he was left with the aftermath of his decisions. And she was gone.

The harsh winds were picking up and together with

waves pushing closer to shore, they howled an urgent warning for him to take cover. This storm would be epic, but Jack was ready. Not because he was terribly prepared, but because dangerous storms no longer worried him. Sure, he was used to unpredictable and strong New England storms and had seen his fair share of them, but these days fear simply had no place in his world. What exactly was there to fear? Dying alone? No. Living with regret and dire loneliness was far more terrifying than the nor'easter growing dangerously strong, just south of Kennebunkport.

At 60 years old, Jack stood about six feet tall, green eyes still twinkling beneath obvious sadness, and his weathered and quiet demeanor still classified him as ruggedly handsome, although he certainly didn't recognize it in himself. He adjusted the hood of his reliable yellow L.L. Bean rain jacket before beginning a slow retreat to the car. With the wind pushing against his back, Jack wished he could walk the two miles to the cottage. Typically, he made the walk in any weather, and as much as he liked to punish himself, it would be a treacherous hike in the current conditions.

As the familiar and normally serene Cape Porpoise Harbor came into view, thoughts drifted to his only daughter, Meghan. The waves in the typically calm and protected harbor were growing stronger as the fishing boats thrashed about. She called that morning from New York City to make sure he was ready for the storm and had what he needed in the house. "Dad this storm is going to be a rough one. Please be careful. Make sure you have what you need for a few days, just in case."

He assured her he was fine. "You worry too much. I'm

completely prepared. Seen more of these storms in my lifetime to consider myself an expert. I'm fine, sweetheart. Promise." He would weather this one alone and refused to make even one visit to a grocery store. Not even a quick trip to Bradbury's Market at the end of his road. He would not participate in the mad dash and long lines for unnecessary provisions. What he had at home would suffice.

Once home, Jack peeled off his cold, wet clothes, took a steaming hot shower and dressed in his softest, oldest thermal shirt, faded jeans, and layered a blue plaid flannel for warmth. If he needed to be indoors for the duration of the storm, he might as well be comfortable. As he buttoned his shirt, it briefly occurred to him he was buttoning the very same shirt he was wearing the day he learned the news. He closed his eyes to ease the pain of the memory racing back like a runaway train.

By evening, the storm intensified and snuffed out the power to the village of Cape Porpoise. Jack lit a single lopsided candle, had his large flashlight ready, and vowed to stay up throughout the night to be sure there would be no damage to the house. He thought of the residents in beach houses along the open ocean and was glad he was tucked more safely on the back side of the harbor. The storm was expected to cause serious damage. The winds, intense and howling at almost 50 miles per hour; blizzard conditions were underway. The late March storm that started out as rain and sleet was turning to a heavy, wet snow, and a foot or more would soon blanket the earth at the beginning of mud season in Maine. Power was already out, and once the tree branches fell due to the weight of the fallen snow, roads would likely close, and homes and small businesses in the village would lay damaged in the wake. But they would clean up and recover, like they did after each storm.

Although he assumed it impossible to sleep with the sound of the old windows rattling, projectiles hitting the roof, and the wind battering the worn shingles, Jack dozed off in his favorite chair beneath a large handmade quilt. The same multi-colored patchwork quilt his mother made when Meghan was a baby. The worn but practical quilt had weathered more than one storm in Jack's life. A few literal blizzards of course, and more than a few personal cyclones. Sadly, his mother didn't live to see his daughter's tenth birthday, but Meghan spent her childhood wrapped in the warm embrace of her grandmother's quilt, making forts in the living room, and hosting tea parties for her teddy bears atop grandma's careful stitches.

The storm finally took its turn out to sea, but not before it ravaged the New England coastline. Jack awoke to an eerie stillness and the early dawn peeking optimistically over the horizon. It was as if the innocent budding new day had no idea the town had experienced mother nature's wrath just hours before. He grumbled to himself as he tossed the quilt to the ground, a bit angry he slept through the tail end of the storm, candle still slowly burning on the kitchen counter. After blowing the flame out with a huff, he slipped on his boots and grabbed his coat that hung lazily by the front door. Twigs, limbs, and trees were down everywhere. One massive branch narrowly missed the front porch. His screen door was shattered, possibly from the wind, maybe from a flying branch, shingles were torn from the front side of the cottage, and part of the roof, just above the porch, would need to be replaced. Otherwise, he and his small home weathered the storm, relatively unscathed. Jack wondered how the rest of the town faired and planned to drive through the neighborhood later in the day. Hands on his hips, he looked out toward the harbor and could hear the sound of a chainsaw starting in the distance, just as the sun rose.

Two
1990

Not every story read like a fairy tale with a happy ending. Sometimes, even the best stories ended badly, Elizabeth concluded. Cinderella didn't always meet the prince. Heck, maybe Cinderella didn't even need a prince. Alone on the king-sized bed she once shared with her husband, Elizabeth Bennett pointed the remote toward the television and felt guilty for not feeling sad. She took an oversized bite of pepperoni pizza, eyed the take-out box sitting lopsided upon Brett's side of the bed, and grinned because she knew he would never, ever tolerate food in bed.

Elizabeth reconciled the years of verbal abuse, the intense jealousy, and the isolation from family and friends, with the fact that Ashley and Conner existed. Without such pain and hardship, they would not have been hers. And she certainly couldn't imagine her life without her children. Therefore, it was all meant to be. Not much of a fairy tale. But the tale was hers.

At 9 years old, Ashley was outgoing and bright, and good at most everything she did. Life came easy to her. If you threw her a football, she caught it and returned it with a perfect spiral. If you put her in a room full of strangers, she held her own in conversation with both adults and children. She was an old and confident soul, Ashley Lynn. But lately, she was visiting the school nurse almost every day with complaints of headaches and stomach aches. After multiple trips to the pediatrician, it appeared even strong and independent Ashley was struggling with the divorce. Conner, at the age of 7, loved animals, and was more sensitive and emotional than his sister. At times, his behavior was unpredictable, and he kept everyone on their toes. He required more snuggles and herculean amounts of patience, but he also understood less of what was going on. Maybe that was for the best. Brett never connected to Conner the way he did with Ashley. Maybe that's because independent and capable Ashley made things easy for him.

"Mom, I can't find my spelling homework," Ashley shouted from her bedroom. Week day mornings were a challenge in Elizabeth's house.

"It's on the kitchen table. Let's get going," she shouted above the din of the morning news. Although Ashely was up and ready to go each day, Conner had to be begged and bribed to wake, dress, and occasionally he even agreed to eat breakfast. But this particular morning wasn't like other weekday mornings. It was the day of Elizabeth's first job interview since the divorce. As she hurried the kids out the door, she stuffed Ashley's spelling homework into her backpack, and made one last attempt to adjust her navy suit and crisp white blouse in the reflection of the refrigerator.

Harborside Academy was an exclusive prep school providing exemplary educational opportunities for the best and brightest. It was the type of place that changed people's lives and afforded elite and competitive students an even greater advantage on the world's stage. All she wanted, was a chance.

———————◦((◦))◦———————

As Elizabeth entered the *Harborside* welcome center in Alexandria, Virginia, she was greeted by a lovely middle-aged receptionist who spoke in a kind whisper and invited her to take a seat while she waited to meet the headmaster. She chose a perfectly appointed leather sofa and inhaled the scent of privilege. With a freshly minted master's degree and high school teaching certification, she was ready to leave her job as a dental receptionist and begin a new career. She waited nervously, looked out toward the terrace, and the view of the expansive Potomac River in the distance took her breath away.

"Miss Bennett?" called an older gentleman, obviously, the headmaster.

If his bold confidence didn't give him away, his argyle sweater vest and seersucker bowtie telegraphed his role. As Elizabeth rose from the chair, she suddenly felt the earth shift beneath her feet. The room began to spin, and she grabbed the arm of the sofa to steady herself. Was that nerves? Quickly regaining her balance and composure, Elizabeth shook the hand of the man who would decide if she was suited to teach literature to high school students preparing for the ivy league. Still with an unsteady gait, she followed him out of the lobby, and glanced at a graceful crystal candle holder, an unexpected sign of grandiosity in a school, she thought to herself. And before her eyes, without explanation, the candle spontaneously lit as she passed. Amazed at how anxiety could affect her worldly perceptions, she returned her attention to the headmaster, who was already asking about her recent student teaching experience.

Later in the evening, over a steaming cup of herbal tea, Elizabeth reflected on her interview questions and second guessed more than half of her answers. She answered all of the questions honestly and thoughtfully but was concerned that she had no idea what an elite prep school looked for in a teacher. Elizabeth's education took place in middle class public schools that looked and felt nothing like *Harborside*. Although she told herself to wait patiently until she heard whether she would be invited to become part of the faculty at *Harborside Academy*, Elizabeth Bennett didn't have a history of being a good listener.

She put her mug in the sink, proceeded to wash her face and brush her teeth, and finally tucked herself into bed. As Elizabeth's head hit the pillow, she whispered to no one and to everyone, "Please let me get that job."

Three
2016

At twenty-five years old, honest, predictable, and loveably neurotic Meghan was at a crossroads. New York City had been her home for the past seven years. It was where she had graduated from NYU with a degree in journalism and where she had met and fell in love with William. Blonde haired, blue-eyed, smart, confident, William. Now, the idea of life in the city without him seemed unbearable. It had been three weeks since William came home from work one rainy Monday evening and told her it was over. They had just returned from a long, relaxing weekend at his sister's house in the Hamptons, hadn't been fighting at all, and in her mind, everything was great. Except it obviously wasn't. Apparently, William met someone at work, someone he was now crazy about, he explained. He stood emotionless, with his hands placed nervously in his pockets. He claimed he wasn't looking for it, wasn't planning it; it just happened. Meghan wasn't even sure he apologized at any point during his awkward speech. And then, he left. Walked out of her life with two months left on their lease in their one-bedroom upper west side apartment and left. He offered to pay the last two months of rent and to return during the day while she was at work to pack his things. "How gracious," she thought.

Since surviving emotionally and financially in the city wasn't a good option, Meghan decided to pack up and return home. Her freelance writing job at the newspaper was a dud and she was only plodding along until a better opportunity presented itself. This seemed like the right time to make a change and to retreat to the comfort and safety of home. But could she envision living in Maine once again after so much time in New York City? On her meager salary, she certainly couldn't afford a place of her own, and the break-up was more than she could bear, so she packed her things slowly and methodically touching every item she would have to say goodbye to. With a deep breath filled with bravado and sadness, Meghan took an emotional inventory of their third-floor, impossibly small apartment filled with thrift store finds used to transform the space into a cozy, eclectic place they affectionately referred to as *the nest*. There was a time, when together, they celebrated every item as if they had uncovered the bargain of the century. There was the stout, wide, cobalt blue two-dollar vase she used for hand-picked flowers, the worn but comfortable seventeen-dollar leather reading chair, and the bizarre but free oil painting they scored after a stoop sale ended in their neighborhood. Every interesting trinket made her feel alive and proud to be part of a city they both loved. It pained her to donate the items, but she knew she would only be able to take so much with her. With tears streaming down her face, she gathered what remained and left the city she loved and wondered if moving back to Maine would save her life or drive her mad. It could go either way.

⸺◦⟨◉⟩◦⸺

Meghan Murphy's view from the porch that faced Cape Porpoise harbor in Kennebunkport, Maine was so tranquil that it mattered little that her back ached from the long drive north from New York City, the contents of her life neatly stacked in her mother's old Subaru. She hadn't driven in years, but the Subaru was reliable, even with over one hundred and fifty thousand miles on it.

Grandpa's home sat sideways on the small lot, its wrap around porch facing the calm harbor only yards away. Its weathered brown shingles held secrets from the past and added a sense of character and mysterious charm that made the house and town almost fictional. Maine. She inhaled the clean salty air she missed so much, never taking the feeling of home for granted. Maine provided her with an idyllic childhood and she was thrilled when her father decided to sell his house in Biddeford and move to the quaint cottage in Cape Porpoise, after her grandfather passed away.

As Meghan sat cross-legged on warped boards in need of repair, she rummaged through a few boxes she stashed in the car for her unexpected move north. Memories from college and her relationship with William, mostly. She decided to bring her boxes to the attic for safekeeping before her Dad arrived home from school. Meghan's gazed turned toward the fishing boats bobbing up and down in the harbor before carrying the boxes up to the attic. She planned to sift through them more carefully, once the pain wasn't so fresh. As she stood to enter the cottage, boxes in hand, the breeze blew gently, comforting her with the security and safety of home.

The narrow stairs to the attic were steep, and although she was barely able to stand beneath the sloped roof, she found an empty corner, and carefully placed her boxes against the wall. With a small bedroom and closet, she decided to store most of her belongings in the attic until she figured out how long she would stay. She hoped to find a job and her own place at some point, but her father seemed happy to have her, so there was no rush. With a deep sigh, she turned to exit and spotted an old photograph tucked into the rugged wood planks that made up the dark attic walls. Meghan curiously plucked the photo from the wall and recognized her father at once. A much younger version of her handsome father stood behind a woman that wasn't her mother. His arms were wrapped around her, both staring contently at the camera, smiling, and unmistakably in love.

Searching for clues, Meghan stared at the picture, her head fitting just barely beneath the beams of the attic ceiling. She always suspected he once loved someone. Growing up, she saw it in his eyes when he appeared to remember something special, or by the way he smiled when he saw something beautiful. Her father was a man of few words but wore his heart on his rolled-up-to-the-elbow, flannel sleeve. As a little girl, she imagined his one true love as a smart, beautiful woman, and her imagination took the three of them on adventures. Now, at twenty-five years of age, Meghan wondered if this image was that woman in her daydreams. Was this her father's once upon a time? She turned the picture over, and in her father's familiar slanted and purposeful handwriting, the inscription read, *Jack Murphy & Lizzy Bennett.* The date was faded from time, and possibly sadness, and all she could make out was the first two numbers of the year, 19... "Meghan, are you up there?" Jack bellowed, bringing Meghan quickly back to reality.

Meghan hastily shoved the picture back in its place, bolted down the attic stairs, and replied, "Hey Dad, I'm up here checking out the size of my closet, which might hold two pairs of shoes and maybe a shirt!"

Meghan rushed down the stairs and entered the dated but charming kitchen to find her father unpacking groceries with the quiet determination of a man ready to make this his daughter's home. Noticing a few new wrinkles around his still sparkling green eyes, she thought to herself, his silent and rugged demeanor had a calming effect on her. At 58 years old, he still had a full head of sandy brown hair, which was now considered salt and pepper and was in a perpetual state of disarray. She smiled lovingly as she realized how much she appreciated him in that moment.

"I know this place is small," he said, "but that view makes it all worth it." He nodded out of the kitchen window, looking toward the harbor. The window served as a picture frame for a breathtaking piece of natural art. Right outside the window, the American flag blew proudly in the breeze against the cloudless blue sky, and yards away, the fishing boats rocked ever so slightly against peaceful waves.

Meghan's breath was still heavy from her attic encounter, and as if on cue, a bulky seagull floated effortlessly on the horizon, and as he turned toward the house, she was almost certain the bird added a careful wink and a purposeful nod in her direction. He squawked loudly, welcoming her to the neighborhood. Meghan blinked twice and shook her head in confusion, convinced her overactive mind was playing tricks on her.

Her first dinner back in Maine consisted of steamed lobsters at Langsford's Lobster and Fish House, only a few houses away. The lopsided lobster shack, covered in faded wooden buoys, served the freshest seafood in town, and only the locals knew you could sit out back on a weary picnic table and eat off a plastic tray overlooking the harbor. As they cracked open the bright red lobster tails and peered out over the harbor, it occurred to Meghan that she missed the place she took for granted as a child. Being gone had allowed her to appreciate its fairytale qualities. The idea that one could live in a fishing village, devour books by the ocean, and eat lobsters plucked from the very wharf she sat upon, seemed almost absurd when compared to the hustle and bustle of New York City. With the glorious scent of every ocean breeze, the chaos of her previous life with William began to drift away.

As they walked home, Jack and Meghan caught glimpses of the boats in the harbor and inhaled the quiet charm of New England. Most tourists had yet to descend upon Kennebunkport for the summer and Jack and Meghan agreed that their harbor walks should become a habit. Each home that lined the street had more charm than the next. Some had welcoming front porches with rocking chairs ready to be sat in while enjoying an afternoon lemonade, some were adorned with American flags, but all had an interesting story waiting to be told. Some hadn't changed a bit from years ago when she would take the same leisurely walks with her grandfather.

With sunset still over an hour away, Meghan settled into the worn hammock on the porch where she once read for hours as a teenager. She grabbed her copy of *Tolstoy and The Purple Chair*, and quickly decided this hammock would be her place of refuge, much like Nina Sankovitch's purple chair. If she could finish the book tonight, she could write her blogpost in the morning. Books about reading was Meghan's latest brilliant idea for her blog. Let's face it, reading about reading was every bookworm's dream. What could be better? Well, maybe writing about reading about reading. "But then again, that's probably why I'm single and living with my dad in a town no one has ever heard of," she thought to herself.

Meghan looked across the yard at her father casting a pole effortlessly under the late day sun. He deserved this seaside cottage after a long and satisfying teaching career. This would be his last year of teaching art at the local high school and this little house would afford him a peaceful and quiet retirement. She only wished he had someone special to share it with. Seemingly out of nowhere, a plump seagull circled above her dad and Meghan wondered if this was the same creature who had greeted her earlier. She smiled to herself. The salty air and gentle breezes were already causing feelings of comfort and belonging to stir. As the hammock swayed and the sun began to set over the fishing boats in the harbor, Meghan thought to herself, *if there is a God, she lives in Kennebunkport.*

The faded photo in the attic briefly came to mind. The

idea that the woman in the picture could be her father's long, lost love was simply her own fantasy; the result of an unhealthy obsession with Kevin Costner movies and sappy love stories. But then again, why after all this time, would that picture still be there? Maybe she would just ask him.

She pushed the photograph from her mind, because in that moment, a hammock, a good book, and a setting sun felt comfortably magical.

———●———

While walking through the town of Kennebunkport in the height of the summer, it wasn't hard to identify the tourists. They wore cameras around their neck, ready to document the charm of the small town. Land Rovers arrived from New York and Connecticut filled with blonde, sun-kissed families dressed in embroidered lobster shorts, Lily Pulitzer prints, and large brimmed straw hats. The town buzzed with activity and people stood in line for lobster rolls and lemonade at The Clam Shack, open only in the summer months.

Meghan liked the feeling of anonymity as she pushed her way through the crowded sidewalks. It reminded her of her college days in New York, where at any time you could be anonymous yet still be around people. Lonely, but not alone. This obviously had a different feel, and the small quintessential town would always feel more like home than New York ever could.

She stopped for an iced coffee at Dock Square Coffee

House and ducked into a few shops listening to the sounds of New York and Boston accents competing for the title of loudest or most annoying. She decided the contest ended in a virtual tie. Meghan biked home via Ocean Avenue and ogled the strong waves as they crashed upon the expansive rocky coast. Her senses were on high alert as she felt the warm sun and the mist of the cool ocean on her pale skin. She listened intently to the rhythmic sounds of the sea, as the expansive Bush compound at Walker's Point came into view. Since the flag was proudly waving from the presidential flagpole, she wondered which family members might be at home. She always imagined she and Jenna Bush would be great friends if the opportunity presented itself.

Jack was making dinner, and Meghan was excited about the pasta primavera with homemade alfredo sauce, garlic bread, and the salad she was tasked with assembling. Starving after her afternoon in the Port, she appreciated her father's domestic skills more as an adult than she ever did as a child. As they sat on the porch, eating and chatting in the late day breeze, Meghan thought about the photo in the attic, and her thoughts drifted effortlessly to the smiling young woman with long blonde curls and bright mysterious eyes.

A steady evening rain began to blanket the quiet fishing village and Meghan retired early to her room to continue the job search and to catch up on her reading. The sound of the rain tapping upon the roof and the smell of a new coastal candle lulled her gently to sleep before the sun went down. The ocean air always had this effect on her.

Her sleep was deep and the dream so vivid, that when she

awoke in the middle of the night, she breathlessly grabbed her journal to record what felt so real, she assumed it held special meaning.

Lizzy Bennett was walking away from her as Meghan yelled her name repeatedly, but there was no response. Thunder rumbled as the earth shook beneath her feet and a heavy rain fell steadily. The only two walking through a beautiful tree-lined park, Meghan was drenched, but Lizzy walked through the storm and the lightning strikes without as much of a rain drop upon her. "I can't see her face, but somehow, I know it is her," Meghan whispered to herself in her dream state.

Meghan continued to call her name to no avail, and when Lizzy was finally out of sight, a welcoming bench appeared for her to rest upon, the skies suddenly cleared, and the sun warmed her chilled skin. Miraculously no longer wet, Meghan welcomed the summer sun, as a seagull landed by her feet. The beautiful bird stared up at her, and in the dream, it mattered not that he spoke, or maybe she could just hear his thoughts.

"You have a special magic growing within – the same magic your father held but never accepted." As the bird flew away gracefully, he reminded Meghan not to turn her back on the magic. Whatever that meant. And when she looked down at the inside of her wrist, Meghan noticed a tiny tattoo of a seagull in flight.

She woke, convinced she had just emerged from the bench in the dream. Her skin felt balmy to the touch from the sun and the soles of her bare feet were warm from the park's pavement. Finally, she checked the inside of her wrist for a tattoo that wasn't there.

The dream mystified Meghan, but still not nearly as much as the photo in the attic.

Meghan kept her journal ready at her bedside, waiting for another dream. But wanting to dream, she learned, didn't result in another meaningful trance. She assumed she dreamt of Lizzy because she was simply curious about the photo. That seemed like a reasonable explanation. Her mind was innocently taking her to a place that the subconscious translated into a dream. She wondered if she was getting too wrapped up in the idea of her father's past. Girlfriends happen. Just because her father once had a girlfriend, didn't mean there was a story to be told. Even still, she couldn't help but wonder if his quiet sadness and occasional far off gaze had to do with the woman he held close in the faded photograph.

Four
1990

The shiny brass name plate that adorned the wall outside the classroom simply read *Ms. Bennett, Literature,* but stood as a powerful symbol of perseverance, accomplishment, and a newfound freedom. Elizabeth stared at it longingly, until she was interrupted by a young, energetic teacher named Charlotte who smiled as she said, "Welcome to Harborside. They don't give you a brass name plate like that in public school." She extended her hand and introduced herself as a second-year history teacher, and her gentle humor and warmth declared them immediate friends. Elizabeth was impressed by Charlotte's trendy short blonde hair and her 'I'm single and I spend all my money on clothes' sense of style. She oozed confidence and fun, two things Elizabeth was sure she lacked as a newly single mom. It would be nice, however, to have someone to go to with questions, and was relieved to find Charlotte's classroom directly across the hall. As a new teacher, the enormity of the position was overwhelming for Elizabeth and it was easy to question whether she would be an effective instructor, whether her lesson plans would keep her students awake, or if she would be perceived as a tough teacher or an easy grader. Similarly, she was equally worried about the little things, which resulted in a lot of worrying. Would she be able to work the copier? Where was the copier? She had already spotted the teachers' room and a coffee maker, thank goodness, but wondered, "Do I bring my own coffee or is it provided by the school?" First things first; she'd decided to solve the coffee mystery and let everything else work itself out. Elizabeth poked her head into Charlotte's classroom and asked, "I hate to give you the wrong impression by this being my first question, but do we bring our own coffee or does the school provide it?"

Charlotte laughed as she tossed her head backward and said, "Oh, we're going to be friends alright. And no, we don't have to buy our own anything. Coffee is provided. There's even an espresso machine if you fancy that sort of thing. We have everything but our own barista." When she saw Elizabeth's eyes widen, she added, "Welcome to *Harborside*," with a sly smile.

The faculty was large enough that Elizabeth still hadn't met everyone, but small enough that she had learned all about Mrs. Jay's husband being brought up on tax evasion charges, how it was common knowledge that Mr. Clarke did very little work but got away with it because he was married to the headmaster's cousin, and how people were generally convinced that Mrs. Jenkins and Mr. McCann slept together on a class trip to Philadelphia, and returned home to their spouses as if nothing happened. Apparently, Harborside gossip ran as deep and as murky as the Potomac River it sat beside. Elizabeth quite enjoyed the drama and joked with Charlotte that the school should have its own tabloid magazine. *The National Enquirer of Harborside.* Or maybe someone should write a tell-all book. She was convinced either would be wildly popular.

The first weeks of school were a big adjustment. Ashley and Conner sensed their mother's soaring stress levels and although Elizabeth worked full time previously, they weren't used to her being distracted by grading papers and writing lesson plans in her free time. There was a lot to balance with their homework, soccer practice, piano lessons, and endless piles of laundry. Her hope was that the first year would be the toughest, and they would all eventually settle in, and things would get easier. The good news was, Elizabeth was happier than she had been in years and loved being part of the *Harborside* school community. "It's all going to work out," she chanted twice to herself for good measure, brewing a strong cup of coffee at 7 p.m., in a dimly lit kitchen.

⸺●⸺

"Please remember that your essay is due on Monday. As we conclude *The Color Purple,* by Alice Walker, you will choose two diary entries, one from the beginning of the book, and one from the end. Be sure to explain how each play a critical role in one of the major themes we've discussed. Please don't resort to summarization to fill your page limit. This is an AP class, my friends. Questions?"

As Elizabeth wrapped up her last period class and noticed her students' waning interest, she felt her confidence growing after only eight weeks as a teacher. One after school meeting left to go, and it would be time for the weekend to begin. Ashley and Conner were spending it with their dad and Elizabeth was looking forward to sleeping in and wearing nothing but sweat pants for two glorious days. The cool, crisp air would make for a wonderful weekend of rented movies, books, and naps. It was amazing, and a little thrilling to have no plans or commitments.

The weekly Friday faculty meeting had been spent considering new applicants for the few remaining spots at the school, reviewing the curriculum requirements of each department, and hearing about upcoming school-wide events. The *Harborside* Harvest Gala was only a week away and was apparently the most important annual fundraiser of the year. Elizabeth made a note in the margin of her spiral notebook to ask Charlotte what she was supposed to wear for such an event, having never been to a "gala" before. The word itself implied she should be shopping for a dress, fancier than those already hanging in her closet. As Friday afternoon turned into early evening, she struggled to keep her focus on the meeting. She thought about the traffic she would encounter on the ride home, what she might pick up for dinner, and the fact that she didn't have to rush home to get the kids. One glance around the room and she noticed other teachers beginning to daydream, too. Mr. Murphy, the art teacher, appeared to be sketching something, while looking up to make eye contact with the speaker frequently enough to simulate a convincing interest. He wasn't overtly handsome, but he had kind eyes and a gentle demeanor. He was 30-something, she presumed. His shoulders were broad, and his sandy brown hair rarely combed, but this worked in the role of art teacher at a prep school. He seemed to care little about what people thought of him and kept out of the faculty drama. She wasn't even sure he had a friend at the school. And no wedding band either. This was also noted in the margin, under 'ask Charlotte.'

After the meeting, Elizabeth tidied her classroom and prepared her lesson plans and handouts for Monday. She liked the school best when the expansive halls were quiet, and she could think clearly. In the richly paneled teacher's room, she noticed Mr. Murphy engrossed in his work. He was oblivious to the fact that she was standing a few feet behind him at the copier. He must have no one to rush home to, she surmised. Standing this close to him, without him knowing, caused her to feel a little uncomfortable, but she enjoyed the feeling of warmth and comfort that washed over her. He smelled like a delicious combination of musky cologne and chalk dust, when he surprised her by turning around and saying, "I'm sorry, I thought I was alone. Didn't mean to hog the copier."

"Oh, no problem," she uttered, "just trying to get a jumpstart on next week."

As he stepped aside to let her copy her first *Animal Farm* assignment, he crossed his arms in front of him, leaned confidently against the counter, and his quiet but full attention on her caused her to chatter, nervously.

"My least favorite book to teach," Elizabeth said, pointing to her copy of *Animal Farm*. "But it's required reading."

"Is *Pride and Prejudice* your favorite?" he asked with a crooked smile. She assumed he was referring to her namesake, the notorious protagonist, Elizabeth Bennett.

"Well, *Pride and Prejudice* was my mother's favorite novel, hence the name," she added timidly.

They worked quickly, sharing the copier, stepping aside and chatting while each completed their work in a quiet building, normally known for its buzz and activity. He asked where she taught last, and she explained that this was her first teaching job. He learned that she was newly divorced and had two children. She learned that he had been seeing the same girl for years now but was ending that relationship on not-so-fabulous terms. He had never been married and had no children. It's hard to believe they learned that much about each other while standing over a copier in a messy, albeit grand, faculty lounge. They said a causal goodbye as they got in their cars to leave work behind and make their way to their respective homes. Elizabeth turned the radio up, sang to her favorite songs, and wondered what it was about Jack Murphy, the quiet, rumpled art teacher, that made her feel so darn delightful.

Once home and wearing her favorite flannel pajamas, she was halfway through her shrimp fried rice, and re-reading *Animal Farm* to prepare for the following week when the phone rang. She jumped up to answer it, always worried about the kids when they were with their dad. Jack's voice on the other end of the phone surprised her, asking if she were free for coffee this weekend. When she said that she was, he replied, "That's great news, Lizzy Bennett."

No one called her Lizzy except for her parents and a few childhood friends. The giddy teenager inside her wrote down the time and place where they would meet, before hanging up with a contented smile.

Five
2016

Growing up, Meghan was a quiet child who loved to dance, read books, write stories, and play make believe. Julia, her imaginary friend, accompanied her on all her adventures and kept an only child company when her parents couldn't entertain her. They played dress up together, drew pictures to hang on the refrigerator, and even rode bikes on chilly fall afternoons, meandering through the neighborhood's tree-lined streets. Meghan's parents allowed Julia to come along on most travels until about the age of five, when they gently explained to her that Julia was simply a product of her creative imagination and would likely need to disappear soon. At the time, Meghan didn't understand why Julia had to leave, but if nothing else, Meghan was a rule follower, even at five years old. So, she did what her parents told her to do, and asked Julia to leave. As an adult, Meghan wasn't left with any concrete memories of Julia, but instead, a mighty sensation of warmth and safety stayed with her always, thanks to a vague feeling of Julia's presence that resurfaced at times of distress.

Meghan grew up, sharing time between her parents, who separated when she was a baby. Although her parents never married, they each told a romantic story that they were in love at one time, however she always suspected the tale was exaggerated for her benefit. Her mom and dad lived in the same town of Biddeford, Maine, making the transition between houses easy enough. She never wished her parents would get back together, mainly because she saw them as two very different people who could never live together in harmony if they tried. Many of her friends' parents fought, kept secrets, eventually divorced, or lived with a partner they detested. She never thought of her life as odd.

Meghan spent as much time with her dad, Jack as she did with her mother, Mella and her childhood felt predictable, safe, and completely normal. She knew her parents argued at times, but they were careful not to include Meghan in their battles. Mella, Meghan's mom would sing, dance, and create plays for them to act out. The memory of her mom's long, dark hair swinging freely as they danced in the living room, made Meghan smile to this day. Unfortunately, Mella also stayed in bed for days at a time, when she became tired or overwhelmed. Meghan remembered her father or her grandparents coming over to help when her mom wasn't feeling well. As a child, Meghan thought nothing of her mother's episodes, but as she grew older, she was able to identify when Mella became sad, emotional, and fatigued, and simply needed a few days of rest before returning to her normal, playful self once again. Meghan's father, Jack, was quite different from her mother. He was less emotional, but steady and reliable. She always knew where she stood with him. He was loving and supportive, but not the free spirit her mother was. With her father, she fished, went on hikes with Sampson, their energetic Golden Retriever, and knew she could count on him for a ride whenever she needed to be shuttled back and forth to music lessons or school events.

To Meghan Murphy, her parents were perfectly opposite, but that suited her just fine. She never thought her family was that bad.

However, she never expected that as an adult, she would one day question the very foundation and truth of their tiny flawed family.

⸺·«(●)»·⸺

After just a few weeks of sifting through the online classifieds, Meghan landed a new job as a multi-media journalist for a local television station in Portland, about 40 minutes from home. It was a regular 9 to 5 job that kept her busy most days, having less time to daydream, and consequently, less time to interpret her dream and think about the life her father might have had. She spent her days writing script for local news and was in charge of web content for hometown stories in the Portland area. She covered restaurant openings, community events, festivals and fairs, and any hometown story she was handed. It was an entry level position but could someday lead to her dream job as a reporter for a major newspaper. She was determined to impress everyone that saw her work and was prepared to put 110% effort into her small-town role of small-town coverage.

Meghan found it interesting that her new job in Maine paid more than her New York City job and considered it a possible sign that her life was on the upswing. And with a year or so under her belt, she would find a small apartment in Portland and create a new life for herself. Minus William, and minus New York City where she, at one time, assumed she would live forever.

Her father would soon be retired from a 30-year teaching career and might finally spend his days doing the things he loved most: painting and fishing. A career spent in the classroom educating America's youth earned him the right to a peaceful retirement, she thought. He grew up in Maine and spent his college years and the beginning of his teaching career in Virginia before returning home to New England. He was more than ready to leave the classroom but also concerned about being bored in retirement. "You know I can't just sit around. I'm not sure how this retirement thing is going to go," he joked with her one evening. He loved Maine, so didn't consider leaving. Plus, he could never part with grandpa's cherished house that sat upon the harbor and was built as a wedding gift to her grandmother. No, that could not be sold to a stranger. Maybe her father would consider traveling, but certainly would not be moving.

An early riser at heart, she knew sleeping in and lounging around the house would not be part of his retirement plan. He had several close friends in town, and to Meghan, he seemed happier than she had seen him in a long time. Father and daughter had settled into a nice groove at home and enjoyed each other's company despite their busy schedules. Jack was enjoying having his daughter home once again, and

Meghan appreciated the company and the security her father provided at a time when she could use the support.

Summer had turned to fall, and Meghan welcomed the bright colors of autumn, the cool crisp temperatures, and even the dark and dreary days that lent themselves to quiet introspection. Of all the things she missed most about Maine, fall topped the list.

As the leaves began to turn their vibrant colors of red, orange, and yellow, Megan thought of her mom. One of their favorite things to do in the Fall was take nature walks, collect leaves in a small brown paper bag and opine about their color, shape, and type before taking them home for their many projects. Some days they would trace the leaves and draw in their veins and colors, slowly and accurately. Other times they would place a leaf beneath an ordinary sheet of white paper and use the side of a crayon to bring about beautifully shaded leaves, big and small. But her favorite activity was placing the leaves ever so gently in between layers of wax paper and watching her mother carefully press them into prosperity for Meghan to hang on her bedroom walls. The smells, colors, and memories of autumn were her favorite. Meghan knew she selected only the positive memories of her mother to replay and offer her comfort, when needed. There was no good point in reliving the more difficult times, growing up as Mella's daughter.

Autumn weekends in Kennebunkport were quieter, yet

still pulsed with locals and a few tourists moving about in anticipation of another long winter. Mainers took special care in their winter preparations, unwilling to let a harsh, snowy season sneak up on them. They were well prepared and celebrated fall with an exuberance that matched their readiness for winter.

Tour buses filled with folks admiring the breathtaking colors of autumn in New England, leaf peepers they were called, filtered through the town, keeping local businesses open, at least for the time being. Some locals missed the warmth and excitement of the summer, but Meghan preferred the chilly days that allowed her to take a deep breath and relax in the calm that settled over coastal Maine. It was easier to feel connected to the rhythm of the changing seasons in New England. New York city never seemed to pause to notice the gradual shift of earthly seasons. Here, she could quiet both mind and soul and feel the shift while riding the slow wave of seasonal change. She grabbed her favorite Ethiopian coffee at *Morning's in Paris* and decided to sit on the patio for a few moments before taking on the last of her errands. Surrounded by fading and slightly tarnished yellow potted mums and a chalkboard that announced the fall specials and mulled cider, she wrapped her red plaid scarf around her face and pulled on fingerless mittens to fend off the cold. The only one sitting outdoors with her coffee, she welcomed both the solitude and the brisk energizing air. She was focused on the beautiful scent of the cool, salty air, and while thinking about the air quality in Maine, she suddenly felt like someone was watching her.

And sure enough, without warning, a curious elderly

lady stood directly in front of her. Closer than a stranger might stand, Meghan quickly tried to assess the situation and couldn't tell if she was an eccentric artist walking about town, or a vagrant. Her close proximity was unsettling; unreasonably intimate. Meghan looked around for other patrons but found herself unwittingly alone with her surprise visitor. She had never seen the woman before and after she spoke, she wondered if she would ever see her again. The woman was not very tall, stood slightly hunched, and her gray hair was long and wiry. A tad unkempt and wearing a long green coat with oversized pearl buttons, she had the brightest blue eyes, which appeared to flow directly from ocean currents. Meghan felt unsteady in her chair, while the woman looked at her as if she had known her forever. She desperately tried to place her. Was she an old friend of her grandfather's? Someone she should recognize from her childhood? Although their interaction lasted only a few seconds, it felt as if something significant had happened.

"Magic lies within you, sweetheart. Don't be afraid. Embrace it. Look for the signs my Meghan, and you will see." Her voice was calm, convincing, and filled with a familiar tenderness Meghan anxiously attempted to recall.

The same message from her dream. "This can't be real," she whispered. Meghan's mouth hung wide open while the mysterious stranger with eyes that held the secrets of the sea, simply smiled an all-knowing smile and held her gaze steady. When Meghan finally closed her mouth and put her coffee down, she blinked, and without warning, the woman was gone. She looked down Western Avenue, looked up Western Avenue, and even looked across the street at the small amount of activity at the King's Port Inn. But she was definitely gone. In a moment, she had vanished. A few shoppers continued their tasks, and a jogger wearing shorts and a winter hat proceeded on his route, passing without a glance, keeping a strong and steady pace. "Where did she go?" Meghan asked aloud. More importantly, she wondered, where did she come from?

Lightheaded, bewildered, and unsteady Meghan planned to sketch the fascinating woman and record all the details from memory in her journal. She even picked up colored pencils and a sketch pad at *Colonial Pharmacy* before heading home. She reminded herself to include the wrinkles and creases by her sparking blue eyes, her long green coat, her timeworn leather boots, her considerate smile. Meghan wasn't the artist her father was, but she inherited some of his abilities and her interpretation of the mystical encounter was accurate enough. And of course, she included the stranger's spoken words. As Meghan sat upon her bed, she sketched freely, doodled and thought, "She knew my name. But even if she hadn't said my name, I am certain she knew me. But I didn't know her, did I", Meghan spoke aloud to her empty bedroom. Something felt intensely familiar about Julia, but she couldn't put her finger on what it was. She couldn't explain it. Just like she couldn't explain the dream.

Six
1990

E lizabeth didn't want to show up like she assumed it was a date. It was just coffee. She had washed and blow dried her hair and decided not to fight the waves and natural curl. After adding mascara and a light pink scented lip gloss, she decided she was satisfied enough to meet the teacher, Mr. Murphy, for coffee. Elizabeth then changed her clothes three times, eventually deciding on jeans and a bulky beige sweater with casual flat brown boots and concluded the worst thing she could do was try too hard.

This wasn't her first date since the divorce. There had been a blind date with a chef her neighbor set her up with. After a few phone calls, Elizabeth thought the chef might be "the one." She fantasized about coming home to seafood risotto and homemade cheesecake. The food fantasy was fleeting, after she met him in person. Then there was the date with the younger, very handsome plumber who showed up for happy hour in dirty clothes, fresh from a full day of plumbing. And when he called the waitress "honey," she checked out. Dating as a single mom was hard. But she was willing to at least try to find her soulmate. She considered having coffee or going on a date with a coworker could be a very bad idea. The reasons were too many to list, so she didn't. She simply applied a second coat of lip gloss and set off to meet a coworker.

They met at a small but crowded coffee house filled with interesting people. Some were reading or writing their novels, engrossed for hours. Others appeared to be happily reconnecting with long lost friends, and still others sat alone on a Saturday night. Everyone had a story and Elizabeth wondered what others would think their story was. Brother and sister? Coworkers? Old friends? Long lost lovers? Or most likely just an awkward first date. No reason to romanticize it. Jack arrived first and grabbed a small table, which allowed them to talk over the din of the eclectic Saturday night crowd.

Jack Murphy of the coffee house was not the Jack Murphy of Harborside. He was still quiet and reserved, and he listened more than he talked, but he smiled more, too, and there was something about the way he looked at Elizabeth when she talked, that insisted he didn't want to be anywhere else. Something so sincere and warm. Something familiar, but she couldn't put her finger on it. They talked for hours about their families, friends, and even their past relationships, normally a taboo subject on a first date. But this did not feel like a date. It was void of awkward silences, and instead, filled with laughter. It was, obviously, missing the wondering whether or not they would see each other again.

About two hours in, they decided they were both hungry, so they jumped in Jack's car and traveled to Rose Marie's in a strip mall. The small Italian restaurant was deserted at 7 p.m. on a Saturday night, but the comforting smell of garlic and freshly baked bread filled the air. They joked that the food must not be very good if only a few tables were filled with patrons, but they didn't care. As Elizabeth ordered her first glass of wine, she made herself a solemn promise not to exceed two glasses since she had to drive home.

They ordered pasta dishes and devoured the warm bread and butter on the table as they waited, drinking red wine slowly over steady conversation. It did not go unnoticed that because they were seated at a tiny table in the corner, their knees slightly touched beneath the table. But Elizabeth didn't mind and didn't move away. Neither did Jack. They ate without the first date jitters and spent all the while gossiping about their coworkers at Harborside. As the hours passed, their knees moved ever so slightly closer. It felt safe and perfectly natural.

Elizabeth was proud of herself for keeping to the two-glass agreement made a few hours prior, and the feelings of drunkenness were not the result of the wine. Jack brought her back to her car, and although the evening itself presented no awkward moments, the goodbye was intensely awkward. Jack looked at Elizabeth like he wanted to kiss her, but he didn't. Their eyes locked, and as much as she wanted him to kiss her, she was torn about this being an actual date; about the possibility of dating a coworker. She was curious about how he was feeling. They got along so well, she was worried maybe they were destined to be the best of friends and nothing more. It was that comfortable. But in the moment of clumsy goodbyes, he pushed the hair out of her eyes and held his hand by the side of her face a moment longer than would have been expected, and said, "Lizzy, you are a beautiful surprise."

In her shock, all she could manage was a smile and to mutter, "Bye, Jack" and then she climbed quickly into her car.

When Elizabeth finally walked into her kitchen at midnight, she placed her purse on the counter and decided to pour herself that third glass of wine while silently and happily reconstructing the details of the night with the strong, quiet art teacher. As she put the cork back in the bottle of red, she wondered how a second date could top that.

———◦《●》◦———

"Wait, tell me everything. Don't leave one tiny detail out." Charlotte was bouncing with curiosity and excitement in the corner of the empty teacher's room. "Really, Mr. Murphy? Okay, well I don't see it, but maybe."

Elizabeth tried to downplay the feelings she was having for Jack, maybe for Charlotte's benefit. Maybe for her own. "I think we're going to be great friends. We talked about everything. It was like talking with a best friend. No topic was off limits. I felt like I'd known him forever, maybe in a past life or something. But we didn't even kiss, so this clearly isn't a romantic thing." When Elizabeth finally took a breath and stopped babbling, Charlotte raised an eyebrow and folded her arms in front of her.

Elizabeth went about her busy teaching schedule, savoring the moments she could cross paths with Jack. A slight touch at the coffee maker, a knowing glance across the crowded lunchroom. It was final exam time and the students and faculty were stressed. She envied Jack for having final exams that consisted of clay and acrylic paints while she poured over text looking for quotes for students to analyze and find essay questions they had not previously prepared for.

Jack and Elizabeth spent most nights talking on the phone after the kids went to bed. They logged hundreds of hours of effortless conversation, learning everything there was to know about one another. She learned that although he and his girlfriend Mella had broken up, he felt responsible for her depression and recent hospitalization. Her family didn't live locally, so since the breakup she felt lonely and isolated. He wanted to be there for her and her family. Since they had been close for so many years, he felt like it was the right thing to do. Apparently, Mella and Jack grew up in Maine where they dated as teenagers, and she moved to Virginia a year after Jack so they could attend college together. Now Mella was having trouble adjusting, he explained. Elizabeth stayed busy with the kids and tried not to judge but felt the talk of Mella was frequent enough to be mildly concerning. She wasn't completely convinced they were over. But her ex-husband, Brett had become less reliable with his weekends with the kids, which meant Elizabeth had less time to focus on the feelings she had for Jack, whatever they were. However, it was undeniable to everyone at Harborside that Jack and Elizabeth had become inseparable.

One afternoon, after a long day at school, they took a walk along the water. It was a rare occasion that Brett wanted to pick the kids up from school and take them to dinner on a Wednesday night. Ashley and Conner were so excited that Elizabeth hoped Brett wouldn't cancel, disappointing them. Walking off the stress of the school day, Jack and Elizabeth moved at a brisk pace as they talked about anything and everything. Neither of them ever addressed that awkward goodbye in the car that night after the Italian restaurant. Instead, they continued to talk, flirt, and get closer than two people could be without being romantic. In some ways, it was the best possible scenario. A safe and comforting relationship that made Elizabeth feel warm and fuzzy inside, without any of the complications. On the other hand, she was confused about her feelings. They were strong. And she felt much more than friendship for Jack. He was exactly the kind of guy she should have married in the first place. The kind of guy she wished would have fathered her children.

They came upon a small pier and stopped to catch their breath, leaning on a railing that overlooked the river. Although about six inches apart, Jack moved closer and they found themselves touching ever so slightly. They gazed out at the water, avoiding eye contact, but immersed in the moment. And once again, a feeling that could only be described as electric stood between them. They stayed like that for what seemed like minutes, or maybe longer. Maybe even hours. Time stood still, and they didn't move, so it was hard to tell.

It was as if they were talking, but without words. Sharing a feeling and a moment they didn't want to end. Time passed, and they finally stepped back from the rail and looked at one another. Jack pulled Elizabeth close and held her. It was their first hug; a long-awaited embrace. His strong, capable hands held her head close to his chest, and suddenly Elizabeth began crying softly, without understanding why. She wasn't sad, and she wasn't happy. She was just overwhelmed with an emotion she couldn't name. Jack touched her chin gently and lifted it to meet his gaze. "Why are you crying?" he asked with great concern.

"I don't know," she blurted with a little chuckle.

It did seem bizarre that she would be crying for no reason at all. Except that as a woman, she couldn't handle the emotion she was experiencing for the first time, ever. An emotion Elizabeth would never experience again with any other man in her lifetime. She just didn't know it at the time.

"Lizzy, I don't know what's going on with us. There's this strange electricity between us. It's so strong it scares me. I feel like if I could stop time and hold on to you forever, it wouldn't be long enough." He took a breath, "My God, I hear myself saying these things and it sounds ridiculous. I sound crazy," he added, only half joking. "What the hell is going on with us?"

She looked at him with a little fear but a lot of love, and all she could do was shrug her shoulders, dry her eyes, and summon the courage to say, "I feel it, too."

Suddenly and unexpectedly, a large seagull floated above them, closer than a bird should get and they were forced to shift their bodies, avoiding him and his impressive wing span.

As he landed on the railing, they both looked at the beautiful silver and white creature and laughed because he was clearly intruding on a very personal and important moment. As they giggled, the bird stood perched and motionless, watching their every move. Interestingly, Elizabeth thought she saw one of the bird's eyes twinkle, with a silver spark aimed in her direction, but she shook her head in disbelief, knowing that at this very moment, she was an unreliable observer in her own life and nothing appeared as it was where Jack Murphy was concerned.

Before they began their walk back to school, Elizabeth leaned her body into Jack's and as he held her face in his hands, he leaned his forehead against hers. Their lips just inches away from one another, their eyes closed, relishing the moment. Finally, he kissed her; the softest, slowest, deepest kiss. There on the pier, with the wind blowing ever so gently between them, wonderfully unaware of pedestrians, seagulls, or other earthly distractions, they were completely lost in the moment. It was the kind of kiss that made Elizabeth unstable on her feet, yet blissfully content. It was the kind of kiss Jack didn't want to end and left him wanting more. It was the kind of kiss they would each re-live and miss when they were apart, now and for decades to come.

Seven
2016

December in Kennebunkport felt a little like July, except for the frigid temps and dreary skies. The quintessential seaside town began to buzz with the excitement of summer once again as locals decorated for Christmas and shoppers returned to Dock Square. Meghan tried never to miss Christmas Prelude in Kennebunkport, almost always making the drive from New York City when she could. She felt fortunate to be back to celebrate with her father. The shops and restaurants that had previously closed for the winter, re-opened for a few weeks to celebrate Christmas Prelude, a two-week winter wonderland extravaganza that rivaled any Hallmark or Lifetime holiday movie. It seemed every lamppost was adorned, and store windows were decorated with festive signs of the holiday. Even *Scalawags*, the boutique pet store in town had hundreds of perfectly crafted white snowflakes hanging from their ceiling, and their window advertised holiday treats for the most discriminating canine. Emma, the bartender at *Alison's* convinced Meghan to come to the annual tree lighting and stop in for a drink afterward. *Alison's* was one of the few restaurants and bars that stayed open year-round for the locals. They were famous for their craft beers, solidly good food, and Friday night karaoke. There would likely be a crowd after the tree lighting ceremony, but Meghan promised to try and stop by.

She invited Jack to come to the tree lighting with her. They had been busy with their own lives as of late and had not seen much of each other. When Meghan first moved back to Maine, they made it their business to have dinner together a few times per week but had since settled into eating on the run and passing one another on the fly. Jack often cooked and left a plate of leftovers in the refrigerator for Meghan since he knew she couldn't be bothered with digging the leftovers out of containers. For a moment, Meghan wondered whether it had been easier for her to avoid him and busy herself, than to confront him and simply ask him about the picture in the attic of a woman from his past named Lizzy Bennett. She had, however, researched and found an Elizabeth Bennett living in Virginia. She was the author of two books, and lived with her husband, an Alexandria attorney. She had two adult children who were unnamed in her basic biography. Elizabeth didn't appear on any bestseller lists, but her books, both historical fiction, got good online reviews from her devoted readers. She had a very basic author's website, from which one could glean little personal information. She didn't have a Facebook page that was easily found. No Instagram, no Twitter. What did anyone do before Google? How did anyone ever track their ex before the internet? Inconceivable.

They bundled up in their warmest winter wear and arrived early for the tree lighting to be sure they would get a parking spot. While walking through town, they escaped into stores like Daytrip Society, giving out hot chocolate, spreading holiday cheer, and offering a moment of warmth from the cold temperatures. Adults and children of all ages wore reindeer antlers, tall Santa hats, and blinking Christmas tree lights strung around their necks. Christmas carols were being piped through the town via large speakers and Meghan had to admit, this place was pretty magical. As they stood on the sidewalk, the spot they determined would be the perfect vantage point for the tree lighting, Meghan snuggled into her dad, linked her arm in his and reminded herself how lucky she was that he was hers.

The town's high school choir arrived to sing carols and the crowd joined in. Meghan took a few pictures for prosperity and looked forward to including this bit of Christmas magic with her media coverage of southern Maine's holiday celebrations. She suddenly realized, with a quick scan of the crowd, and just minutes until the tree lighting, hundreds, maybe thousands of visitors, locals, and neighborhood Labradors had quickly filled the streets, now belting out *Santa Clause is Coming to Town.* Suddenly, Jack looked down at Meghan and said to his daughter, "It's hard to believe this place is real sometimes."

The light snow flurries that began to fall reminded Meghan not to turn her back on the magic, because with one look around the picturesque little seaside town celebrating Christmas, she understood she was meant to be there, and no other place could feel more like home. Meghan looked up at her father and agreed, "How lucky are we?"

"Five, four, three, two, one," the town sang in harmony and the enormous tree positioned perfectly in Dock Square was lit in celebration with thousands of white lights. The buoys and lobsters that hung from the tree were now illuminated and the crowd began to quickly disperse. But before the night was over, a series of the most breathtaking fireworks were lofted over the town and Jack and Meghan stopped in their tracks to take it all in.

————)((◍)) ————

The town library was quiet on a chilly Saturday morning and Meghan was lucky enough to find both of Elizabeth Bennett's books on the shelf. Dressed in her oldest and most comfortable NYU hooded sweatshirt, she carried the books to an empty table in the library's sitting room and held them in her hands, trying to connect to this mystery woman and feel the magic. When you grow up believing libraries are sacred spaces, you assume any magic you may have been granted would manifest in the most hallowed halls. When Megan was growing up, every Saturday morning, she couldn't wait for her father to pick her up and take her to the local library to discover new books that she would devour over a week's time. But now, while waiting for mystical but questionable powers to come, she felt nothing but the smooth jackets covering two ordinary library books and she let out a deep sigh.

One of Elizabeth's books took place on the Titanic and was a fictional account of a family traveling with small children. All family members perished on the sinking ship, except the youngest child, an infant at the time. The story took the reader through his life as a sole survivor. Her second book, also fiction, was set in 1920, and the main character, a lonely young woman, found a series of journals written by one of the Brontë sisters and unraveled romantic mysteries encrypted in the journals. Meghan flipped through the pages hoping to find a character named Jack, or a love affair lost to tragedy. But nothing at all connected Elizabeth Bennett to Jack Murphy in the pages. At least not in the few hours at the library. It was possible there was no meaningful relationship. It was possible she was creating a love story where there was none.

She decided to get a library card at the *Graves Memorial Library* and take the books home where she could read them from cover to cover and look for signs of a love affair with her father. The smiling, round, 70-something librarian had her fill out a form to check the books out. Her hair was gray with a hint of lavender and her scarf covered in tiny ladybug prints. As she slid the books toward Meghan, she inserted a bookmark labeled with the name of the library, *Graves Memorial Library*. She thanked her warmly and noticed a logo; a sketch of a small seagull in the upper right corner of the bookmark. Another seagull. But hardly unusual in a coastal community, she thought. The unusual and miraculous part was what happened next. Without warning, the seagull flapped its wings off the page and as if in slow motion, returned to its inanimate state. Meghan stopped and looked up at the librarian with wide eyes, who simply winked and said, "Have a magical day, sweetheart," with a knowing grin. Feeling completely dumbfounded, and once again lightheaded, Meghan paused, and turned to leave, unable to respond.

Eight
1990

The *Harborside* Winter Formal was only a few days away. An event for parents, junior and senior students, as well as faculty to dress up, attend a fancy dinner, raise money, and mill about exchanging niceties. Jack and Elizabeth would be attending together. Well, not together as a couple, but simultaneously. Dressed up. Near each other.

Elizabeth decided to up her game as far as dresses went, and asked Charlotte to take her shopping for a classy yet sexy dress that would stop Jack in his tracks. She chose a navy off-the-shoulder, A-line velvet dress that was simple and elegant, yet fit snuggly in all the right places. She added navy heels and her grandmother's pearls and felt amazing. Elizabeth arrived at the school, and a valet was unexpectedly present to park her car. The school had somehow quickly and expertly been transformed into a candlelit affair, worthy of the status of its affluent and powerful guests. She accepted a glass of champagne from a fresh faced white-gloved waiter, felt a bit like Cinderella entering the ball, and circled the room until she saw him. He was wearing a navy suit, with a white shirt and a red and white pinstriped tie. His shoes were brown dressy loafers and he looked more like a young, wealthy, handsome parent than an art teacher. Only his still tousled hair gave him away. As Elizabeth approached, Jack caught her eye and looked at her like they were the only two people in the room. Both suddenly remembered there were students, parents, the headmaster, and colleagues milling around. The rumors were starting to fly that something was going on between them. They had to be responsible. After a few minutes of sipping drinks and wishing they were anywhere else, they separated to circulate and search out their place cards for dinner.

Elizabeth found herself at Table 7 and was the first to arrive. She set her purse down and introduced herself to a couple who sat down next to her; Dr. and Mrs. Cunningham. They had freshman twins, a boy and a girl, at *Harborside*. Others arrived and the guests at the table listened politely as the Cunningham's spoke proudly about the twins' aspirations for medical school and about their "modest" summer home at the beach. A moment later, Jack unexpectedly arrived at the table, showed Elizabeth his card that read *Table 7*, and sat down beside her, placing his hand on her knee without anyone seeing. Seated at the same table. What were the chances? During dinner, a parent seated across from the pair asked Jack and Elizabeth where they were from and how old their children were. Confused at first, Elizabeth finally answered, "Oh no, we aren't together, we're both teachers here."

The woman tilted her head and replied, "Well, if you aren't a couple now, you should be. You're perfect together."

Jack smiled politely and looked at Elizabeth with eyes that sparkled and a shrug that meant, "She must be right." Meanwhile, placing his hand a bit further up her thigh, he sent chills throughout her entire body.

The night ended promptly at ten o'clock, mainly because it was the responsible thing to do with students in attendance. As they retrieved their keys from the valet, they assured the uniformed gentleman they could manage their own vehicles. As they walked toward their cars, Jack grabbed Elizabeth's hand. Before they reached their destination, he stopped. "You know what, I don't want this night to end. How about a dance, just the two of us? We can sneak into the art room. I have my key. What do you say?"

Excited, to finally spend some time alone with Jack, they tiptoed around the outside of the East building that housed the art room and let themselves in. With the lights turned off to be sure no one would spot them, Jack gently placed his hand on the small of Elizabeth's back. His touch was more than she could handle. He popped a cassette into his portable stereo and with the music playing softly, he grabbed her hand, spun her around, and pulled her close. They danced, slowly and intimately, in the dark, with the moonlight shining in through the classroom as he played with her hair and gazed into her eyes. Elizabeth tried to remind herself not to get lost in the moment and to drink in every last detail, so she could recall it someday when she was old, someday when her grandchild would ask about the most romantic moment in her lifetime. The music stopped, their breathing irregular. Jack gently but firmly led Elizabeth to the back wall of the large art room, held the back of her head in his hand, and pulled her hair just hard enough that her mouth naturally opened, letting him kiss her, over and over. His hands traveled over her body as she held his dress shirt tightly, when he suddenly stopped. "We can't. Not like this," he said.

She disagreed. "Yes, we can. No one will see us," she said, out of breath, practically begging him to finish what he started.

But it wasn't meant to be. Jack walked her back to her car, their clothes rumpled but still in-tact. He spoke first. "You're far too important to me, to have our first time be like this. In a classroom. It's ridiculous. I completely lost my head. But there's something you should know. I should have told you this a while ago, but I've been afraid. With everything going on with Mella and with you only just getting over a terrible divorce, I didn't want to complicate things. But Lizzy, I'm in love you."

—((●))—

First thing Monday morning, after first period, Elizabeth decided she couldn't keep what happened to herself. She left a note on Charlotte's desk that said only, "Need to talk. Soon. J.M. update." She added multiple exclamation points in an English teacher's red pen, for dramatic effect. It was a busy day at school and Charlotte was in charge of the college fair being held in the gymnasium, so she was hardly in her classroom. When she finally saw the note, the school had emptied out and she looked exhausted.

"This better be juicy; my life is entirely too boring for my liking."

"It's pretty good," Elizabeth teased and invited her to come over for dinner with her and the kids.

For someone who didn't have, nor want children, Charlotte was amazingly patient and fun with Ashley and Conner. They loved when she came over, because she sang, danced, read stories in full character voices, and always brought a delicious dessert. Elizabeth decided it should be a taco night and kept things simple. They shared a bottle of wine as a welcome addition to a Monday night, much deserved after a long day of school. Once the kids were finally bathed and in bed, Charlotte grinned from ear to ear and said, "Dish. Now. Everything," as she took a large bite of her brownie sundae. Elizabeth replayed the night as they finished off the bottle of red and tried to remember to include every last detail.

"Not adding up," Charlotte blurted with a shake of her head. "There's not a man on this planet that wouldn't have taken that opportunity to have sex. Not a man alive that would have walked away from that moment. Especially with you in that dress. For goodness sake, I couldn't resist you in that dress," she joked. "Unless, of course…"

Elizabeth interrupted her and shouted, "What?" a little too loudly.

Apparently, Charlotte went on to say she believed that Jack Murphy was leading a double life. Still caring for and sleeping with his supposed ex-girlfriend, while enjoying all the benefits of having someone to flirt with at work. She said it was the only thing that made sense. Elizabeth felt deflated as she wanted nothing more than her best friend to participate in her excitement and her soon to be fairytale. Elizabeth thought it sounded like an unlikely conspiracy theory. But as the months went by, Charlotte's words played like daunting background music and serious doubt and suspicion began to take over.

By mid-December, the students and faculty were readying for a two-and-a half week break, and Elizabeth summoned the nerve to ask Jack about Mella. He assured her that their relationship was over and had been for some time. Elizabeth felt somewhat better until he added, "I do stop in to check on her occasionally. But it's just out of concern. Her parents live in Maine and they rely on me to help them when Mella becomes depressed and spends days and sometimes weeks at a time in bed."

The creepy background music may have quieted somewhat, but it still played ever so slightly in the distance.

Nine
2016

J ack decided to take a trip to D.C. for New Year's Eve and celebrate the arrival of 2017 with some old friends from college. Meghan noticed he had been more relaxed and carefree than ever before, with retirement near. Every Saturday morning, he met three of his friends for breakfast and they casually talked about the tides, the quality of the fishing, and neighborhood happenings. He was also painting again. And he was reading a lot, too. Mysteries and spy novels seemed to be his current favorites. He was even talking about eventually getting a part-time job at the art gallery around the corner. It warmed Meghan's heart to see him happy and planning his future. He was retiring at a young age and she wanted to be certain he had some fun in this next phase of his life.

He had been gone for a few days and since the house was quieter than usual, Meghan found herself looking for things to do. With an impending snowstorm about to hit southern Maine, the first one of the year, she balanced her time with reading, writing, snacking, and movies. Not a bad existence, she decided, but thought she should venture out for a bit since the storm might keep her home for a few days.

"I'll have Port fries and a vodka and soda with extra lime," she said to Emma, pushing the menu back, without looking at it, in her direction.

"You've got it. I'm hoping we close early due to the storm," she said. Meghan was the only one sitting at the bar at Alison's except for an older man at the opposite end, who looked like a local fisherman, retired from the trade. Steady flurries were starting to fall outside the window and the white lights on the storefront's window made the scene look like a shaken snow globe. The only thing missing was the childlike music usually wound from beneath the globe. The beauty of the beginning of a snow storm never got old. She read a chapter in her book, *The Ocean at the End of the Lane,* while at the bar, indulged in her dinner, and was about to ask for the bill when a stranger walked in, shaking off the snow. Clearly not a local, he was dressed in rumpled, but expensive khakis, and a tailored black winter jacket. He was about her age, Meghan thought, maybe a few years older, and wore a grey scarf tied fashionably around his neck. His light brown skin stood out in the mostly white New England town. Of all the things she didn't miss about New York City: the crowds, the smells, the fast-paced vibe, she did miss the diversity. A town consisting almost only of white people was now odd to her. Seeing a stranger who didn't look like a typical Maine fisherman, landscaper, or contractor, was intriguing.

The cute stranger sat two barstools away from Meghan and introduced himself as Elliott, a local, at least for a few years, while he worked on a grant at the University of New

England in Biddeford. Since he had just completed his Ph.D. in Marine Biology, she calculated he might not be that young. She found herself delaying the paying of her tab as the snow outside started to fall harder. They chatted casually about their work and what brought them to Maine. Elliott grew up in the suburbs of Boston, and his parents, both academics, still worked at universities in the city. She learned he was part of a research team, studying the sustainability of ocean foods and was renting a tiny, one- bedroom apartment in town. He was on foot as the snow began to fall and he would be able to walk home without the worry of slick roads. Before conditions became dangerous, Meghan said goodbye as Elliott's burger arrived. She paid her bill and drove the two and a half miles home, slowly and carefully. As she drove, she noted the stark differences between Elliott and William. There were the obvious physical differences, William being blonde-haired and blue eyed, and Elliott's dark brown eyes and warm brown skin that set him apart in Maine. But there was more. William was always confident and a bit boisterous whereas Elliott was gentle. Very friendly, but less animated and overpowering than William. "Maybe I will start dating again. And maybe, just maybe, I should be looking for the opposite of William," she thought to herself amidst the falling snow.

Meghan slept in and awoke to find ten inches of snow had blanketed the neighborhood overnight. She was glad Jack arranged for them to be plowed out since he wasn't home to help with the shoveling. A foot of snow wasn't a big deal in Maine, but she wasn't in the mood to dig out. She noted a few cars grinding up and down the street and the neighbors already hard at work, shovels in hand. She continued to gaze out the window and was convinced, even after a snowstorm, this place read like a storybook.

Coffee was brewing, and Meghan enjoyed the aroma as she pulled her favorite oversized mug from the cabinet and noticed an older woman trekking through the snow, bundled up and walking toward the market and the church. There was something familiar about her and it certainly seemed odd that a woman of her age would be walking to the market alone in the snow. But folks in Maine were hearty. Her grandparents did the same thing, well into their eighties. As the woman lifted her head and looked toward the house, her blue eyes glistened, and Meghan realized it was the very same woman who had vanished before her eyes on the sidewalk of the coffee shop in the fall. She hurried to pull on her snow boots and grabbed her coat, dashing out the door. She awkwardly threw on her coat, mid-run, bounding through the light, fluffy snow. By the time Meghan reached the mailbox, she was gone. Again. Frustrated, she slapped both hands on her thighs and bent over slightly from being winded, partly from cold air, but mostly from the race through the snow. Suddenly, she noticed a small package on the ground at her feet. A small silver box shimmered in the sun, somehow untouched by the storm. Could the old woman have left the box and hurried into a neighboring home? Meghan thought this woman could be her neighbor. But did she really just vanish into thin air, once again? She carried the box inside and laid it on the counter as she kicked off her boots and removed her jacket. Inside the box was a small hand-painted seagull carved delicately from wood. And on the bottom of the seagull were the initials, EB. There was no note and no clues. With a deep sigh, she placed the mystery gift on the kitchen windowsill, faced him toward the harbor, and asked aloud to her miniature seagull, "Where did you come from?"

Two cups of coffee later, she placed her empty mug in the sink, began to wash out the coffee pot with warm soapy water and suddenly wondered if EB could be a connection to Elizabeth, or Lizzy Bennett. Or was she officially losing her mind?

※

Meghan spent her first New Year's Eve back in Maine alone at home, happily watching Ryan Seacrest and his celebrity friends ring in 2017. She didn't need to buy a new outfit and didn't waste money on a lukewarm, over-priced meal. During her freshman year at NYU, her friends insisted on dragging her to Times Square on New Year's Eve to see the ball drop, and after spending one sleepless, tipsy night trying to get back downtown to her dorm room, she was miraculously cured of any desire to be in Times Square on New Year's Eve, ever again. Someday, she hoped to spend New Year's with her handsome husband and their adorable 2.5 kids, ordering Chinese food and playing board games in the suburbs. For now, however, cold leftover pepperoni pizza and light beer would have to do. At about 11:30 p.m., she picked up her phone to call her father and wish him a Happy New Year, when a text message appeared from a number she didn't recognize. It was Elliott from the bar. Apparently, he was at *Alison's* and got her number from Emma.

"Hey, Meghan. It's Elliott. We met at *Alison's* last week. I wanted to wish you a Happy New Year and wondered if you wanted to meet for a drink some time? We could even do dinner, if you're up to it."

Interesting. She wondered if she might run into Elliott again. Now it looked like she would. She thought for a few moments and typed back an equally friendly message, "Hey there. Happy New Year to you, too! Sure, let's get together."

———————◦((◦))◦———————

Meghan always believed New Year's resolutions were silly and reserved for unattainable goal setters and overzealous humans bound to set themselves up for failure. But this year would be different, she vowed. This was the year for resolutions, for so many reasons. Meghan used her journal to try and makes sense of her life. She separated her goals into three categories, personal, professional, and family. Neatly crafting three columns, she began to take notes and make lists. Personally, she knew she had a lot of work to do. She was still reeling after the break-up with William and had to refrain from calling him or texting him in moments of weakness. She would get over William in 2017 and focus on building more confidence and finding hobbies in Maine. Easy enough. She considered adding healthy eating habits and abruptly stopped herself. No reason to be ridiculous. Professionally, she planned to impress her boss at the station and make a name for herself in Southern Maine. It would take time and effort, but she was up for the challenge. And as for her family, well, she really should have titled that category, "Dad." She wanted to know more about her father's past and more about the woman he loved enough to keep her picture after all these years. And then, as an afterthought, she added a fourth category in a large bubble at the top of the page and wrote, "mystery woman."

Meghan closed the journal and began to focus on all of the strange happenings since arriving back home in Maine. Although she briefly considered that she might simply be crazy, or completely stressed due to the break-up and the move, Meghan knew what she saw and heard. And now there was the mystery gift of the hand carved seagull, making her delusions more tangible. She would be busy trying to find answers in the new year but was also beginning to question what was real and what was fantasy.

—— •((◑))• ——

Sadie was the town psychic. It's wasn't as if every town had a psychic, but in the seaside town of Kennebunkport, tourists made their way to a staircase at the center of Dock Square, which led them to a mystical loft overlooking town, advertising chakra, tarot card, and palm readings; Seaside Psychic. The sign glowed in the mid-day sun. Never would Meghan have imagined paying hard-earned money for such a service, unless, of course, she was desperate. And desperate, she was. She had reached a point in a series of her own personal fever dreams, that required intervention. There was the wild dream and messages she couldn't explain. She had questions about Lizzy Bennett. Questions about the old woman who appeared. There was a lot she wanted to know. And she hoped Sadie could help.

She wouldn't admit to a living soul that she made an appointment to see Sadie, but she felt like she needed her. Meghan entered the loft a few minutes before the scheduled appointment, sat patiently on a soft, oversized white chair, and found herself surrounded by muted colors, white lights, crystals, and a large Buddha watching over the space. She could hear her heart beating and tried to calm herself by taking a few cleansing breaths when Sadie appeared from behind a heavy pink velvet curtain. Instantly struck by her appearance, she was not at all what she expected. She looked like anyone else walking through Anytown, USA; like the 6th grade teacher you run into at the mall or the gentle woman who helped you select cinnamon rolls at the bakery. Her grey hair was pulled back into a long, untidy ponytail and her dark clothes fit loosely on her larger than average frame. Her large, brown eyes were kind and compassionate and welcomed her like an old friend. Meghan sat down nervously and waited for her to speak first. A moment of silence passed between them.

"First and foremost, you're going to need to relax. I start by reading energy and honey your energy is intense. It feels dizzying to me. Does that make sense?" Sophie asked.

"Yes, it does. I'm very nervous. I've never done anything like this before. But I'm also confused and feeling anxious lately," she admitted. She kept to herself the part about her always being anxious. Not just lately.

Sadie closed her eyes, took a long deep breath, and proceeded, "Okay, let me start by saying this. You need to accept the things you cannot change. So, if you are…" She paused and tilted her head gently to the side, choosing her words carefully, "experiencing things that aren't easily explained, or a bit outside the norm, you're better off embracing them. Accepting them. Does that make sense?"

Meghan answered quickly as she placed both hands firmly on the table in front of her, "Does that make sense?" she huffed sarcastically. "If you mean constantly seeing things that aren't there? And oh, I don't know, like having seagulls follow me? Or, meeting an old woman who appears at random times while I'm awake? The woman who appears and disappears?" She could have gone on but instead took her journal out of her bag and threw it open revealing her sketch of the woman in the green coat who followed her in her daydreams and sometimes in her reality.

"So, I see you've met Julia," Sadie said calmly, with a slight smile, clasping her hands in front of her.

Meghan lowered her voice, embarrassed by her uncontrolled rant. Her hands both now in front of her on the table. "You know this woman?"

"Julia is somewhat famous in town. As the story goes, she has appeared to a few lucky residents and tourists. She has been known to leave gifts, give advice, and comfort those who are hurting. Anyone who believes this town is enchanted, believes in Julia."

"How do you know this is Julia?" she asked, pointing to the mystery woman sketched upon the page from her own memory.

"Let's just say I have met her more than once," Sadie smiled gently and added, "Julia is thought to be the wife of a prominent ship builder in town, from the mid-1800s. She never had children of her own, but her husband's mistress had three. At that time in history, many townspeople believed Julia practiced witchcraft and went on to cast a spell on her husband's mistress, leaving her with pneumonia, which resulted in a slow and painful death at the young age of 27. Julia, however, denied ever using her gifts to harm anyone and later raised the children as if they were her own. In fact, she was so in love with them that she granted each child powerful abilities and healing gifts under a waxing crescent moon. Some in town secretly met with her for healing magic, and many more others considered her dangerous and capable of dark magic and evil spells."

"Do you really believe in Julia? Do you believe this town is enchanted?" Meghan asked her questions quickly and with a sense of urgency as she stood and paced about the small room.

Sadie looked up at Meghan with compassion. "It doesn't matter what I believe. What matters is what *you* believe, Meghan. If you have this gift, you have a choice. You can either accept it, or not. If you fight it, however, it may be difficult for you. You're already feeling anxious and on edge. My advice to you is to try and accept your experiences with an open heart and an open mind. It's possible that one of your parents has a similar gift, for lack of a better term."

Suddenly, she remembered the dream. The one where the seagull gave her a message that her dad turned his back on the magic. Meghan inhaled deeply, "I think it was my dad, but he never talks about it. And possibly my grandfather.

He always told elaborate stories of magic about the town of Kennebunkport. As much as I loved his stories, I thought he was just good at making up fairytales." Meghan, still confused and bewildered, sat back down and stared intently at Sadie.

Sadie reached across the table and took both of Meghan's hands in hers, "Honey, it's not a bad thing. Just remember, acceptance. With an open heart and an open mind. Stop worrying."

Easier said than done, Meghan thought to herself.

After almost an hour of absorbing Sadie's messages, Meghan left the session with a feeling she could only describe as a relieved sense of exhaustion. She didn't have the opportunity to ask all of her questions but considered returning another day. A wave of calm washed over her as the sun was about to set. She stood on the sidewalk, overlooking Dock Square and for a moment allowed herself to appreciate the enchanted little town set out before her. The late day sun bounced off the brightly colored buildings filled with New England charm and nostalgia of times gone by. The town her grandfather loved so much stood before her like an oil painting, telling stories of the past and the present. The town her grandfather shared magical stories of that she assumed were simply childhood fairytales. Maybe Grandpa knew something she didn't and how she wished he was still alive today.

Rather than run home or check her phone for messages, she simply took a cleansing breath and focused on the scent of the clean air she had once again come to love and decided to at least try to have an open heart and an open mind.

Ten

1990

Elizabeth was looking forward to Christmas break with the kids, so they could sleep in and spend some time together without the stresses of homework and school activities. As they hung the ornaments on the artificial tree, Ashley pointed out, "We always used to have a real tree." Understanding she meant before the divorce, Elizabeth explained this one would be easier for them to put up and take down, with the advantages of not having to water it or clean up the needles. She omitted the part about not having the energy to traipse through the local tree farm and figure out how to pull a 7-foot tree from the car into the house. Some things were best left unsaid.

"Dad's getting a real tree and he said we can help him put it up with Florence," added Conner excitedly.

With her back turned to the kids, she hung an ornament and rolled her eyes like an angsty teen. Of course, Brett was dating and had already introduced the kids to Florence who might or might not already be living with him. Brett couldn't be alone, so she wasn't surprised by the development. And who had a name like Florence, in her 30s? That was just unfortunate. Either way, the kids seemed excited to see her. And their far superior Christmas tree.

Elizabeth made sure the kids picked out and wrapped gifts for their dad and his new friend and suppressed the urge to ask questions about what Florence looked like. Or what she did for a living. The curiosity was killing her, but she didn't want the kids to have to answer such ridiculous questions from their mother. They said they liked her, and she was nice to them. And they added since she didn't have children herself, she could buy *them* more Christmas presents. Maybe with Flo around, they would now get a good meal at their dad's.

Ashley and Conner were spending the weekend before Christmas with their dad and his new lady friend, so Elizabeth invited Jack to a Christmas party thrown by a friend from high school. The party was in the neighboring town and since the kids were with Brett for the weekend, she considered this a good opportunity to see how Jack operated as boyfriend material outside of school. Until then, weekend dinners were always only the two of them. She wasn't ready to introduce Jack to the kids yet, but a trial run as a "couple" seemed fitting.

Elizabeth was dressed and ready to go when the phone rang. It was Jack explaining he wasn't going to make it. Apparently, Mella was missing, and her parents had called him in a panic. He said he needed make sure she was safe.

"I'm really sorry. I promise to make it up to you. I'm worried about Mella and her parents are counting on me to help," Jack explained.

Elizabeth believed Mella and her drama were no longer Jack's problem and now questioned whether Charlotte had been right all along. Slow tears of disappointment began to fall as she hung up the phone. She took off her clothes, kicked off uncomfortably high heels, and climbed into flannel pajamas. But after ten minutes of pouting on the couch, Elizabeth scolded herself for allowing Jack and Mella to ruin the night. She swiftly picked the party clothes off the bedroom floor, got dressed again, reapplied the mascara washed away by the tears, and headed to the party. Alone.

The first Christmas party as a solo divorcee could be a bit intimidating. Almost everyone there was part of a couple and there were very few singles. But Elizabeth was determined to make this a positive experience. When handed a large glass of wine, she circulated, reconnected with a few old friends, and jumped into as many conversations as she could without spending much time in a corner by herself. It took effort and practice, but she was determined to appear confident and perfectly happy to be single at Christmastime in a room full of couples. While refilling her glass, a much younger man, definitely in his 20s, stood behind her and introduced himself as Michael, the younger brother of the host. He was so good-looking it was distracting, and she couldn't help but focus on his perfect teeth and the way he smiled when he talked. His white dress shirt was perfectly tailored and clung to him, letting everyone know how much time he spent at the gym. He invited Elizabeth to join him outside while he smoked a cigarette. As they chatted and shivered on the front porch, she realized she had never found the act of smoking sexy. But this man could make anything sexy.

The party was winding down and Elizabeth could feel the effects of the wine so decided to get going. Michael asked if he could walk her to her car and she obliged. She said her goodbyes and thanked the hosts before walking outside into the chilly night with a virtual stranger. They leaned against her car and were suddenly close enough to kiss. And kiss they did. Intoxicated by the smell of cigarettes and his chiseled beauty, they made out like teenagers for about ten minutes before Elizabeth got in her car and drove away, giggling to herself. Job well done, she thought. First successful Christmas party as a single person.

"That will teach ya, Jack. I gave a very sexy stranger my phone number and I made out with him. And liked it. So there," she thought to herself.

Luckily the drive home only took about ten minutes. Her feet hurt from wearing non-sensible shoes, and her brand-new sweater smelled like smoke. She pulled into her dark driveway and was dreaming about climbing into comfy flannel pajamas, when her jaw dropped in surprise. Jack's jeep was parked in her driveway. At 12:30 a.m. When he rolled down his window, he looked exhausted, smiled apologetically, and said, "I needed to see you in person to apologize for letting you down tonight. Do you mind if I come in?" Elizabeth thought to herself, *sure... but do you mind if I just made out with a delicious 25-year-old?*

Jack carried a bottle of wine into the house and they stood in the kitchen while Elizabeth took glasses from the cabinet. He explained somberly about finding Mella in the emergency room after a motorist stopped his car and talked her down from the ledge of a local bridge. She was threatening to jump but later admitted to the treating Psychiatrist she was just crying out for help. That she didn't want to end her life, she simply felt hopeless. She didn't think anyone would miss her. Luckily, she was safely admitted to the hospital where she would stay for an evaluation. Whether it was the wine or the thought of Charlotte's likely smirk when she told her the story, she wondered if Mella was playing everyone just for the attention. Abruptly, Elizabeth stopped herself, ashamed at the thought and conjured some compassion for Mella.

"I stayed with her until she was admitted into a room. I wanted to be sure she wasn't alone. I wanted to be certain she got the help she needed. I can't be the kind of person that simply walks away. It's over between us. It's been over. But I don't know what I'd do if she hurt herself."

Jack looked tired and beaten down, and for the first time since she had known him, Elizabeth was sure his relationship with Mella was over. She felt sad for Mella, lying all alone in a hospital bed. And sad for Jack, not knowing exactly how to help her, considering the circumstances. Now she was clearer about why he continued to try and help Mella, and she was glad he was the type of man who wouldn't turn his back on someone in pain. At that moment, Charlotte's suspicions and conspiracy theories angered her and Elizabeth promised herself she would no longer doubt Jack's intentions.

That night, Jack lit the fireplace and at 1 a.m., they carried their wine glasses to the couch, wrapped themselves in a blanket, and talked about the future. "So, here's a big question." Jack took a long sip of wine and paused before he continued. "Do you think you would want more children someday?"

Although Elizabeth had decided after the divorce that she wanted to focus on her career and did not in fact want more children, she was surprised by her own response. Her heart leapt from her chest, and without thinking, she replied, "With you. I'd have another baby with you."

"I only have one sister and she moved to Seattle when she was in her early 20s. She rarely returns to visit family and I don't have much of a relationship with her. She's a very successful art curator. I always wished we were closer. And always wished our family was closer. And bigger. I guess what I am saying is, I could see myself with a few kids. Maybe even a houseful." Jack laughed as she imagined a loud, rollicking house filed with kids. Lizzy's two, and theirs together.

The late hour contributed to their fatigue, but his kiss ignited a passion they could no longer deny. And as the fire died down, their wine glasses now placed upon the coffee table, illuminated the light of the fire. As Jack and Lizzy took in the moment, knowing they were about to make a promise to one another, their gaze lingered, and their hearts smiled. It was a promise of love, passion, family, and future. They were both ready. His green eyes sparkled with the reflection of the flame and she silently asked the universe to please grant her one wish. "Please keep Jack Murphy close to me, forever," she begged.

Little did Elizabeth know the power such a request would have.

He took her hand and led her to the bedroom. That night was the most perfect night. Life seemed to make sense. They professed their love, made love endlessly and repeatedly, and didn't fall asleep until the sun was about to rise.

———— ((◉)) ————

Although their relationship was moving forward, Elizabeth decided not to introduce Ashley and Conner to Jack yet. They agreed springtime would make the most sense, giving them time together as a couple and time to consider ways they might ease the kids into a new life with their mom's boyfriend. Jack was incredibly sensitive to how they might react. Flo was still in the picture and although they hoped that relationship would help to ease the transition, the kids might feel anxious all the same. Ashley and Conner spent most of their time with Elizabeth and were used to getting all of her attention.

———— ((◉)) ————

Elizabeth bought Jack a watch for Christmas. It took days and multiple trips to the mall to find the perfect one. She floated through the stores like a woman in love, humming to Christmas music and basking in the healthy glow of a new relationship. But this was more than a new relationship. It was a refreshing change of pace. Jack listened to her, trusted her, shared common interests, and most importantly, laughed at her jokes. Eventually, Elizabeth settled on a watch with a light brown leather band and a large silver face adorned with the etched image of a compass. She wrapped it carefully in heavy gold paper and topped it with a red velvet bow.

By the time they exchanged gifts it was almost the New Year. The kids had a nice Christmas with both families, collecting the numerous gifts purchased to compensate for their first major holiday spent as children of divorce.

Brett picked the kids up an hour late on a Friday night, so Jack spent time circling the block and waiting for the all clear.

"I hope you like your gifts," Jack said as they sat huddled next to the Christmas tree. The homemade hot chocolate they whipped up in the kitchen was the perfect accompaniment. It was hard to believe life could *be* like this, they agreed. Friendship, companionship, love, and lust, all wrapped up in one relatively drama free relationship. Almost too good to be true.

"You got me three gifts?" Elizabeth scolded him, but secretly loved it. The first package was wrapped in plain white paper and was personally illustrated with books, pens, and literary images. It must have taken him hours. "I don't want to rip the paper," she said. "I want to save it." After carefully lifting the tape, the most beautiful copy of *Pride and Prejudice* slid out of the wrapping.

"It's an edition you don't have. I checked all your bookshelves. It's a vintage copy from the 1800s." The beautifully bound book was in incredible condition. When she cracked open the binding, she noticed it included exquisite illustrations throughout. Elizabeth hugged him through a few happy tears. Never had she received such a thoughtful gift. "Elizabeth Bennett should have the finest copy of *Pride and Prejudice* a teacher can afford," he said with a sexy smile.

Next, she opened two smaller boxes. One held a lovely paperweight, decorated with a pressed daisy and her initials. The other held a delicate bangled bracelet with a silver book charm. Jack was a thoughtful man who understood her bookish obsessions. True love. There could be no other explanation.

Elizabeth handed Jack the gold box and he commented on the near-professional wrapping job. "Open it, open it," she said to him with the excitement of a child. He began to open the box but stopped unexpectedly.

"Before I open this, I want to say something. I want you to know how happy you make me. I want you to know that having a relationship like this is new to me. One that is fun and thoughtful, and well, simple. I've always had complicated and difficult relationships with women, especially Mella. I didn't know it could be like this. And I'm glad it is."

He kissed her passionately beneath the lighted Christmas tree and feelings of happiness and contentment flowed through them like the healing effects of bright summer sunshine in the middle of a dreary and chilly Friday afternoon. When he finally opened the watch, he stared at it for so long she was worried he had one just like it. Or worse, he didn't like it. Quietly and slowly taking in all the details, he finally looked up with genuine appreciation and tenderness in his eyes and professed, "It's perfect. I love it."

Eleven
2017

S adie planted seeds of both intrigue and doubt that plagued Meghan since her visit to The Seaside Psychic, but she blamed herself for being confused. What did she expect from a psychic in business, making money from tourists? Half the time, she disregarded the entire experience as foolishness and took Sadie for an entertainer who played into the details Meghan shared with her. The other half of the time, she believed her completely and whole-heartedly. There was unfortunately no grey area and Meghan's confusion only intensified.

Either way, Meghan decided she needed to find out once and for all who Lizzy Bennett was. There was the dream she couldn't shake, an old woman who appeared out of nowhere, and mysterious seagulls seemingly sending cryptic messages. Grandpa always told her Kennebunkport was enchanted. And she knew how much he loved the little town, but she always assumed the magical stories he crafted were fantasy that fed into her active imagination. Now she wondered what was real and what wasn't. She climbed the steep attic stairs once again, hoping to find another clue or a simple answer to quiet her busy mind and fantastical delusions. She hoped to put an end to the dreams and bizarre feelings the state of Maine had imposed upon her since her return.

Just before reaching the top step, a vivid memory returned without warning. For a moment, Meghan was unable to move. She was about ten years old, visiting her grandparents in this very house. Her grandfather held her on his lap, rocking in his chair overlooking the harbor. It was springtime and although only a memory, she could smell the flowers blooming as the seagulls soared overhead, calling out to one another. "Meggie, Did I ever tell you the story about Kennebunkport's guardian angel?"

"No Grandpa, tell it, tell it."

"Well it's not a story many people know. You have to promise to keep the story close to your heart, and to only share it with people who love this town as much as we do."

With wide and curious eyes, Meghan crossed her ten-year-old heart.

"A long, long time ago, a very beautiful and kind woman who lived here in town had magical powers. She loved every corner of this town, especially the tidal pools you love to play in, the walking trails filled with amazing flowers and tall trees, and of course the ocean we are all lucky enough to call home. She had the kind of powers that could help people when they were sick, make them happy when they were sad, and just by placing her hands upon a sick animal, could make them well again."

"What did she look like, Grandpa?" Meghan asked. "Did she have a magic wand?"

"She had long, flowing brown hair and it often had flowers woven in here and there." He demonstrated by showing Meghan on her own hair. "I don't remember a magic wand, but she had captivating blue eyes and the most beautiful thing about her was her heart. People knew they could go to her with their problems and she never turned anyone away."

"Was she your friend?"

Meghan's grandfather laughed and continued to rock slowly in his chair, "No, I wish. But I have seen her a few times here in Cape Porpoise. I never knew her name, but when an old fisherman told me the story when I was just a boy about your age, he called her the guardian angel of Kennebunkport."

"Is she still here, Grandpa?"

He looked out toward the stillness of the harbor and said, "I believe she is Meghan, I believe she is. You just have to believe in her, and maybe, just maybe, you will be lucky enough to meet her one day."

Meghan, now holding on to the attic railing, was amazed at how quickly she was transported to her childhood and how vivid the experience. The memory left her light-headed and bewildered. Unexplainably, she was able to relive the experience with almost perfect recall and felt the loving hands of her grandfather on her head as he showed her just where the guardian angel wore wild flowers. The magic in the air around her ten-year-old self was palpable. Maybe there was good reason to believe in Julia, after all. Taken aback, she finished her journey to the top of the attic stairs, hoping to find answers to her many questions.

Meghan, photo in hand, marveled once again at the happiness emanating from the picture taken so long ago. Jack held Lizzy in a room unfamiliar to Meghan, and she knew her father went to college at James Madison University in Virginia, so it was very possible the photo dated back to his years following college. After anxiously digging through three of her father's boxes and finding nothing, the fourth box contained something completely unexpected. There at the bottom of a box that held his college degree, old family photos, and a portfolio of his sketches, sat an envelope. A letter, she assumed, addressed to Lizzy Bennet of Virginia. Of course, she knew she shouldn't violate her father's privacy by reading the letter, but she needed to solve the mystery once and for all. For her own mental health. Unable to help herself, she quickly turned the envelope over, only to find it was sealed. The letter to Lizzy was sealed, addressed, and stamped, but never sent. It made no sense. Why would he write her a letter, but never send it? She had to know. And she had to know now.

The guilt lasted only a fleeting moment, before Meghan ever so carefully lifted the letter out of its envelope, ignoring the warm temperatures in the cramped attic. Although the night air had been perfectly still before this moment, an unexpected ocean breeze floated through the open window and wrapped its arms around her in a gesture of kindness and support. Grateful for the charmed embrace, she silently thanked the soul of the wind for its sudden friendship.

Twelve
1991

A shley's soccer practice ended late on what was supposed to be an ordinary Wednesday night. Little did Elizabeth know as she ushered two dirty, cranky, bickering kids into the house, this Wednesday night would soon change the course of her life and go down in her personal anthology as anything but ordinary.

The kids talked their mother into a trip to McDonald's after practice and they pulled into the driveway behind the typical bath time and bedtime schedule. It was after 9 p.m. once two exhausted kids were finally tucked in, and the house was blissfully quiet. Elizabeth stepped out of the shower and wrapped herself in her favorite faded pink bath robe, and suddenly heard the phone ring. She thought about letting the answering machine pick up but didn't want to wake the kids.

It was Jack.

"I really need to talk to you."

His tone was serious and his voice low. She sat down on the side of the bed, still not completely dry from jumping out of the shower.

"Okay, the kids are asleep. I can talk. What's wrong?"

"I've spent the afternoon dealing with something and I have no idea how to tell you this," he stammered.

"Just tell me, Jack." But he didn't respond. "Jack, are you there?"

After an awkward pause, he said, "Lizzy, I have a child. A two-month-old baby girl. Her name is Meghan. Apparently, Mella had planned on keeping this from me, but she changed her mind and wants my help. Mella moved to Maine to be with her parents, and now I know why."

The silence was deafening, and as the seconds passed, Elizabeth's chest tightened, and she felt like she was going to be sick. Before this moment life was too good to be true. Mella had moved to be with her parents, Jack had no contact with her and their lives were almost perfect. Even Charlotte was optimistic when she learned the news and said, "Maine, well that's perfect. She's practically moving to Canada. She'll certainly be out of your hair." How tragically wrong she was.

"How is this even possible, Jack? Does the timeline match up? Are you definitely the father of this child? Could she be lying to you? Obviously, anyone could be the father."

"Trust me, I've spent the last five hours trying to get to the bottom of this with her. The hard truth is yes, it is possible. Just before we broke up, about a year ago, we were together one last time. I'm so sorry but it seems like yes, the baby is mine. And I told her that the minute I arrive in Maine, I'll be getting a paternity test, just to be sure. She insists she hasn't been with anyone else."

All Charlotte's conspiracy theories and doubts about Mella and Jack rushed violently to the forefront of her mind like a runaway freight train. She trembled as she spoke. A sharp pain landed squarely in the center of her forehead. She told him it couldn't be true. She told him she didn't think the baby was his. She peppered him with questions about the last time he spoke with her and demanded details about the last time he slept with her. For the first time since they had known one another, they shouted, argued, and talked over each other. After a grueling exchange, a few moments of silence settled between them. Elizabeth could feel tears begin to stream, uncontrolled, down her face. He was the first to speak, possibly hearing or sensing the quiet sobs on the other end of the line.

"Listen, you don't know how sorry I am, Lizzy. You don't know what the last five hours have been like for me. I tried to convince Mella to move back to Virginia, but she refuses. I thought about asking you and the kids to move to Maine, but they can't leave their father. And if I were Brett, I'd never consent to that anyway. Conner and Ashley deserve their father. And now, Meghan deserves hers. I played out every possible scenario. Nothing works." He paused, before sharing the unthinkable. "I've decided to leave *Harborside*, give my notice, and move up north to take care of my baby girl."

"What? Why? There are plenty of ways you can co-parent with Mella. You're only a plane ride away from her and the baby. Or a long car ride. If the baby is even yours, that is. Have you seriously decided to move for a baby that might not even be yours? To Maine?" Elizabeth's voice was filled with desperation and dread.

"Lizzy, I'm pretty sure the baby is mine. And I'll get

confirmation as soon as I arrive. But I have to be there. It's a ten-hour car ride, at least. Flights are expensive, and you know we would start out with the best of intentions, but we wouldn't be able to sustain that. I won't exactly be around the corner. And if I stayed to be here with you and the kids, I'd miss raising my daughter. This is something I have to do. I'm so sorry." His voice was somber but eerily confident in his decision.

She didn't remember the last words they said to each other before they hung up the phone. He didn't tell her he loved her, that much she recalled. Elizabeth, feeling like her world had been tipped upside down, cried herself to sleep. On top of her bed, the covers untouched, in a damp robe, in the fetal position, on what was supposed to be an ordinary Wednesday night.

The emotional pain was more than Elizabeth could bear, and she called in sick the next day. A substitute teacher would take her place and her students would be thrilled to have an extra day to prepare for their quizzes, papers, and tests that were scheduled. Ashley and Conner were told she had a terrible cold and sinus infection, which explained their mother's red swollen eyes. And since she looked and felt like she had the flu, the story was wretchedly believable. Elizabeth made the kids a breakfast of scrambled eggs and bacon and promised to drive them to and pick them up from school herself. They were thrilled with the surprising arrangement and chattered away as if nothing at all was wrong. She drifted through the morning like a zombie and came home to an empty house where she climbed back into bed and slid beneath the covers, fully clothed, until it was time to pick the kids up from school. If she didn't have children to take care of, she would have stayed in that faded bathrobe, looking and feeling like she had the flu, for many more days. Maybe Charlotte had been right from the beginning. Mella had played her cards just right.

The very next day, in a fit of anger and disappointment, Elizabeth impulsively scribbled a short note she left on Jack's desk he would take with him on the day of his departure.

> *Jack–*
> *You are right. This could never work. Mostly because you seem to be focused on getting to Mella as quickly as possible and aren't even willing to come to a reasonable compromise. You have decided to become a dedicated father to a child you are not even 100% certain is yours.*
> *I am mad at myself for investing so much into a future we will never see. And as much as I love you, I agree that walking away completely is probably best. And although I am incredibly disappointed, I wish you and your new family nothing but happiness. And I wish the same for myself. Now that I know what happiness looks and feels like, I only hope I will be able to find it again.*
> *Goodbye, Jack–*
> *L*

They hadn't spent years spent building a life together, so why was the idea of Jack leaving so devastating? In the end, it wasn't a tragic loss of a man who entered her life and helped raise her kids. In fact, he had not yet even met Ashley and Conner. It was that, for the first time in her life, she was truly happy, felt loved and respected for who she was, and had felt sure she would spend the rest of her life with Jack Murphy. Her soulmate.

But it wasn't meant to be.

Thirteen
2017

C overing her devious tracks, Meghan was careful not to disturb the seal of the envelope so much that she couldn't effectively put it back together. She worked slowly and methodically to unglue an almost thirty-year old secret.

Dear Lizzy,

Maybe this letter is just an inexpensive way to work through my emotions, regrets, and fears. A private and cowardly way to tell you things that need to be said, I suppose. Yesterday, I found out that I have a child. A two-month old baby girl, who lives more than ten hours away. The hardest thing I ever had to do was tell you. In retrospect, I shouldn't have told you this news with a phone call. You deserved to learn this in person, but I wasn't thinking clearly. Though, I am glad I didn't have to look into your eyes and see the pain I had caused. Knowing that for the first time since we had known each other, I not only couldn't help you with your pain and disappointment, but I single-handedly caused it. I could hear the tremble and anger in your voice. I know you think there is another way to solve this. But there isn't. Our children need to come first and a long-distance relationship would never work. Even you agreed to that. If Brett would agree to you and the kids moving to Maine, or if Mella agreed to come back to Virginia, we could have worked this out. But the harsh reality is, we will be ten hours away from one another, raising our kids who are the first priority.

Lizzy, you need to know that I had plans for us. I imagined us getting married and growing old together. I imagined loving your children as if they were mine. I imagined being there for you like Brett never was. And protecting you. Not that you need protecting. You are strong and smart, and you will move on from this and do amazing things. You will probably marry a great guy. A man I will look at from afar with envy. Knowing that should have been me.

You will always be my only true love and my biggest regret. I love you more than I deserve to say given our circumstances. To be fair to you, I have made the solemn promise to never again tell you that I love you. I will think it, I will record it here, I will whisper it before I fall asleep. But I will never speak the words aloud to you. It would be unfair because you need to move on. And If I want for nothing else in this world, it is for you to be happy.

I will be leaving Harborside and I think it is best that once I leave, we don't contact one another. You deserve so much more.

There is only one week left before I pack my belongings and move to Maine to raise my daughter with a woman I don't love. Only my love for Meghan drives this decision and all future decisions. She may be the only child I will ever have, and I will dedicate my life to her safety and well-being. Mella is not stable. I need to be there to pick up the pieces if she decides motherhood is not for her. I need to be by her side to make sure she takes parenthood seriously and stays healthy.

Mella and I loved each other at one time, but not now. All we have done is fight since she called me to tell me about Meghan. Apparently, she intended to keep the pregnancy and the baby from me and decided only recently that I should bear the responsibility. She has decided I should be supporting her and Meghan. She doesn't even love me. It is going to be a long road. I am angry and sad, but at the same time, amazed and excited about the idea of being a father.

Working in the same school, on the same campus, will make the next week painfully difficult. I woke up this morning with the thought of catching a glimpse of you teaching your 9th grade AP literature class or bumping into you at the coffee maker. Today I noticed you were wearing a new sweater and I wanted to wrap my arms around you and breathe in the scent of your shampoo, but I fought the urge. I felt that same indescribable electricity we experienced that day on the pier. That crazy exciting energy, which I didn't know could exist between two people. That feeling will travel with me back to my home state and will have to carry me to my new life.

I am a father now. Although I wish with every fiber of my being this baby was ours together, I cannot turn my back on my child.

Missing you already,

Jack

Meghan's heart ached in her chest because she realized

that after all this time, the woman he loved, or possibly still loved after all these years, was his greatest regret, because of her. Would he have lived happily ever after with this woman if she hadn't been born? Is this Lizzy his beautiful, free-spirited soul mate she pictured as a child? Now her dad was lonely and possibly still missing this mystery woman. All while her yogi mother enjoyed her most recent jaunt to Costa Rica with her long-haired boyfriend, 15 years her junior, without a care in the world. It hardly seemed fair.

But there was another confusing detail. He wrote that he found out about her when she was two months old and didn't know he was having a child before that time. How was that possible? The letter was dated almost exactly two months after the day Meghan was born. Was her father not present for her birth? How did he not know her mother was pregnant? Her head spun with confusion.

It took Meghan one sleepless night and a full day to decide what to do next. She wanted to talk to her dad, but she wanted answers from her mom, too.

She texted Elliott and asked him to meet her in Bidderford Pool after work, where the small beach and tidal pools would be less crowded. It was off the beaten path and they would have fewer tourists milling about. It was after six o'clock by the time he got out of work and evening had settled over the coast, but the sun was still warm, and the pale blue sky remained littered with the fluffiest white clouds.

Meghan brought the letter with her and read it for the one hundredth time, this time aloud to Elliott. Patiently, he let her finish before he said, "Do you really think reading the letter was a good idea? It seems like it has created more

THE MAGIC OF MISSING YOU

questions than answers." He grabbed her hand and squeezed tightly, letting her know he was there for her.

"I desperately needed to read the letter. How could I not? In fact, I dug through the attic for a few more hours hoping to find another letter, pictures, more clues, anything. But I found nothing else. A single letter, and a single photograph, leaving me wondering if my life is a lie. Leaving me wondering how my father did not know about me until I was two months old." Elliott tilted his head away from the sun and shaded his eyes with his hand, "I guess anything is possible. But I don't think you should jump to any wild conclusions," he said in his typically calm and annoyingly logical manner.

Elliott and Meghan had been dating steadily for about five months and when he and Jack hit it off fabulously, she knew Elliott was a keeper. He was smart and easy-going, flexible and kind. He even invited Meghan to Boston to meet his Indian parents, who may have wanted him to meet a nice Indian girl, but they were kind enough to never say so. They were gracious and lovely, and made jokes over dinner. Elliott said his parents were quite modern and didn't hold to traditional standards. She could see that Elliott got his calm and steady personality from his father, and his thoughtfulness and good looks from his mother. His calm demeanor had yet to rub off on Meghan, but she remained hopeful.

"I need to talk to my parents. Soon. And separately. Get their answers, understand what happened and try to move on from this, so I can stop seeing and imagining things. Maybe even forget about Lizzy. Dad must have."

They stopped at the edge of a tide pool and watched a few crabs scurry through the pools at low tide on the breezy day. Meghan bent down to pick up a piece of sea glass, pale blue in color, in the shape of an almost perfectly formed heart, and wondered if it was placed there to remind her how much her parents loved her. Or, if once again, she was creating an alternate universe wherever she went, seeing common things in uncommon ways. It was dizzying being this confused.

As she stared intently at the sea glass and ran her fingers over its smooth surface, Elliott said, "Do you think it's possible that finding that picture and the letter has clouded your thinking? And now to finally learn that your life's story isn't exactly as perfect as you thought it was has taken its toll on you?"

She shrugged sadly, and accepted Elliott's warm embrace as the inviting sand and the icy, cold Maine water ran through her toes and grounded her to the earth in a way that was not only stabilizing but comforting. She buried her head in his chest, and as she exhaled a deep breath, Elliott allowed her to cry quietly for as long as she needed to. He held her tightly in the late day sun while she thought to herself, "Everyone needs an Elliott."

As a seagull circled above, she no longer wondered why he was there.

————)((◉)) (————

She waited until she knew Dad would be at his painting class for a few hours and checked the time in Cost Rica. After four rings, she was about to give up when her mom finally answered, "Hi baby girl, how are you?"

"Hi Mom, I'm good. How is everything in Costa Rica? It has been a while since we chatted. Rather than text, I thought I'd call."

"Did you get the pictures I sent you of our new yoga studio? It's perfectly amazing."

"I did. It looks great, and so do you. You look tanned and relaxed and your hair is longer."

"Oh Meggie, I love it here. I wish you'd come visit."

Since it was physically painful for Meghan to participate in small talk, she quickly summoned the courage. "Mom, there's something pretty serious I need to talk to you about, so if this isn't a good time, or if you aren't alone, maybe we can do it another time."

"No, no Meghan, now is fine. I'm sitting on the patio. Alone. Marcus is teaching a class, so I have time. What is it? Are you okay in Maine?"

"It's about you and Dad. I want to know how you met and how you had me and why you never got married."

Mella sighed, and her daughter could tell she didn't understand where this was coming from but went on to explain a version of what she had already been told as a child. That she and Jack met at a neighborhood block party and fell in love immediately. "We dated for four years before we had you. Our parents were friends and we had many mutual friends and neighbors. In the end, though, we decided not to marry because we tried living together, and as you know, your dad and I are very different people. So, although we were both excited to have you, we ultimately decided to raise you separately."

"Mom, I know all of this. But I'm confused about

something and I expect you to tell me the truth. Why did Dad not know about me until I was two months old? How is that even possible?" A long and awkward silence journeyed from Costa Rica to Maine and back again. "Mom, are you still there?"

"Meghan, I don't understand. Where is this coming from? Did you talk to your dad about this?"

"No, Mom, I haven't talked to Dad yet, but I will. I wanted to call you first and beg you to tell me the truth about when and how I was born. And why Dad didn't know you were pregnant."

"How, I don't understand how..." She couldn't get the words out.

Meghan's voice softened. "Mom, it doesn't matter how I know this. But I do. And no, Dad didn't tell me; he doesn't even know that I know. So please, just tell me the truth."

"Megan, your dad and I had just broken up before I found out I was pregnant with you. It was a bad break up. We'd been fighting for months. I was struggling with depression at the time, so severe, I couldn't get out of bed for days at a time. There were times I even thought about taking my own life."

Meghan could hear the pain in her mother's voice and had to interject. "Mom, how could you have not told me this before?"

"Gee Meghan, I don't know, maybe because it's not something I'm proud of. Those were dark days. I made a ton of mistakes, but I was sick. And no one treated depression like an illness then. You didn't have depression, you were just lazy. Or worse, crazy. At times, I'm sure I fought people who tried to help me. I was young, and I didn't know what I know

now. So, when I found out I was pregnant I was afraid to tell your dad. I didn't want him to feel obligated. I didn't want him to be with me just because I was pregnant. And I knew that's what he'd do."

"So, you didn't tell him. But then you did?"

"Exactly. I thought I could take care of you and raise you myself. Nanna and Poppie said they'd help, and they did. They convinced me Maine was the best place to raise a child and insisted I come home to live with them. But once you were born, it was hard. Really hard. Especially financially."

Meghan couldn't help but think the worst. "So, you wanted Dad to be involved because you needed money to raise me?"

"My God, Meghan is that what you're getting from all of this? Of course not. But it was hard for me to hold down a job at the time, and your grandparents could only do so much. I decided your father should know about you and share in the raising of his daughter. I made a mistake not telling him and I decided to fix it."

She could hear Mella begin to sob. She clearly never expected to have this conversation with her only daughter. While Meghan's heart was partially breaking for her mother, she was also furious for being lied to. Her next words came so quickly, Meghan couldn't take them back even if she wanted to. "Is Dad even my biological father? I mean, can you even be sure of this?"

She held her breath in anticipation and regret for even asking. But she needed to know.

"Mom, are you still there?" But all she heard was the empty sound of a dial tone.

———◉———

Two days after Meghan's conversation with her mother, Mella began to call and text. Meghan couldn't find the strength within to answer her. Maybe she didn't want to know the truth. She had a deadline at work and focused her efforts in a small cubicle on the third floor, looking out over downtown Portland. But her mother persisted, and when an email from her arrived in Meghan's inbox, she opened it with a single click. There in her office cubicle, filled with fluorescent light and crippling doubt, she shook her head and silently snickered to herself as she made a mental note of her email: MindfulMella@costayogi.com. Oh, Mom.

My Meggie-

I don't know why you haven't taken my calls, but I wanted to be sure you had all the information you need and are looking for. I wish you would talk to me, Meghan. I know you must be confused, but the answers to your questions are actually quite simple. Your dad and I loved each other when you were conceived. There was no one else in my life and it is physically and biologically impossible for anyone else to be your father. I promise you this. Yes, your father and I broke up and one week later I found out I was pregnant. If I could do it all over again, I would have told him immediately. We would have worked it out. I have grown to understand that your father is a fair and reasonable man. But, at the time, we were fighting and had broken up for good. I knew he wasn't in love with me anymore and I was depressed and stubborn. I thought I could and should raise you alone. When I realized how wrong I was, you were already two months old. I decided I didn't want you to grow up without a father. So, it was then, at two months old, that I held you in my arms, crying tears of exhaustion from sleepless nights, and phoned your dad. There are absolutely no other details. A few weeks later, your dad moved to be near us, and settled in his tiny home on Grand Street, with the swing out front that you loved so much. We raised you the best we could even though we agreed on almost nothing, but that you know. Please, Meghan, come to Costa Rica and we can talk as much as you need to. I miss you and I am sorry I never told you the whole truth. There are many things in life I regret, but having you was never one of them. You are the thing I am most proud of. Please believe me. Please trust the love I have for you.

    Missing you,
    Mom

Meghan's eyes filled with tears as she looked at the computer screen and realized that she believed her. At least she hoped, with every fiber of her being, that her mother was telling the truth. And if her dad did what he said in the letter, he got a paternity test and became her dad. Just eight short weeks later than she assumed. For the first time in a year, the mystery Meghan created was beginning to make sense. And as Elliott would likely rationalize, there wouldn't have been good reason for either of her parents to share this information with her. With this mystery solved, she quietly wondered if her life would go back to normal. Before the dreams, before the seagulls, before her mind created and imagined magic. Maybe the voodoo foolishness would finally come to an end.

But it didn't. Meghan woke up in her bed on Sunday morning in a cold sweat; another powerful dream. In the dream, she didn't recognize her mom at first. She was standing in the kitchen of Dad's house on Grand Street in Biddeford, trying to help her with her homework. Meghan couldn't make out her face and her voice was unfamiliar. Meghan was about twelve years old and trying to do math homework, but the problems kept disappearing from the page. She called to her mother for help, but the faceless, ghostly woman didn't respond. Her father entered the room and calmly said, "Just ask Lizzy; she can help you." Mella screamed out in anger and vanished. Standing her in place was Lizzy, the beautiful author from the photo in the attic; from her father's past. The same woman from the park in her first dream. This time, her features were clear and when she called her name, she answered. Lizzy lovingly sat down next to Meghan, set a hand on her shoulder, and the math problems appeared on the page, perfectly solved. Jack beamed with pride and handed Lizzy a gift. A small wooden seagull, he had carved with a tiny knife. In the dream, he handed her the same painted seagull, with the initials EB, that sat upon Meghan's windowsill overlooking Cape Porpoise harbor. The same seagull left by her magical visitor.

Fourteen
1994

The literature classroom at *Harborside* had changed little over time. Students came and went, desks occasionally repositioned, posters on the classroom walls updated, but the curriculum, the academic expectations, and the high stress environment to be the best of the best had not. And almost three years had passed since Elizabeth last saw or spoke with Jack Murphy. It felt like both a minute and a lifetime had passed as she gazed out her classroom window. She felt decades older and wiser. When they agreed not to contact one another, emotions were high, and Elizabeth never expected either one of them to keep such a ridiculous promise. But that was three years ago. Every day she thought about calling him or trying to find him. She spent hours writing him letters she would later tear up or toss hopelessly into the fireplace. To this day, none of it made sense to her. She could only guess that he found out the baby was his and decided to stay in Maine. Even if that were the case, they could have found a way. Unless, of course, Charlotte was right all along, and he simply returned to Mella and was raising his family in Maine.

The sun's rays shone brightly through the classroom and although it was still March, the temperatures were seasonably warm in Virginia. The last period bell rang, and within three minutes the halls were joyfully silent. Elizabeth walked slowly through her now empty classroom, gazed down the wonderfully empty halls, and wondered how was it possible for something to be the best thing that had ever happened to you and also the worst thing that has ever happened to you? Elizabeth imagined Jack walking through the door more times than she could count, waited for the phone to ring, and checked the mailbox for a letter that never came. While she missed him terribly, anger was an even stronger emotion. She thought about Meghan and assumed she was a healthy toddler, talking up a storm and giving everyone a run for their money as three-year-old's do. She wondered if she had Jack's messy, sandy brown hair and green eyes. She pondered whether Jack and Mella were married. She supposed they were.

Charlotte's head suddenly appeared in her doorway, "Hey lady, I can't believe in just a few months you aren't going to be haunting this school and this classroom anymore. What am I going to do with the old man they're replacing you with?"

"He's not an old man. He's probably in his early 50s. That doesn't qualify him for Medicare just yet. He seems lovely."

"Yeah, yeah, well either way I can't expect him to gossip and share a bottle of wine with me on a school night."

"Or can you," Meghan said with a sly smile and a giggle. She was going to miss Charlotte the most. They had already agreed to stay in touch, but she was worried. Charlotte was single and free to travel and explore the world on school breaks. Her weekends were filled with scandalous experiences she didn't have to plan or apologize for. If she didn't have this time with her in school, she was afraid they would simply drift apart.

They plopped down on classroom chairs across from one another and shared a huge piece of coffee cake left in the teacher's room by a thankful parent who had just learned of her son's acceptance into Harvard. "We still have more than two months until the end of the school year," she reminded her, "so I suggest we make them count."

They raised their coffee mugs and Charlotte added, "Cheers to that."

The last few months of school flew by and Elizabeth didn't share her uncertainty with anyone about the decision to leave Harborside. She had conflicting feelings about leaving what had become a safe and predictable job, and some close colleagues and friends. Just when she was hitting her stride, she decided to take a chance and leave the comforts of *home* to teach night school in Alexandria. There were whispers of judgement in the teacher's room about what a tragic mistake it was. Of course, it was hard to admit to them and to herself that she wanted an opportunity to begin again and leave the images, feelings, and longings for Jack Murphy behind.

The last day of the school year was emotional. As students threw their graded final exams in the air in celebration, they left campus in busses and cars with windows down, shouting exclamations of joy. Elizabeth packed her final belongings in two cardboard boxes and stopped to look back at the classroom that began her teaching career, but more importantly gave her a fresh start at life. Now it was time for her to move forward, rather than stay stuck in the past.

As she walked out to the almost empty parking lot, boxes in hand, she hurried to beat a storm about to roll in. Very fitting because a massive cloud of self-doubt had been following Elizabeth for the past few months, like a silently brewing storm, waiting to unleash the fury of wind and soaking failure. Suddenly, a white delivery van pulled up alongside her car and the man inside asked if she knew a Lizzy Bennett. Resting the boxes upon the trunk of the car, she confirmed her identity as Lizzy and he handed over a beautiful bouquet of wild flowers with a pleasant smile and quick goodbye. She was shocked, but assumed the flowers could only be from her parents since no one else called her Lizzy, except of course…

She tore the envelope open and the tiny card's message was typed,

Good luck, Lizzy. Believe in yourself and bring magic to all you do.

There was no signature and she didn't think to get the name of the florist who had already sped off to his next delivery. As soon as she got home, she called her mom and asked if she sent flowers to *Harborside.* He mother sounded surprised as and jokingly asked Lizzy if she had a secret admirer. She assured her she did not. Next, she called Charlotte and a few friends, but no one admitted to sending flowers on the last day of school. She couldn't help but wonder, if after three years, Jack Murphy had finally sent her a message. However, she could not comprehend how he could have known she was leaving her job.

The wild flowers, vivid yellows and oranges, died a few weeks later, but Elizabeth saved the anonymous card and tucked it inside her wallet where she carried it with her, for good luck.

Elizabeth Bennet accepted a job teaching English at an alternative public night school in Alexandria. When she first saw the job positing in the newspaper, she didn't think it would be possible to take a job that would keep her out of the house at night. But at almost 13 and 11 years old, the kids thought it was a good idea, too. They all decided there would be great benefit to having breakfast together that did not consist of a rushed granola bar or a barely toasted frozen waffle on the run. She would make a proper breakfast, like a real mom, and drive both kids to school while still having some daytime hours to herself. Maybe she would write. She had always wanted to write.

Their next-door neighbor Jennifer, a sweet 17-year-old with a driver's license, came to be the perfect babysitter. And the truth of the matter was, the kids got their homework done happily and more efficiently with her at the helm than with their mother, the teacher. Brett even stepped up and offered to take the kids to dinner on Wednesday nights. Cautiously optimistic, Elizabeth decided to keep Jennifer at the house on Wednesdays in case Brett was late or had to cancel. She said she could help with some laundry and light housekeeping while the kids were with their dad. They had a solid plan.

Fifteen
2017

E very time she considered talking to her father about her birth, with the hopes of confirming Mella's story, she realized that doing so would be admitting to a true violation of trust and privacy. Could he forgive her for reading the letter in the attic; his personal property? Should he forgive her? As Meghan walked into the living room, coffee in hand and deep in thought, Jack was putting the finishing touches on his latest painting, crafted in Cape Porpoise. His easel and paints occupied a small corner of the room, overlooking the harbor; a view neither of them ever tired of.

"That's really beautiful, Dad."

"Thanks, honey. It's almost finished. It's missing something, but I'm not sure what."

Tilting her head to the side to examine it further, she added, "Well, it looks perfect to me. Is this scene from the fishing pier?" A photo was clipped to the side of the painting with a tattered clothes pin and appeared to be taken from the end of Pier Road, known for its working fishing boats, lobstermen, and magnificent sunsets. She imagined the panorama at the end of Pier Road must have been the most photographed place in Kennebunkport.

"Yep, by far my favorite place in town." He stepped back and put his hands on his hips to critique his work further.

The painting perfectly captured a lobster boat called the *Mamma G* at sunset, bright yellow lobster traps placed upon the dock, and on the corner of the well-used trap sat a seagull, residing proudly over the early evening's events.

"Dad, have you ever noticed how the seagulls always seem to be hanging around you?"

Before he could answer, the church bells from *The Church on the Cape* that rang on the hour clang seven times, reminding them both that they missed dinner. Recently Meghan read a book, *Peace is Every Step*, by Thich Naht Hanh. Her favorite passage in the book reminded its readers to use church bells to practice mindfulness and to appreciate the present moment. Naht Hanh wrote, "When we hear the bell, we can pause and enjoy our breathing and get in touch with the wonders of life that are around us—the flowers, the children, the beautiful sounds. Every time we get back in touch with ourselves, the conditions become favorable for us to encounter life in the present moment."

Accept life with an open heart and an open mind. *I am trying, Sadie, I am trying.*

They decided to grill steaks and fresh corn from Bradbury's Market and enjoy the cool late summer evening. As Jack grilled, Meghan sat on the porch with her laptop and decided to Google the meaning of seagulls as symbolism.

She stumbled upon a few passages that she decided to copy and save for later.

> *Seagulls symbolize communication with spirit guides. They demonstrate the need for friendship, love, and relationships. Seagulls can teach lessons of resourcefulness, cooperation, and enlightenment. They emphasize important connections to both the physical and spiritual worlds.*
> *These spiritual messengers mate for life.*

Meghan closed her laptop as Jack carried their dinner to the porch and Meghan made a mental note to re-read *Jonathan Livingston Seagull.*

The next day, Meghan walked to her car in downtown Portland after a long day at work and heard her cell phone ring repeatedly but couldn't seem to fish it out of her purse with a coffee in one hand and a notebook in the other. While walking at a brisk pace, she didn't want to slow down since she was already going to be late for dinner with Elliott. She tried to shove the notebook under one arm and feel for the phone, likely at the bottom of her bottomless purse, but it was a struggle. She decided to let the call go to voicemail.

They were having dinner at *Pedro's* and she had she been dreaming about homemade guacamole and a burrito for the better part of the day. There was little Pedro couldn't fix with a burrito and a margarita on the rocks. Mexican food filled her soul with joy. Once she got to the car, she would text Elliott and tell him to grab seats at the bar and have a drink since she would be a few minutes late.

She scurried up the stairs to the third floor of the parking garage, rather than wait for the elevator, and as she started her car, she remembered to check her phone for a missed call or a message. Hopefully, whoever it was left a text message and would save her some time retrieving a voicemail and returning a call. Like she suspected, the phone was buried at the bottom of her purse. Unfortunately, there was a voicemail from a number she didn't recognize. Possibly from outside the country. Meghan intended to drive while listening to the message, however, that wasn't possible. Just before she put the car in reverse, she strained to listen to an unthinkable message. Meghan was frozen at the wheel of her car, alone in a sunless parking garage, while a woman with broken English and a Spanish accent spoke words that were easy to understand but difficult to comprehend.

Hello, Miss Murphy. My name is Sylvia and I am a nurse at Limon Hospital in Costa Rica. I am calling because your mom has been in a serious accident.

The rest of the words were impossible to retain since she was already frantically dialing and trying to reach Costa Rica. The hospital gave her very little information, except that Mella was hit by a car while riding her bicycle. She asked to speak with her mother but was told her condition was serious and she was unable to speak on the phone. Marcus' phone went directly to voicemail each time she tried to reach him, but the nurse assured her that Marcus was with her and her mother was not alone.

Both Elliott and Jack had trouble understanding her

when Meghan called, because she was inconsolable, and her words completely muffled by sobs. Still sitting in the parking garage, unable to move or make sense of the information she just received, Meghan felt helpless. Both her father and Elliott insisted on going with her to Costa Rica, but she needed to go alone. She needed to get there quickly and didn't want a single person to console her. Plus, the last thing her mother needed to deal with was Jack, her ex-boyfriend, or Elliott, a man she had never met.

Before leaving Maine, Meghan decided to stay in Costa Rica for as long as it took to help her mother heal and she needed to be alone for that. Elliott booked her flight and drove to Portland to rescue her from behind the wheel of her car and escorted Meghan to the airport. Slumped in an uncomfortable chair at the airport, she waited impatiently for her flight to board, so she sent her boss at the station an email and explained that she would need to take a leave of absence to be with her mother. She detailed the seriousness and urgency the best she could with few details to fill in the blanks. And as she hit send, she realized she didn't care if she lost her job over it.

The flight was excruciatingly long. Although Meghan tried to will herself to sleep, she was unable to even close her eyes. Rest was brutally and cruelly elusive. She tried to read, listen to music, clean out her purse, anything at all to pass the time, but nothing worked. She shifted herself in her seat repeatedly, but the minutes felt like hours and the hours felt like days. Meghan couldn't help but wish that she had returned her mother's email. Or called her to talk and let her know that she understood. That she forgave her for keeping their little family secret. A secret that hardly mattered now. She would fix this.

A middle-aged cab driver with a kind face shuttled Meghan to the hospital, and although he spoke little English, he understood the importance of arriving quickly by the declaration of the destination and Meghan's terrified demeanor. The hospital was stark, bright, and difficult to navigate. Megan suddenly wished she had taken Spanish in high school rather than Italian, which she rarely found helpful. When she finally arrived at the nurse's desk on the floor of her mother's room, she learned, in broken English, that her mother had been in a coma since her accident and she would not recover from her head injury. Marcus interpreted the details with as much compassion as he could muster considering his own pain and shock. Apparently, a truck was blinded by the afternoon sun and was unable to see Mella riding her bike home from the farmer's market. He explained, "I insisted that the medical team wait to take your mom off of life support until you arrived. I wanted the two of you to have the chance to say goodbye." Meghan clung to Marcus, a man she barely knew, and thanked him for being there when she couldn't. She wasn't sure she could ever forgive herself for letting her mother die thinking her own daughter despised her.

At her mother's bedside she held her mother's hand in hers and whispered, "Mom, I hope you can hear me. I want you to know how much I love you and how mad I am at myself for not calling you back. You and Dad were the best parents, and I know now you did everything you could for me." Through her tears, Meghan hugged her mother, put her head on her chest, and said goodbye. "This is not how it was supposed to end, Mamma. I am so sorry."

Marcus invited her to stay at their home while funeral arrangements were being made, but Meghan explained to him that she desperately needed to be alone and promised to call if she needed anything. He drove her to a small hotel in town, where she would have her own bed, coffee maker, and four white stucco walls that would shelter her from the outside world but would fail to protect her from her own guilt and oppressive sadness. She shed more tears in a few days than she had in a lifetime.

The ceremony was small but beautiful. Marcus did an amazing job planning a sunset ceremony on Mella's favorite beach. She would not have wanted a traditional ceremony, they both agreed. There were candles, shells, family pictures, and the most beautiful tropical flowers Meghan had ever seen, in colors so bright and vivid, they called more for a celebration than a funeral. She didn't know any of the thirty or so people in attendance, but they all told wonderful stories about how they met Mella when she came to Costa Rica and how she introduced them to Yoga at her studio. As the sun set and the candles struggled to stay alight in the wind, Meghan took solace in the fact that her mother found peace and happiness in this beautiful paradise and was able to leave behind the difficulties she faced as a young mother. Now that she was gone, Meghan believed she might never understand the depth of her mother's experience, though she promised to try.

Once at the airport, Meghan faced Marcus and held both of his hands in hers, "I can't thank you enough for everything. Mostly for loving my mother the way she deserved in a place so stunningly beautiful. And for the service. I know she was there. And I know she loved us both." After a long embrace, Meghan boarded a plane with a large bag of keepsakes and memories of her mother, mere hours after spreading her ashes in the Caribbean Sea.

Sixteen
1998

Teaching night classes to students studying for their GED in a dilapidated town building that stood vacant during the day had surprisingly resulted in a renewed energy and fresh perspectives on education and life itself. While Harborside would forever boast high academic standards and challenged the brightest, the wealthiest, and most privileged, the city of Alexandria produced hardworking adult students who had seen difficult times and had not been born to privilege nor prestige. Elizabeth was impressed by their dedication to their studies and the pure resolve that drove them to improve their lives, and in turn, the lives of their families. She was challenged to find new and creative ways to reach students who found learning difficult in the inner city. Most students were there voluntarily, working to better themselves, but some were there as a requirement of the court or justice system. Four fast years in the city made her a better teacher, but more importantly, a better human being. Or so she thought.

Night school was also single handedly responsible for

bringing her Jonathan. A friendly but somewhat reserved attorney, walked into her small, dusty classroom one Thursday night to check on a student as a favor for a colleague. He needed to be sure that the student, who was in the juvenile court system, was attending classes with regularity. At first, she dismissed Jonathan as a handsome, but stuck-up attorney who wore round-rimmed glasses and corduroy blazers with elbow patches. She turned him down the first two times he asked her to dinner, but he eventually wore her down and convinced her to meet him for drinks on a Tuesday night. He was persistent. Simply put, he was not only a good attorney, but he was good at being kind, good at falling in love, and wonderful at being in a committed relationship. He was good at most things he did. And being with Elizabeth was no exception.

They shared many things in common. They were both divorced, both had children, and both had too many hysterical dating stories to count. The two were engaged a year after they met and married one more year later in a small ceremony with only their kids by kids by their side in a lovely mid-day ocean side ceremony at The Madison Waterfront Hotel. Ashley, almost 18 years old, was getting ready to head off to Boston College for her freshman year, and Conner, a rowdy and sports-loving 16-year-old, had just gotten his driver's license. Both were happy and supportive, but it was obvious they were each more involved in their own lives than in their mother's, which Elizabeth assured herself was developmentally appropriate. Audrey, Jonathan's daughter, stood with Ashley and Conner as a 22-year-old graduate student enrolled at George Washington law school, following in her father's capable footsteps at his alma matter.

Elizabeth's wedding dress, made of champagne-colored lace, was boat-necked and knee-length, and tied at the waist with a wide pale pink satin sash that perfectly matched her strappy sandals and small bouquet consisting solely of large pink roses. Elizabeth wore her mother's pearl earrings and she never felt more beautiful and more loved than she did on that day. Never once did she doubt Jonathan's love, commitment, and friendship. At 41 years of age, she finally learned that love should be free of drama. Love should be reliable, steady, and something you should be able to count on. She would always be able to count on Jonathan. As they turned to one another to say their vows, Elizabeth looked into Jonathan's eyes and didn't think it was possible for a man to possess so many of the qualities she had dreamt of. He was everything she had ever asked for. He was everything Jack wasn't.

After returning from a honeymoon in Italy, Elizabeth opened a series of cards and gifts from family and friends with unpacked suitcases still strewn about. Charlotte sent a beautiful card and a Lenox picture frame, perfect for her favorite wedding photo of her and Jonathan on the beach ready to say their vows. Jonathan's sister from Seattle sent a lovely gray cashmere blanket, perfect for reading books on the couch by the fireplace on a fall day. Since they decided to find a home that would be theirs together, they were boxing wedding gifts and packing up her home and Jonathan's apartment all at the same time. "It will be nice to bring these gifts to our new home. A fresh start and new beginning," Elizabeth turned to Jonathan. "Now, all we have to do is find a place to call home."

"How does it feel to be a married woman?" Jonathan

walked up behind her, wrapped his arms around his beautiful wife, and placed teeny kisses on her neck, giving her butterflies as she organized bills, gifts, and two weeks' worth of mail.

"It feels amazing, but it'll feel even better when we're finally settled in our new home," she said with a smile. "I can't believe how hard it has been to find the perfect place."

"Let's hit some open houses this Sunday and consider getting a new realtor. I'm not impressed with that lady your mom recommended."

Elizabeth agreed and left the newspaper out with local listings and open houses, so they could go through them over dinner. "How's Chinese food for dinner tonight?"

"Sounds good to me. I have to run to the dry cleaners and to the post office. I can pick it up on my way home," Jonathan added.

Her stomach growled as she waited patiently for both the shrimp fried rice and sesame chicken she ordered, realizing they had both skipped lunch. Changing into pajamas early on a Friday night was a guilty pleasure, especially after a well-orchestrated yet simple wedding and two weeks of blissful but tiring travel through Italy. Life was good, and Elizabeth had no complaints. It felt good to be home.

Over take out containers and half empty glasses of wine, they flipped through the real estate listings, weighing the pros and cons of a townhouse or a single-family home, and reminded themselves they would need enough room for all three kids when they visited. At the moment, only Conner was living at home, but time was flying by and they would likely become empty nesters in a few years.

Jonathan tossed the nearly empty containers in the trash and gave his new wife a peck on the cheek before heading upstairs to take a shower. "I'll finish up down here and head up to bed in a few," Elizabeth promised.

She tidied the kitchen counters and just beneath the scattered sections of newspaper, it appeared she had missed a card addressed only to her. The handwriting was familiar, and when she realized why, the room began to spin, and her heart leapt. A card from Jack Murphy? There was no return address, but it was post marked from Maine, so she ripped it open quickly, and sure enough, found a short note from Jack. Ten years had passed, with not a word, a call, nor a note. And now a small, plain white card adorned only with black ink and his handwriting. Handwriting that, in one abrupt moment, brought her back to dancing in a classroom, and the scent of his skin on hers.

> *Dear Lizzy,*
> *I know it has been years, but I wanted to congratulate you on your wedding and wish you a lifetime of happiness and joy. You deserve nothing but the best. I think of you often and hope that all your dreams come true.*
> *All my love,*
> *Jack*

"All my love? All my love? No way. Not now, not after all these years," she thought to herself. Almost a decade of silence had passed and out of the blue he had the nerve to send a card. She tossed it in the garbage in a fit of bewilderment and anger. But as the card landed upside down in the trash can, she noticed a personalized illustration on the back of the white notecard. A riverside scene was sketched that looked hauntingly similar to her wedding. And perched upon the rail of what looked to be the Madison Waterfront Hotel, sat a single seagull, ready to take flight. Reaching back into the trash, she lifted Jack's illustration out, unable to throw it away.

She headed upstairs but before tucking herself into bed next to her husband, she stuck the note in her purse. "Damn you, Jack," she said to herself.

Seventeen
2017

A small package propped inside the screen door on Langsford Road, caught Meghan's attention. She chuckled to herself, because in Maine that's where deliverers leave packages, whereas in New York, they consider that breaking and entering. She grabbed the package and realized that Marcus had sent something. Probably a few more of her mother's personal items. After a long day at work, she decided to grab a diet soda out of the refrigerator before unlocking a new series of painful memories.

She opened the package using a kitchen knife and removed a note that read:

Dear Meghan,

I hope this note finds you well as you return home with fond memories of your mother. I miss her dearly as I am sure you do. I stumbled upon your baby book and thought you would like to have this keepsake. You were your mother's most cherished keepsake.

Love and Light,

Marcus

Tears of happiness and sadness fell as she took in the once-white, but now yellowed, book with a pink and green spotted giraffe on the cover. Before opening it, she ran her hand over the book she held hundreds of times. She flipped through the pages where her mother recorded her first word (Dada), and that she took her first steps on her mother's birthday when she was 14 months old. Some of the photos were secured with yellowed tape and others were placed in the book, unattached. She lifted one picture of her mom holding her as a newborn in the hospital. She looked young, fresh-faced, and beautiful. She was smiling as Meghan's tiny hand wrapped around her finger. Her mother was beaming. There was no doubt Mella was happy in that moment. The photograph could not lie. Not a single sign of regret or sadness to be found. As she continued to flip through the rest of the book, she noticed there were no pictures of her dad at the hospital. No newborn pictures with her father. By now, she understood why.

Being back home was more difficult than Meghan anticipated. She expertly and stealthily avoided both Elliott and her dad. She extended her work days well into the evening and found little time for either of them. She suspected they didn't understand she was simply waiting for the tidal wave of grief to pass before being ready to talk to anyone. Before being ready for life again. But they were intensely worried. She moved through her days like a hollow, lonely ghost, without a purpose, haunting only herself. She doubted she would ever be able to forgive herself.

"You don't understand," she exclaimed to Elliott, while

sitting on a blanket at Colony Beach. They chose a spot furthest from the few people there enjoying the rocky coastline. "The last words I spoke to Mom were hateful. I asked her if she was sure my dad was my biological father. She hung up on me, and rightfully so. Then, when she tried to reach out to me, I dodged her calls and never answered her email. I was going to write back to her. I just needed time. Now I have to live with the fact that I didn't have time, and let my mother die alone on the side of the road believing her only daughter despised her."

Elliott pulled her close. "Meghan, I think you need to see a therapist or a grief counselor. This is a lot to carry around and you need to heal. I want to help you every step of the way and be there for you, but you've been shutting me out. Besides, I'm not a professional. I'll support you, always, but let's find someone who can really help."

The sounds of the strong waves were deafening as the sun was about to set. "If I could sit here in this place, listening to the waves and leaning on you for eternity, I would. But the rest of the world feels like a threat. It's hard to breathe some days."

Meghan knew she was not the only one who had experienced loss, but it felt that way.

She agreed to seek out a therapist and work with someone who specialized in grief. Maybe it would be easier to talk about her feelings of guilt and shame with a complete stranger. She wished Julia would visit, but even that wish felt ridiculous.

On Sunday, Jack insisted they have breakfast together. She knew her father was trying to help, and she appreciated it. He made his famous pancakes with crispy bacon on the side, which was Meghan's favorite combination as a kid. Even Jack had been sad and more silent than usual; both having taken the shocking loss of Mella hard. Jack didn't know if he was sad for Meghan, for him, or for the two of them collectively. He thought a nice breakfast together might help them both.

"So, I know I've been pretty quiet lately; pretty shut down," Meghan said to Jack as he placed her breakfast in front of her and took his seat at the kitchen table.

"I understand. Losing a mom at your age, unexpectedly, it's devastating. You take all the time you need, honey. We can talk when you're ready. You know I'm a patient guy," he added with a slight smile, meant to make her feel better.

"Dad, I have a question for you."

"Shoot, baby girl. Anything," he replied, casually.

"Well, Marcus sent me my baby book that Mom kept. It starts when I was born and ends on the first day of kindergarten. I remember seeing it growing up, but it's been years. I'm glad I have it now."

"Marcus sounds like a stand-up guy."

"Why is it that you aren't in any of the pictures at the hospital? There are newborn pictures of me with Mom, and others of me with Nanna and Poppie, but none with you." Meghan desperately wanted to tell him all the details about her phone conversation with her mother, because in that moment, keeping that from him felt dishonest. But the only way to get to the truth was to see if their stories matched. She waited while he decided how to tell her his version of the truth. "I need to know, Dad," she probed further.

"The truth is, Meghan, I didn't know I was a father on the day you were born. It's a day I wouldn't have missed, and it tears me apart that I wasn't there."

"You didn't know Mom was pregnant?"

"I didn't. We'd been broken up for a while. I hadn't seen your mom in a little over a year when she called to tell me about you."

"Were you upset?"

"Sure, I was. Upset, confused, and we fought a lot, your mom and me. I came to meet you soon after I found out. When I held you in my arms, everything in the universe aligned for me. It was a happiness, to this day, I can't put into words. You were perfect. I moved to Maine from Virginia where I was teaching to be closer to you and your mom. And the rest is history. A very happy history."

"Why did you and Mom keep this from me?" she asked suspiciously.

"It's funny, because neither one of us ever spoke about it. We never kept it from you intentionally. Maybe we were both pre-occupied with the best way to raise you and we never found the right time to tell you. I doubt either one of us were particularly focused on reliving that. I guess we felt our past mistakes shouldn't affect you and your happiness."

"Dad, if you hadn't seen Mom in a year, how can you be sure that you're my father?"

"Oh, Meghan," Jack said with sincerity as he stretched his arm to reach his daughter's, "You're mine. I'm as sure of it as there's a sun in the sky and water in the oceans."

"Did you have a paternity test? You know, just to be sure."

He thought about his response for what seemed to be

minutes before he answered, and when he finally did, the mystery she was hoping would soon be over, was clearly just beginning.

"I meant to. But when I held you in my arms and looked into your eyes, there was no doubt. You were mine and I was yours. I never needed a test to tell me what was so obviously true."

Eighteen
1999

After moving into their new home, Jonathan convinced Elizabeth to take a year off from work. She had been getting unexplained headaches and after a series of tests, all the neurologist could come up with was 'non-specified migraines.' Since they purchased a modest townhome in a neighboring suburb, they could afford a year without her salary. He was convinced the stress of work and all the life changes could be cured with some well-deserved down time. She only agreed because she was truly exhausted. They moved Ashley into her dorm room and Elizabeth drove back and forth to Boston more frequently than she cared to admit. Conner totaled his first car and was lucky to escape with ten stitches on his forehead but fought with his parents about reinstating his driving privileges. Elizabeth took on a few extra adult education classes and everything had proved to be way too much. Jonathan helped with dinner and shopping, he hired a housekeeper every other week, and did everything he could to help, but the troubling headaches persisted. When she finally agreed to take a leave of absence, he looked relieved, but still worried. What Elizabeth didn't share with him, was that she had been having dreams, which started the night Jack's note arrived. More than once, she threw the note in the trash, convinced it was causing her to relive memories of Jack and the theatrics of their time at *Harborside*. But every time she tossed it away, she travelled back into the garbage, recommitting herself to the memories. And the dreams.

Much to her surprise, Elizabeth had little trouble adjusting to life without a job. Although she asked Jonathan to get rid of the housekeeper, he insisted on keeping her, reminding Elizabeth the point of the year was to rest, not to scrub bathrooms and mop floors. She acquiesced and allowed herself to sleep until 8 a.m. and sip coffee in her bathrobe for at least an hour before starting the day. Since morning television proved to be less entertaining than she had expected, she started having the newspaper delivered to the house and developed a nice morning routine of reading while having coffee and toast with Jonathan. Once he left for work at around 8:45 a.m., she would shower and start her new work, writing. Thankfully, the headaches were becoming less severe and less frequent. The dreams though, not so much.

Her love of historical fiction began when she was a teenager. Elizabeth was fifteen years old when she first read *Jane Eyre*. The idea that a book could transport you to another time and place felt like the greatest adventure one could take without leaving the house. As a child, she would become completely absorbed in her books and treated reading like an out-of-body experience. She was lucky enough to have a mother who loved books as much as she did, and they spent every Saturday morning at the local library.

The thing she loved most about writing historical fiction for adults was the research. You couldn't just throw a few words on the page and hope people liked your book. You couldn't rely on personal experiences or hastily borrow flawed characters from your own complicated life. The trick was to immerse yourself in research, transport to another time, and become an expert on the time-period, or in the event you decided to cover. It felt self-indulgent to bury herself in research and history while avoiding her personal realities, but it proved to be a healing and transformative experience. Once the research was complete, she began crafting her story at the local library and wouldn't leave until she wrote at least five pages per day. When she hit a wall, or had writer's block, she created timelines, outlines, brainstorming webs, and character charts to accelerate the writing process. Her old teaching strategies came back to visit like a helpful old friend. She edited, revised, re-read, and re-wrote until every character felt alive. Allowing the characters in the story to travel with her to the pharmacy and to the grocery store meant they took up permanent residency in her psyche. She knew she looked distracted or as if she was daydreaming, but the truth was, that for the better part of six months, Elizabeth Bennett was living in a creative corner of her own mind, in 1912 with a family travelling aboard the doomed Titanic. Every family member made a separate sacrifice to save the youngest and sole survivor, baby Samuel. Elizabeth treated the novel like a full-time job and finished her first book, *Saving Samuel,* in a little over ten months.

Although the headaches came less often, the dreams arrived with relative frequency. Jack visited her dreams in odd ways. Once, she was teaching a class in a large lecture hall, and he was sitting in the back row. Jack's hand was raised high in the air, eager to say something, and every time she called on him, he disappeared into thin air. In yet another dream, Elizabeth was boarding a plane and every other passenger was Jack, but there were no empty seats. She kept walking and walking to reach the back of the plane, but it continued into infinity. The recurring theme was that Jack and Elizabeth shared some space and although they tried to connect, they couldn't. She felt dreadfully guilty about dreaming about Jack and never mentioned the dreams to Jonathan. She told herself that they didn't mean much, since they never did connect or even touch in her countless dreams. Elizabeth chalked the dreams up to a vivid imagination and shooed Jack into the recesses of her mind, replacing him with 284 pages of fictional prose.

Four rejection letters had already arrived, politely thanking Elizabeth for submitting the manuscript of Saving Samuel, when a letter arrived from a lesser known publishing house, offering an embarrassingly small amount of money and a promise to publish the story. She was standing alone in the kitchen, hovering over a half-eaten tuna sandwich when she squealed with delight. She was about to be a published author and couldn't wait to call Jonathan at work to tell him the news.

"I'm so happy for you, baby." Jonathan's excitement was genuine and traveled through the phone lines. "When I read your story, I knew it'd get picked up. You're a talented writer. Honestly, I think it's going to make a great motion picture. Get ready for fame and fortune, Elizabeth Bennett." He laughed. "Just don't throw me by the wayside when you become rich and famous."

Fame and fortune did not follow and there would be no feature film depicting *Saving Samuel*, but the book enjoyed some quiet success and Elizabeth began to settle into her new life as a writer. One weekend, while in Boston, visiting Ashley, Jonathan surprised her by turning one of their guest bedrooms into a comfortable office, and *Saving Samuel* gave her the confidence to continue writing a second book. When Elizabeth wasn't promoting the book, or attending local book signings, she was researching and writing.

Brighton Books was the first local, independent bookstore to promote *Saving Samuel* and Elizabeth was thrilled when they scheduled a Friday evening book signing. She half expected no one to show up but chose her outfit carefully all the same. She wore a crisp new pink blouse and black dress pants that flowed comfortably passed flat jeweled sandals. She added the large silver necklace that Jonathan bought her especially for the occasion. Elizabeth's mom and a few of her friends were excited for the event, so at least it would appear as if she had a following. Much to her surprise, more than a few people arrived. A small table was set up in the front corner of the store and the local newspaper covered the signing with a nice article and photo.

The store boasted floor to ceiling mahogany bookshelves, adorned with handwritten book recommendations for its customers 'who were known to spend hours perusing and shopping. It was energizing to sign copies of the book and

Elizabeth discussed characters with customers who had already read the story of Samuel. Running on pure adrenaline and bliss, she didn't realize how tired she had become as the night came to an end.

Before the evening concluded, one last woman approached her table. She was elderly and downright adorable. She immediately reminded Elizabeth of her grandmother before she passed away. She took Elizabeth's hand in hers and told her she believed she was a gifted writer and had been following her for many years. Although a brand-new writer, with only one book under her belt, Elizabeth decided not to mention the obvious. She simply smiled graciously and signed the last book of the night. *For Julia, Elizabeth Bennett.*

After four hours, 15 copies of *Saving Samuel* had sold, and Elizabeth signed many more, which would be left at the store for future customers to purchase. As the store was closing, Charlotte arrived with a bottle of wine and two glasses. With the door to Brighton Books locked, they toasted to a wonderful evening, years of friendship, and to *Saving Samuel*. It felt as if the moon and the stars had aligned on a perfectly clear night and for the first time in a long while, Elizabeth Bennett felt at ease.

—((◉))—

There was much to celebrate. A few magazines mentioned the book and highlighted Elizabeth as a promising new author. She also did telephone interviews, and one in-person interview on Channel 8's Sunday morning broadcast. *Saving*

Samuel received some positive reviews and Elizabeth was gaining confidence being in the public eye. Considering all of her self-doubt at the time of the divorce from Brett, if anyone told her she would be a published author, retired from teaching in her 40s, she would have thought them completely batty.

Jonathan and Elizabeth planned a long weekend away in New York City where she was asked to attend a writer's conference, *The National Book Expose*. Although she would be tied up for two days at author events, they agreed to stay two additional days at the Marriott Marquis and enjoy the city for a few days. But, at the last minute, Jonathan learned he needed to remain in Virginia and work on an important case. He convinced Elizabeth to keep the reservation and enjoy a few days of rest and relaxation at the hotel. It was disappointing, but she called Charlotte and convinced her to make the trip and meet her for dinner one night, deciding it would be good to get away for a few days.

The sights, sounds, and smells of the city were exhilarating. Elizabeth lofted her large Vera Bradley tote bag over her shoulder and traversed through the crowd at Grand Central Station, finding her way to 42nd street where visitors like herself felt small and insignificant, but aware that people come here to become somebody. After checking into the Marriott Marquis, she voyaged to the 28th floor where the tiny room overlooked a city of flashing lights. She was missing Jonathan when there was a knock at the door. A tray of chocolate covered strawberries arrived with a tiny bottle of champagne tied with a shimmering golden bow. The note read,

I love you more than you will ever know, Elizabeth. I am so proud of you. I'm sorry I couldn't be there with you. Knock em' dead.

Love,

Jonathan.

Life was good. She poured herself a glass of champagne, kicked off her shoes, and threw herself on the ever so comfortable bed, savoring her first night in New York City as a published author.

Nineteen
2017

They stared at their half-eaten breakfast as Meghan said quietly, almost inaudibly, "You know, this means there's a chance you aren't my father." There were no tears left to cry and the thought she could lose both her mother and her father at the same time was inconceivable.

Jack looked heartbroken but remained calm yet serious. "Meghan, there's no way I am *not* your father. I don't know how to explain it, but the moment I held you in my arms and looked into your beautiful eyes, it was as if a spell was cast upon me. A good spell." He smiled and held her hands across the table. "Trust me, we belong to each other. But you've been through a lot. And I'm so sorry you had to learn about your birth this way. If it makes you feel better, we'll get ourselves to a lab first thing tomorrow."

She accepted his offer and told him that although she couldn't take any more days off from work, she would really like to go to the lab on Saturday. And finally settle the mystery she was carrying with her like a lead weight. He agreed to let Meghan choose a lab and he would be there, ready to prove his devotion and his genetic link to his daughter. She felt a bit better, knowing that for once and for all, she would have an answer.

Jack cleared the dishes and just as Meghan was heading back upstairs to her bedroom he called out. "You know what's funny? When I found out you were born, in some ways it was like all my wishes had been answered. You always hear about women wanting to have babies, but as a man, I desperately wanted babies. And a family. Sure, it's true I didn't expect to have a baby with my ex-girlfriend, but I honestly believed then as I do now, that everything happens for a reason. And you, my daughter, were destined to be mine."

Meghan held her tongue when she wanted to ask if he had ever wanted to get married. Ever wanted to have more children. She didn't have the heart nor the energy to bring up Lizzy Bennett. One family secret per Sunday breakfast seemed enough. For the time being.

———— ((•)) ————

Monday nights were therapy night. Dr. Spellman was young but seemed old for her years. Her clothes were dated, and her long, black, loose skirt hid her legs, and likely her nice shape. Her shoes were unnecessarily chunky and safe, although practical for navigating the hilly and uneven brick roads of Portland. She was kind enough, but serious and completely non-emotional. Probably just what she needed, Meghan decided. Her office sat on the second floor of a brick building in the West End and Meghan went to and from her appointments anonymously, as her office always seemed empty. She didn't think being in therapy in Maine was like being in therapy in New York City, where everyone had a therapist on speed dial.

Meghan held a red velvet pillow on her lap for security as she took in the details of the sensibly modern Portland office space, a *Maine Home and Design* magazine sitting upon the immaculate coffee table. Her appointments each week began precisely at 6:00 p.m. and her therapist's penchant for time irritated Meghan for a reason she couldn't describe. She mistakenly envisioned therapy being like having a chat with a new friend. The therapist giving her opinions like a true friend would. In fact, a little guidance would have been nice. But it was nothing like that. Dr. Lucy Spellman, a psychoanalyst trained at the Center for Modern Psychoanalytic Studies in New York City, posed more questions than she answered, and Meghan wondered if this is what therapy was supposed to be like. With only three sessions under her belt so far, she was still committed to the process and promised herself she would keep at it even though she wasn't sure where it was going. Or if Dr. Spellman was the right therapist for her.

By Tuesday, the work week was moving so slowly, Meghan was looking for things to keep her busy. Unfortunately, those things included long Google searches of her parents, their hometowns, their high schools, colleges, and any information that might lead her to their romantic history. The internet was a blessing and a curse at times like these, she posited. She was one step away from searching for her biological father, when she likely didn't need to. "Complete lunacy," she whispered to herself, staring at her computer screen, "Get ahold of yourself, woman," she muttered into the air filling her cubicle. She also researched Lizzy Bennett further, and learned she would be one of four authors speaking at the *New England Literacy Symposium* for writers in Portsmouth, New Hampshire, in just a few months. She zoomed in on her photo on her website and if her dad was in love with her, she could see why. Lizzy had kind and beautiful eyes, and a smile that beamed, but it was her energy and spirit that jumped out at Meghan at 6:30 p.m. on a Tuesday night. She thought she was alone in her office cubicle when she was startled by a voice.

"Go home and get some rest, Meg. You have all week to catch up on your work. No need to burn the candle at both ends. Get out of here." Her boss Phillip carried his briefcase past her with his coat hung over his arm.

"Thanks, Phillip. I really appreciate it. I'm leaving in a few minutes. I swear." But Elliott was in Boston visiting his parents and she was in no hurry to rush home. She impulsively registered for the writing symposium and decided the day-long workshop was technically work-related and a way to develop her own skills as a writer. She even put in for reimbursement for the $125 workshop fee. If she was going to do a little private investigating and hone her writing skills at the same time, she might as well have the station pay for it.

On Saturday morning, the sun refused to break out from behind the clouds, and Meghan wondered if the weather was trying to tell her something as she looked to the sky. The waiting room was dated and looked more like a country inn than a medical office. Ivory ruffled curtains hung on the windows and a solid oak rocking chair sat in the corner of the room. Maine in 2017 amazed her at times. Ironically, the Bee Gee's *How Deep is Your Love*, was quietly playing in the background. Meghan only hoped their medical equipment was more updated than their décor and choice of music. A simple blood draw should be fine anywhere. Right?

"Dad," she whispered, although the elderly couple sitting on the other side of the waiting room likely couldn't hear them. "What will we do if the news isn't what either of us expect? What if, after all these years, someone else is my father?" She anxiously strung her sentences together without taking a breath, hovering over an outdated *People* magazine.

"There's no chance we aren't related. Think about it," he said, trying to convince her to relax, "that freckle on your nose?" He pointed to the identical freckle on his nose and shrugged his shoulders. She smiled and told him the shape of the freckle was totally different. But he continued, "The way we both sneeze in threes," he added. "The way I look at it, a blood test is completely unnecessary." Meghan rolled her eyes at his sorry and untimely attempts at humor.

"Jack and Meghan Murphy," Barbara, the stocky nurse, called while holding a clipboard. She was straight out of central casting and had likely held the job for at least 30 years.

"Game time," Meghan declared beneath her breath.

"I love you baby," Jack uttered, as he squeezed her hand and stood first, bravely facing their uncertain future.

Meghan followed more slowly.

"How accurate is this test?" she asked the nurse.

"About 90-99 percent accurate, sweetie," she insisted confidently, while placing a piece of gauze and a bandage on Meghan's arm.

Their arms linked together as they found their way to their respective cars parked alongside each other in the expansive parking lot. As Meghan turned to hug him, he broke the silence.

"In a few days we'll be able to put all this behind us," he said reassuringly.

"I know, Dad. I know. I just need to keep the faith," Meghan said, faking a mildly positive outlook. "Have a great time at your painting class. I'll see you tonight."

He yelled over his shoulder, "Love you, Meggie-Poo."

She smiled. He hadn't called her that since she was a little girl, and although she hated that nickname as a teenager, in this moment she secretly loved it.

※ ((◉)) ※

Meghan hadn't taken a yoga class since college, but something called her to Village Yoga on Port Road on a Thursday night. Each night after work during the week, she rushed home only to find a mailbox devoid of DNA test results. She hadn't been sleeping well and her muscles were tight and stressed. So today, she decided to drive directly to a restorative yoga class and save herself the torture of the painful mailbox waiting game. She also admitted to herself that she might be desperate to understand her mom on a deeper level and might be trying to connect to her through her love of yoga. Maybe it was a way to say she was sorry.

She arrived early and as she pulled her yoga mat out of her trunk, she felt like she was being watched. She looked around but saw nothing, however the odd feeling persisted and soon a suspicious tingling feeling came over her body, from head to toe. Her senses were on high alert as she closed her trunk and took another look around. Still nothing. She moved quickly toward the building and as she approached the front door of the yoga studio, Julia suddenly appeared, seemingly out of nowhere. She was desperately hoping to see her again, but the surprising way in which she materialized was less than comforting in that very moment. Her heart began to race, and this time Julia reached out and touched her. It was a warm, soothing touch that calmed her rattled nerves. Julia was as vivid and real as any other person she had interacted with that day. And a welcome sight.

Julia's voice was filled with warmth and gratitude. "I've been waiting for you to come here. Why has it taken you so long?"

Her wrinkled hands were crooked from arthritis and she was unable to stand completely upright. Julia looked lovely, wearing the same green jacket. Her twinkling blue eyes didn't leave Meghan's as she tried to adjust from the shock of her.

"You've been waiting for me? I have been waiting for you," Meghan laughed nervously.

Julia reached into her pocket and handed Meghan what looked like a white rock with jagged edges. It was warm from her touch, and once in Meghan's hands, she felt a slight vibration and an overwhelming sense of joy and calm.

Julia's hands remained on Meghan's. "This is selenite," she stated matter-of-factly. "The name comes from Selene, the Greek goddess of the moon." Meghan watched as Julia's eyes moved toward the sky. "Hold this crystal and keep it close to you," she advised. "It will give you peace and help quiet your mind. It will also help you connect to your mother, but you will have to ask. Listen carefully and look for signs. You will need to open your heart and believe."

Meghan stared in wonderment of this beautiful and generous woman and couldn't help but question why she was helping her. Eventually, she found the power to mutter, "Thank you, Julia." Her sparking eyes flickered, and her smile radiated a warm white light in the darkness of evening.

"Oh, and tuck it under your pillow for a good night's sleep," she added with a wink.

Suddenly, Meghan heard the tires of a car pulling into the gravel parking lot and turned toward the sound. Another classmate had arrived. But when she turned back, Julia was gone. This time, she felt her presence like a soft blanket and allowed Julia's generosity, kindness, and warm embrace to fill her with hope. Hope to connect with her mother, to tell her how sorry she was, and to thank her for being her mom. Hope to learn that her father was not a stranger, but the strong and quiet man who taught her how to ride a bike and who gave her crooked braids before school in the morning, was her biological father. Hope... Julia just handed her hope.

"Thank you so much," Meghan mouthed in the direction of the captivating moonbeams, shining down on her from a cold, wintery sky. She tucked the crystal in the pocket of her sweatshirt and was the first to enter class. She set her yoga mat down in the back corner of the studio and decided to leave her sweatshirt on, as to keep the crystal close to her. Even from her pocket she could feel the joy radiating from the misshapen gift, shared with her in a moment of unexpected magic.

The lights had been lowered for the restorative yoga poses and candles softly illuminated the room. Lexie, the young, grounded yoga teacher, informed the eight or so men and women in the room that she would be lighting celestial incense designed to, "Comfort and support you as you escape from your daily tasks, allowing your stress to leave the body, replacing it with clarity and happiness."

"Sounds good to me," Meghan's inner sarcastic-self responded quietly. Although Lexie's voice was soft and rhythmic, Meghan struggled to relax fully. She quickly refocused her breathing, cleared her mind, and reminded herself to take this seriously and to at least try to approach this with an open heart. Meghan slipped her hand in her pocket and channeled the healing properties of a simple, yet powerful crystal gifted to her by a purely enchanted woman.

They stretched deeply, and held poses for extended periods of time, using bolsters, pillows, and blankets to support and calm them for ninety minutes of pure relaxation and bliss. Meghan sensed class was coming to a close and didn't want it to end. Lexie's melodious and hypnotic voice instructed the class to end their experience in Savasana, lying flat, and to " please silently ask each of your own personal angels and guides to provide you with comfort, advice, and joy." At first, Meghan lay there quietly not knowing exactly what to do or what to say. Then, out of nowhere, she felt an incredible warmth radiating from her pocket. The selenite, prodding and encouraging her to follow the directions. So, she did. As awkward as it was, she silently inquired, "Mom, are you there? Will my own personal angels and guides help me? Will you please send me signs and give me comfort?" She even thanked them. She didn't know who she was thanking or what she was thanking them for, but it felt like the right thing to do.

Miraculously, whether real or imagined, Meghan felt the sensation of angel wings. The soft, plush wings of an angel wrapping her in a loving embrace. As she slowly opened her eyes and let her vision adjust to the dimly lit room, she began to hear muffled words of encouragement directed at the other participants. Foggy white auras surrounded people at the conclusion of their Thursday night yoga class. Angels? Spirits? Speechless and frozen in time, she tried to soak in the details of the experience. It was then, she noticed a tall, thin, elderly man surrounded in white light, standing facing the corner of the room with his back to a young girl in her late teens, rolling up her yoga mat. He stood motionless with his head to the wall as Meghan got ready to leave. She passed him and curiously whispered, "What are you doing?"

To which he replied and nodded toward the red-headed girl now holding her yoga mat and grabbing her water bottle before getting ready to leave, "She never asks for help. I'm here for her, but she never asks."

Twenty
1999

After two days of attending workshops, meeting other authors, signing books, and speaking to agents and publishers, Elizabeth was feeling too exhausted to meet Charlotte for dinner, but didn't dare cancel. She was taking the train in from New Haven, where Charlotte was visiting her sister and her new baby, and the two hadn't seen one another since the book signing a few months prior at Brighton's. Plus, they were both excited to meet for dinner in the city. Since Elizabeth had a little over two hours before their reservations, she slipped off her clothes, took a quick but relaxing bubble bath, and put on a favorite oversized t-shirt to take a nap. There was nothing more indulgent and satisfying than a midday hotel nap. She drifted easily into a deep sleep. But that's when the dream came. And this one was not like the others.

Elizabeth was sitting alone on a towel on a white sandy beach, the warm sun tanning her skin, and the ocean breeze gently blowing her hair. She could feel the fine, silky sand as she buried her feet, and heard the rhythmic sounds of waves crashing in the distance. She was alone but heard someone calling her name. Jack. Approaching from down the beach, it seemed to take him forever to finally reach her.

"Lizzy, I've missed you. I told you I'd come back for you and I have," he said as he held her face lovingly in his hands.

"You came back?" she asked him. "I'm confused. I thought you were gone forever."

He looked deep into her soul. "Gone forever? Don't be silly. I'd never leave you. Not in this lifetime."

But before she awoke and left the dream state, they laid in the soft, warm sand and kissed passionately before removing their bathing suits, and there, alone on the deserted beach, they made love. Again, and again.

Elizabeth awoke disoriented, and took a moment to remember where she was, as evening had already set over the city and the hotel room darkened. She checked the clock and realized she had 20 minutes to pull herself together to meet Charlotte for dinner. She quickly dialed her friend's number and with a sleepy voice, admitted she took a quick nap and would be there soon. She decided on a fitted short black dress since it never needed ironing and added a long gold necklace, a Christmas gift from Conner. After forcing her hair back into a soft but curly ponytail, she quickly applied mascara and lip gloss. As she slipped into her strappy heels, perfect for a night out in the city, she glanced at Jonathan's bottle of champagne and felt dreadfully guilty for a dream that wasn't even real.

"How's the life of my famous author friend?" Charlotte joked as the girls tipped their wine glasses to celebrate their fancy New York City dinner in a loud and chaotic restaurant.

"Ah, well not all that famous. Literally no one knows who I am and I'm one hundred percent sure that's the definition of *NOT* being famous," Elizabeth joked. Charlotte was dressed in a fabulous red mini skirt, heels, and a black blouse unbuttoned low enough to catch the eye of more than one passerby. Elizabeth had forgotten how young and stunningly beautiful Charlotte was. How easy it was for her to be the center of attention in any room. When Elizabeth left her hotel room, she felt sexy in her little black dress and strappy heels, but in comparison, she suddenly felt like the 40-something, married woman she was.

"So, how's *Harborside* these days? Any new gossip?" she asked, genuinely interested and missing the drama of the school.

"It's been kind of quiet these days. Not much going on. Oh, except Mrs. Carver, the office manager was fired. Rumor has it she was drinking on the job."

"Scandalous," Elizabeth added with intrigue as she took a sip of wine.

"Not really, I suppose it's only scandalous because she got caught. Apparently, she was tipsy at noon and knocked over a large crystal vase filled with fresh flowers in front of a VIP parent. She was asked to leave at the end of the day and not return. They escorted her to her car."

While Elizabeth listened to Charlotte's stories about school, she wanted to tell her about her dream but as dinner arrived, decided against it. They ate their dinners slowly and ordered a second bottle of wine. "Hey, we aren't driving, and we haven't done this in forever," Charlotte defended the arrival of bottle number two.

They talked about the kids and their families and Elizabeth realized how much she missed her good friend. After draining another glass of wine, she blurted out, "I've been dreaming about Jack lately. A lot."

"Shut up. The ghost of Jack Murphy is haunting you? I have to say, it's a little shocking because Jack doesn't hold a candle to that delicious lawyer husband of yours."

"Charlotte, please. This has nothing to do with Jonathan. I think I'm having dreams because he sent me a note of congratulations on my wedding."

Charlotte took a long sip of wine and looked at her friend over the rim of the glass, "Right, because it's so indecent that he'd send you a card. I bet you received a bunch of cards. He just happens to be someone from your past. No big deal."

Elizabeth sighed and almost agreed. "But he signed it, *All My Love*, Jack."

"Oh, Elizabeth. I think it's normal to have a few steamy dreams about an ex. Don't make too much of it. Seriously, you have everything going for you… a great career, amazing kids, and a hunky husband. You win, my darling," she exclaimed as she lifted her almost empty glass in the air.

Elizabeth felt better, as she usually did, after dinner and drinks with Charlotte. They stood in front of the restaurant, said their goodbyes, and held a long embrace before Elizabeth made sure she was safely in her cab before walking the four short blocks back to the hotel. It was only just after 11 p.m. and a reasonable time to be walking home alone from dinner in New York City.

Still a little tipsy, Elizabeth stepped into the lobby of the hotel and noticed a man holding her book. Focused on the cover design of *Saving Samuel* and still wishing they had let her choose the color of the book jacket, she looked up. The man, now closer, took a step toward her, and as she raised her eyes to his, he was smiling. "Hi, Lizzy."

It was Jack. And it wasn't a dream.

"Jack, what are you doing here?" she asked as the lobby of the Marriott Marquis, possibly the busiest hotel in Times Square, suddenly became much smaller and quieter. She didn't know if it was the wine or Jack's presence that made the rest of New York City disappear into a haze of nothingness.

"I was hoping to get my book signed," he said with a crooked, sexy smile while holding *Saving Samuel* in the space between them. They could both feel the same familiar warmth, electricity, and feeling of total and complete happiness just by being in the same space.

"This is completely crazy," she added, without taking her eyes away from his. "I never expected to see you again. That was our agreement."

"I know, but I couldn't help myself. It's been over ten years, and I decided I'd come to New York to see you. See if you were okay. Happy? I wasn't even sure whether to let you know I was here. But when I realized you were alone, I thought maybe we could talk. Catch up, after all these years."

"Oh, Jack. I don't know." She finally turned her gaze to the floor, and as she shifted her feet, she lost her balance, slightly. When he grabbed her arm to steady her, a jolt of electricity ran through her body and she struggled to stay focused.

"Let's just have one drink, here at the hotel bar. It's great to see you again. I've been following your career and have always been so proud of you. I had no doubt you'd do something amazing with your life. One drink and I'm on my way."

"Until the next ten years?" she asked.

"Nine," he muttered under his breath. "It's been 9 and a half years," he said as if he had been methodically counting the hours, days, and years.

Being next to Jack in the elevator that took them to the 8th floor lounge overlooking Times Square, was equal parts terror and delight. She thought about Jonathan and whether he had left her a message before innocently tucking himself into bed. Their marital bed, just a few hours away from the chaotic moment she found herself wrapped in. As the elevator doors pinged open, they stepped into a crowd of people who moved about as if it was noon rather than midnight. They found their way to a small table for two by the window and sat down across from one another blending in with the New York City nightlife. Beneath them, Times Square pulsated, flashed, and loudly celebrated itself. Elizabeth was uncomfortable and comfortable, sad yet filled with joy, confused but crystal clear. Turning down another drink, she ordered a club soda with lime and was determined to keep her wits about her around Jack Murphy.

Jack showed her pictures of Meghan who was almost ten years old and explained that his little girl was a bit shy but got straight A-grades and loved to read and dance. "She's the best thing that's ever happened to me," he said while looking longingly at a picture of her from a dance recital when she was eight years old. She was wearing a white leotard and a pink tutu with long, dark uncombed hair and large dark eyes. Elizabeth suspected she looked like her mother since she saw little resemblance to Jack.

His words stung as she tried to decode the meaning of such a statement and was still processing memories of his departure when he took her hand in his and looked her in the eye. His strong but soft touch was more than she could handle in the moment.

"Lizzy, I've missed you. I can't tell you how many times I've looked at Meghan and wished she was yours. Ours. I imagined us as a family, taking trips, having dinner together on a school night, reading stories before bed."

Elizabeth interrupted him. "How does your wife feel about that?"

"Wife? Mella and I never married. We weren't in love and didn't pretend to be."

"Then, why..." As if reading her mind, he finished the question she was having trouble generating.

"Why didn't I come back? Why didn't I contact you in all this time? I thought about it, so many times. But decided it wouldn't be wise for anyone. I wouldn't be able to give Meghan or you, or us for that matter, one hundred percent. My daughter deserved the best of me, and you deserved to find someone who wouldn't split their time and raise a child with someone else in another state. You deserved better, Lizzy."

His words didn't make her feel better and she certainly didn't agree with his logic. It made her a little angry until she reminded herself that it didn't matter anyway. She was a married woman. Married to Jonathan, who loved her unconditionally, steadily, and without drama. The Lizzy and Jack of *Harborside* were not meant to be. Jack was still the intense, rumpled art teacher she once knew who had earned a few grey hairs and some wrinkles at the corners of his soulful green eyes, over the course of a decade. The years had been kind to him and he was still the man she fell in love with once upon a time. But now, Elizabeth realized he was not the person she could have built a life with. He was merely the person she needed him to be at that time and place in her life. She wondered if her own desperation and hope created this decade long obsession over what could have been. It would have been far less exciting and tantalizing to admit to herself that Jack Murphy was simply ordinary.

She told him stories about Ashley and Conner and he admitted regretting never having met them. He said he thought about them all the time and often wondered how they were. Again, Elizabeth had mixed feelings because something deep inside of her believed he could have met them. Could have been part of their lives. She reminded herself that he chose not to, while at the same time being swept away by the undeniable chemistry still present, and sitting between them, like an unwelcomed guest. Her dilemma was such that she just couldn't decide if he was ordinary or extraordinary.

It was almost 3 a.m. and they decided the night should finally come to an end. Jack insisted on walking Elizabeth to her hotel room door even as the hotel continued to buzz with activity. They walked slowly and as room 2812 came into view, they stopped to face one another. Goodbyes were always difficult, but this one would prove to be agonizing.

Jack looked tired and vulnerable, so Elizabeth spoke first. "Jack, as tough as this was, it was good to see you. Good to hear your voice and know that you and Meghan are doing well. Maybe we'll do it again in another ten years," she said with a sad little smile.

Jack looked at her like he wanted to say something but didn't. A few moments passed as they stood face-to-face in the hallway of the 28th floor of the hotel, eyes locked, unable to say goodbye.

Twenty-One
2017

The overwhelming positive emotion of the evening allowed Meghan to temporarily forget about the results of the paternity test, even if for a brief snapshot in time. She could no longer feel the support of angel wings but was doing her best to keep the feelings and emotions alive within her like a cherished gift she hoped to carry with her for an eternity. But she remembered that tonight should be the night the test results arrived, as she pulled into the short driveway made entirely of white crushed sea shells on Langsford Drive, and parked the car. Before exiting her car, she could see her father moving about the house in the brightly lighted rooms, standing out against the dark of night. The clear and cold starry sky reflected its quiet loveliness over Cape Porpoise and she felt a sense of calm she hoped wouldn't be stripped away. Jack had already checked the mailbox and retrieved the letter, so when she walked up the crooked, natural stone path to the front door, she was met with the aroma of roasted chicken and rice, and a table set for two. It appeared as if a tiny, happy family lived in the space and she couldn't help but wonder if this was their tiny, happy truth or instead, some warped version of the truth they all agreed to believe 25 years ago.

"Are they here?" Meghan called out nervously.

Jack handed Meghan an envelope that remained sealed, "They're here. I waited for you."

She nervously held the envelope that contained her fate and looked at the only parent she had left with fear in her heart. "Ready?" she asked.

Jack stood with his hands on his hips, his eyes tired. "Ready, baby girl."

She slowly lifted the neatly folded document out of the envelope and saw an array of numbers first. On the first page, there were tables of data and as she scanned the page, she couldn't decode the information quickly enough for her liking. In a rush to truth, she flipped to the second page and read the final sentence of the report. The sentence that would change her life. Forever.

Our conclusion, based on the analysis of the alleged father, Mr. Jack Murphy, and child, Meghan Murphy, is greater than 99.999% accurate. Based on our analysis it is practically proven that Mr. Jack Murphy is the biological father of Meghan Murphy.

Her body, that just moments ago was filled anger and fear, dropped onto a waiting sofa as her head fell to her knees. She expected tears to fall, and Jack waited nearby, but the waterworks never came. Instead, regaining her composure, Meghan shed only a few happy tears and stood to face her father who simply smiled and opened his arms wide enough to wrap them around his daughter, as it was time for their tiny family to put this chapter of their story behind them.

"Dad, I'm sorry I put us through this, I really am," she finally said when she pulled herself away from his tight embrace.

With his hands firmly on her tiny shoulders he insisted, "You have absolutely nothing to be sorry for. You've been through so much and some of this is my fault. If I'd gotten the test when you were born, like I intended, I would have had the answers you needed. I'm so sorry. I just didn't need that test to know the truth."

Meghan told her father how much she loved and appreciated him.

And that she was starving.

———— «(○)» ————

Meghan spent the next day at work, feverishly writing to meet a deadline. Writer's block had suddenly disappeared, and she promised herself it was time to work on those New Year's resolutions and crush some of her personal goals. She would impress her boss with her latest article on the real-estate boom in Portland, a hip city now known to be the ideal place for singles, young families, and entrepreneurs. She also had to somehow thank Elliott for willingly coming along on this outrageous journey with her, so soon in their relationship. Probably not what he bargained for.

———— «(○)» ————

As the water reached a boil and steam rose above the small stove, Meghan added a box of pasta and stirred carefully, enjoying the mundane task. Making a week night dinner in Elliott's tiny apartment helped her return to a sense of routine she had been desperately missing lately. They agreed she would head over to his place, get started on dinner, and wait for him to come home from a long day at the University. Elliott had been patient and incredibly understanding while she spiraled into the depths of despair and confusion these past few months. She didn't even know what words or actions would be sufficient to thank him. The homemade vodka sauce and the fresh flowers she picked up at the grocery store could be a start. Stirring the pasta once again, she glanced around the apartment, and it appeared to her, the cozy apartment was silent. She opened her laptop and played some music that filled the second-floor apartment with an unassuming delight and interesting possibilities. It felt like home, with John Mayer hovering effortlessly in the background. A home to a very normal, very typical young couple. A nice concept.

"Well *this*, I could get used to," Elliott beamed as he walked through the door, dropping his keys on the hallway bookcase that doubled as a table and spotted the colorful wild flowers on the table and the steam rising from his small stovetop.

"It's the least I could do to thank you for helping me through the wildest and craziest months of my life. In fact, there will be many more of these dinners. As proper payback for my crazy," Meghan concocted a crooked but silly face.

Wrapping her in a hug and a quick kiss, Elliott responded, "No need to thank me, Megs. Life isn't always easy. If I can't be there for you in the tough times, I don't deserve to be there in the good times."

Ah Elliott, so damn reasonable. And so damn cute. While he showered and changed into a grey UNE hoodie and black sweat pants, she placed the bread and butter, caesar salad, and pasta with vodka sauce on the table. She remembered to pick up some freshly grated parmesan cheese and stepped back to admire her work and think about how much she liked this simple life with Elliott. Over dinner, she filled him in on the details of the story he already knew the ending to. How she anxiously opened the letter to find out that Jack Murphy *was* truly Meghan Murphy's dad, made a few Maury Povich jokes, and announced that life could now continue on as originally planned.

Well, almost.

Elliott told Meghan stories about his day at the University and how slow the research process was going and how frustrating some of his colleagues were. Meghan was glad to hear more about his day and his life's stressors rather than constantly focusing on her own. As they devoured dinner and tackled the dishes together, she wondered if Elliott might be her future. Was fate at play when she drove up from New York without having a solid plan? Would Elliott someday tell the story of how he met and fell in love with Meghan in this perfect seaside town? Deep in thought, she dried the last dish, placed it in the cupboard, and smiled when she thought about how smart and adorable their kids would be.

Snuggled on the couch, stuffed from a delicious dinner, and wrapped in a blanket, they spontaneously began talking about places they had each traveled to and places they would still like to visit. They discovered that neither of them had ever been to Key West before and it was on their respective bucket lists. Soon the laptop was propped between them as they searched travel sites for their first vacation as a couple.

Since hotels on the island were pricy, they opted to rent a small loft overlooking busy Duval street and booked their flights immediately. Elliott said booking that trip within an hour was the most spontaneous thing he had ever done and jokingly blamed her for intoxicating him with multiple helpings of her vodka sauce.

It was decided. They would leave for the warmth of Key West in a few months and quickly made arrangements for six days off from the station, from the University, and from a rather chaotic and recently messy life. Meghan fell asleep on the oversized couch, in Elliott's arms and had the best night's sleep since moving back home to Maine.

— ((◉)) —

Unexpected happiness was suddenly appearing all over the place. Although it wasn't exactly *his* art show, the gallery on Pier Road was having their annual open house, and Jack's work was being displayed as a new, featured artist. He had four paintings for sale and on display at *The Wright Gallery*. Meghan dressed in a navy and white polka-dot dress, her hair swept up in a loose bun, and felt like a full-fledged adult, as she readied herself for her father's first art show. It was an exciting night and she glanced at her phone as Elliott's text message announced he would arrive in ten minutes.

Since her dad was already there, setting up and preparing to mingle with neighborhood guests and art connoisseurs, Meghan stood alone in their charming cottage, enjoying the clear views of the serene harbor and feeling light, optimistic, and maybe even blissful for the first time since her mother died. She glanced in the mirror and felt satisfied as she put her earrings in. She was eager to have Elliott see her dressed up and hoped he was at least a little impressed.

"You look beautiful, Megs. Wow, really beautiful," Elliott said when he arrived. He spun her around in her party dress and kissed her like he meant it. She hadn't shared much with Elliott about her most recent visit from Julia or how the weekly yoga classes appeared to be connecting her to both her mom and other mysterious forces helping her along. Meghan neglected to explain how much the healing crystal, a gift from a long-dead wife of a local ship builder, was helping her to return to a better version of herself. A version of herself she didn't even know existed. Elliott, the practical and sensible scientist might not understand. She wasn't even sure she understood.

The small gallery was crowded with people sharing wine, stories, and interpretive glances at the gallery's offerings. The wide-planked cedar floors, low ceilings, and overhead beams set a casual and coastal background for the art, so different from either the edgy or the presumptuous galleries of New York City. Jack was mulling about, speaking to patrons about his paintings as well as his background as an art teacher turned retired fisherman and tinkering painter. He was told by many he was being too modest and that his talent stood out as both intriguing and serene.

"What's the symbolism behind the seagull in each of your paintings?" asked one interested gentleman.

Meghan inched closer to try and hear her father's response. The constant din of the room made it hard to hear the conversation, so she continued to move even closer as he told a complete stranger, "I've always felt connected to seagulls and for some reason they always seem to be trying to give me a message." He smiled and chuckled casually, "Of course, I still haven't been able to figure out what that message is yet." She could tell by Jack's response that he might very well understand more than he was letting on about the seagulls in his life. The older gentleman was impressed enough with Jack's work to purchase one of his paintings and the gallery agreed to deliver it to his home on Paddy Creek and expertly hang it in the gentleman's study.

By the end of the night, Jack had sold two of his paintings and earned himself the right to call himself an artist. An artist who sold his paintings in an art gallery. An impressive accomplishment Meghan's father humbly downplayed as, "Not really a big deal." But there was a spring in his step and his confidence blossomed, whether he would admit to his own talent and accomplishments or not. Jack Murphy was officially an artist.

Jack, Meghan, and Elliott walked home under the optimistic light of a full moon on a cold spring night. They chatted about the eclectic gallery guests and gossiped about the quirky neighbors who seemed to attend the gallery open house only for the free food and wine. They laughed and admitted the night was long but enjoyable and how they each planned to sleep in the following Saturday morning. As they came upon the house, Jack said goodnight and thanked them for coming to support him before heading indoors. The evening was more important to Jack then he would admit, but the happiness on his face was apparent and warmed Meghan's soul from within. He deserved the happiness and joy he had just experienced.

As Jack Murphy, the artist, swung open the screen door and settled in for the night, Elliott and Meghan decided to continue on for a short brisk walk to the end of the cul-de-sac. They weren't ready for the night to end. Meghan gladly accepted Elliot's gloves from his coat pocket and they walked hand-in-hand on a beautifully clear night.

"It's good to see you feeling better, Meg. I know how hard the last few months have been," Elliott said as they continued their slow stroll.

"I've really been working on myself. Taking better care of me, from everything to eating better, taking yoga classes, seeing my therapist, and even trying to stay connected to my mom. As weird as that sounds," she added.

"Not weird at all. I think it makes perfect sense. I believe your mom is here with you, watching over you and is incredibly proud of you. I'm very sure all she wants if for you to be happy. All parents want that for their children."

"Well, you make me happy, Elliott. The happiest I've ever been. Plus, you keep me calm and rational, which is no easy task," she said with a levity she hadn't felt in forever.

They stopped at the end of road, which overlooked the harbor boasting an expanse of still water that laid like a thin gray blanket spread evenly beneath a breathtakingly starry sky. Elliott turned to her and with both of his hands on her face he said, "Meghan, I love you and I can't wait for Key West and for all of the other adventures, big and small, I hope we share together."

Elliott kissed her softly but passionately while she felt a sudden stroke of gratitude for the long, winding, and sometimes treacherous road that brought her to this captivating place, at the end of the lane, at that very moment.

Twenty-Two
2000

Elizabeth reluctantly retreated as Jack stepped closer. Close enough to smell his familiar scent that hadn't faded over time. Close enough to take her breath away and possibly lose her mind. And all sense of right and wrong. Her lower back was pressed against the wall for security, her subconscious begging for hidden strength and support. She could hear her own heart beating and it was as if the events of the last ten years had disappeared and she was back in the art room at *Harborside*, begging him to kiss her. She remembered all too vividly what it felt like to be wrapped in his arms, to lay her head against his chest, and to feel his body pressed against her own. Too often she longed secretly for this exact feeling when wrapped in her husband's arms. She tried countless times to recreate it. Never once coming close. Suddenly and strangely, she thought she smelled the ocean and salt water, and was brought back into her most recent dream, although wide awake. A dream where only hours ago they were making love in the sand while the warmth of the sun covered their bodies. Where only the two of them mattered and there was no responsibility to do the right thing. But Elizabeth shook herself back to the present moment where she reminded herself that she was a happily married woman, currently acting like a fool. "Jack," she paused, breathless. "It was really nice to see you. I'm glad we had a chance to talk, even if it took ten years." Her eyes didn't leave his as he sighed, both of them knowing this moment would have to come to an end. His eyes moved to the floor, understanding he was wrong for what he desperately wanted and didn't deserve.

He placed one hand on the wall behind her, possibly to keep them from pressing their bodies against one another. He brought his head even closer to hers, so his forehead was touching hers. Jack closed his eyes, trying to figure out the impossible; how to say goodbye. His other hand moved gently from her neck to the back of her head, until he slowly played with her pony tail. Elizabeth didn't stop him. Their breath was synchronized, and she was frozen. She closed her eyes and begged her mind and body to conspire to do the right thing. But in the moment, as hard as she tried, she had no control over either.

"I've thought of you every day for ten years. I made a mistake, Lizzy. I should have come back. I should have found a way. And now it's too late. But I still love you. Always will."

As their lips touched slightly, both of them knew that with every gentle touch, every sensual movement, they were playing with fire standing in the hallway of a New York City hotel, in the middle of the night. And it didn't go unnoticed to either of them, that an empty hotel room stood ready and waiting, and maybe had been for ten years. The kiss started gently and slowly, and his mouth moved to Elizabeth's neck. Such a familiar feeling, a feeling so strong not even a decade could erase. Their kiss grew more passionate, his hands traveling beneath the hem of her dress, the world around them completely invisible. With her eyes closed, still pinned against the wall with the weight of his body hypnotizing her, she imagined slipping out of her dress, standing in front of Jack Murphy, and reenacting that day's dream that may have been more of a wish. Maybe that dream was a powerful premonition of what was about to come?

"Jack, I can't." She pushed him back gently but the touch of his firm chest beneath his rumpled shirt made her wonder if she needed one more night with him. Maybe more than one. But she kept her thoughts to herself. "I'm sorry, Jack. I have to go." Before she could change her mind, before she could say goodbye with one last word or one last touch, she forced the hotel room door open and closed it behind her. With Jack on the other side of the door, she dropped her purse and keys to the ground and turned to face the door, the awful barrier that stood between them. She pressed her hand and her forehead against the door imagining that Jack was doing the same. And he was.

Elizabeth's tears came easily. It was late, and she was exhausted. And this was an exhaustion like no other. She drank more than she should have and there was a slight buzzing sound that may have been the hotel room lights or may have been the wine. She knew for a fact the exact moment Jack walked away from the door. It was a long and painful ten minutes after she shut it between them. For those minutes, they silently propped themselves against the door telling each other how sorry they were. How much they missed each other, all without a word or a sound uttered. It was easy for them to communicate without words back then. And after all this time, nothing had changed.

Elizabeth brushed her teeth and climbed into bed with just a t-shirt on and accepted sleep might not come easily. Just as she climbed into bed and turned out the light, she noticed the phone alerting her of a message with a red light, blinking with the intensity of a warning. Jonathan. "Oh, my God, Jonathan," she said aloud. She jumped up to listen to his worried message. She anxiously bit her bottom lip hard enough that it began to bleed.

Baby, I'm worried now. It's 2 a.m. and I haven't heard from you. I hope you are just out having a good time, but you promised to call and let me know you were ok. Please, please call me when you get in. Tell me that you are safe. Ok, I love you.

Her eyes squeezed shut while she considered her options. If she waited to call until tomorrow, he would be beside himself with worry, possibly making things worse. But if she called now, she would have to force the lies from her mouth with the taste of Jack still on her lips. Her head dropped as she picked up the phone and dialed. He answered on the first ring, before she could lose her courage.

"Are you okay"? He sounded sleepy and she was relieved that he would likely settle for a quick chat before heading back to his slumber.

"I'm fine. I'm so sorry. Charlotte and I lost track of time and had way too much wine. But I'm completely safe, ready to tuck myself into bed," Elizabeth replied, proud that not one word uttered was a lie.

"Ok, I miss you. Can't wait to see you tomorrow. What train will you be taking home?" he asked, looking for details she hadn't yet considered.

"Not sure. I'm going to sleep in and take a late afternoon train. I have a feeling I'll need to sleep this crazy night off. I'm not much of a city girl, it appears. But I'll call you just before I leave. Promise," her voice filled with equal parts regret and tenderness.

"Ok, goodnight Elizabeth. Love you."

"I love you too, Jonathan."

As she hung up, she wondered if she did truly love Jonathan. Did she love him the way she loved Jack, with every fiber of her being? Without words?

————))((————

The late morning sunlight peeking through the hotel room's drapes frantically shouted at Elizabeth to get up and get home to her husband. As she swung her legs over the side of the bed, she planted her feet firmly on the floor and put her head in her hands while the events of the night before returned with a vengence. It was 11 a.m. when she slowly dragged her tired and guilty body to the shower. As she passed the mirror, she realized she was barely recognizable. Her eyes were swollen from crying and the mascara that had run down her unwashed face was smudged beneath puffy eyes, filled with confusion. She looked horrific and felt even worse. "At least I didn't dream about Jack last night. At least there's that," she thought to herself.

The scalding water felt amazing and somewhat healing,

DIDI COOPER

and as she washed her hair, she tried to convince herself that she did the right thing. She walked away from a potentially disastrous situation. Nothing really happened, she told herself. A kiss wasn't actually cheating was it? As she came out of the bathroom in the hotel robe, her hair damp but her regular-self beginning to take shape, she noticed an envelope had been pushed beneath the door. It wasn't there a few minutes ago, she was sure of it.

The envelope was blank but carefully sealed. Elizabeth quickly opened it and pulled out a single sheet of paper. A note from Jack. She sat on the end of the bed and with one glance at his handwriting, she missed him.

> *Dear Lizzy,*
>
> *I am sorry about last night. I haven't slept at all and I thought about seeing you this morning to clear things up between us but decided it might make things worse. I shouldn't have come to New York. It's too hard to be near you and not hold you in my arms. It's too hard to look at you and not imagine what could have been. I meant everything I said to you last night, but there was something I didn't say. I am happy for you, Lizzy. You have a wonderful life and you are married to a good man. A man who makes you happy, and most importantly, a man you love and who loves you back. You deserve such happiness. You deserve all the things I did not give you.*
>
> *I will see you in my dreams and in all the signs the universe gives me to remind me of you. I will carry you with me, Lizzy.*
>
> *Always missing you,*
> *JM*

Suddenly, there was a light knock at the hotel room door and Elizabeth realized he must have come back. She jumped to her feet and in two fast steps to the door, would throw herself into his arms, accept an apology he didn't need to make, and agree to see him again. As she raced to the door, tightened the belt on her bathrobe, and threw open the barrier that stood between them, relieved they would have another chance.

Much to her surprise, standing in front of her was Jonathan. The man who loved her with all his heart and soul. The man who had never walked away and had never chosen another life.

Beaming with pride for surprising her he said, "You look like you saw a ghost," with a laugh. He reached out to hug her and added, "I knew you'd sleep in, so I thought I'd take an early train and surprise you and take you to a nice brunch in the City." He smiled and hesitated, "Basically, I missed you so much I couldn't stay away."

"You're the best," Elizabeth replied, still in shock. Hating herself for wanting the knock on the door to be Jack, she kept Jonathan in an extra-long embrace to make sure he couldn't read the look of disappointment on her face.

"Boy, it's a good thing you didn't catch an early train back," he added lightheartedly.

Before Jonathan fully entered the room, she grabbed Jack's letter off the bed and slipped it into her duffle bag before he could notice.

They brunched at *Penelope's* on Lexington and the Nutella French toast served with a heaping side of shame, slipped down more easily than expected. Elizabeth turned down her usual mimosa, but the medicinal hot coffee kept coming and the noisy chatter of their close-talking dining companions reminded her how much space they had in Virginia. In the moment, she was comforted by a crowd that protected her from an intimate and honest conversation with her husband and prevented her from sitting with her own guilt. She filled him in on the exciting details of the conference and admitted the pace of the city had been exhausting. They both agreed that living in the suburbs of Virginia had many advantages from real estate prices, to elbow room in restaurants, as well as its proximity to both D.C. and New York City.

"Imagine what we'd be living in here, for the cost of our townhouse," Jonathan chuckled.

His words drifted in and out of her consciousness like a dense morning fog that had settled in her mind and now inhabited her soul. "I'm feeling a little lightheaded," she explained, as they finished their meals.

"You look pale, and it's awfully noisy in here. You must be exhausted. We don't need to spend the whole day in the City. Let's get you home. I'll light the fireplace and you can do nothing but relax with a good book and your favorite blanket, for at least two days."

Elizabeth forced a smile to remind herself how much she didn't deserve the man sitting across from her, always willing to make everything better.

"Besides, I have a surprise for you back home," he added as he rose from his seat. As her eyes lit up Jonathan added, "Don't even ask, because I won't tell. Not a word until we get home." His smile and beautiful face began to replace images of the confusing night before. "Now let's get home to your surprise," he said and took her hand.

One would not think you could sleep soundly on a moving train, with its frequent jolts and stops, but Elizabeth was able to do just that. The dream emerged as she lay there sleeping, her head nestled on Jonathan's shoulder, his full attention focused on *The New York Times*. In her unconscious state, it appeared this dream had no sound and she would pay close attention to the sights, smells, and earthly vibrations around her since the silence was unexpected. The sunlight was bright, and her feet dangled in a slow-moving stream. She kicked her feet, expecting to hear a gentle splash, but no sound was generated. Her legs were unusually tanned, and a warm breeze gently blew her long, cotton purple paisley skirt. She felt his presence before she saw him. She smelled his freshly showered skin before she saw him. As she looked to her right, Jack was there next to her. He was lying on the bank of the river, eyes closed, his face pointed toward the welcoming sun. One hand was behind his head and the other was on her thigh and they sat there together, silently and lovingly. Jack was wearing a white t-shirt and faded jeans and it occurred to Elizabeth that he was more relaxed than she had ever seen him in their real time together. His energy was entirely different. There was nothing weighing on him, nothing keeping him from an innocent and lighthearted joy. When he finally opened his eyes, they both looked to the sky to see their seagull circling above. They chuckled without sound, understanding the meaning behind the gentle bird who had become a symbol of their love, silent communication, and supernatural connection. Just before she woke, Jack sat up, looked deep within her soul, and showed her the inside of his right wrist. A black image; a tattoo of a bird in flight, was imprinted upon his skin. He gently took her hand, turned her palm to the sun and revealed the same tattoo on Elizabeth's own skin. They smiled and as his lips tenderly touched hers, she was awoken by Jonathan, kissing her ever so lightly on the forehead, to rouse her. They had arrived home and she had slept the entire ride.

———⊂((O))⊃———

What she could not have known is that on the same Sunday afternoon, at the exact same time, Jack Murphy pulled his Jeep to the side of a deserted wooded road somewhere in Massachusetts. On his drive from New York City, back to Maine and to his daughter, he decided the fatigue and emotion from the night's events were more than he could handle while behind the wheel of a car. He hadn't slept. He needed coffee and he needed to rest. He decided to take a ten-minute nap in his car and get home to Meghan safely. And nap he did.

Unbelievably, Jack dreamed the exact same vivid, but silent dream, along with Lizzy. An unexplainable, implausible, and purely astonishing shared experience.

One they would not understand for years to come.

———⊂((O))⊃———

As their tree-lined driveway came into view, Elizabeth was elated to return to her comfortable, predictable, and loving reality. With the lines between reality and fantasy recently blurred, she was eager to place her feet firmly on the Virginia earth. Simultaneously, she made a silent vow to appreciate her life and to remain planted in the reality she was so fortunate to have.

Jonathan insisted she stand in the driveway with her eyes closed as she prepared for a surprise she didn't deserve. She complied with his request and before she knew it, she heard Jonathan say, "Okay, now open your eyes." And there in his safe and loving arms, was the sweetest four-month old black Labrador puppy she had ever seen.

"Oh, Jonathan, he's the cutest," she squealed as she reached out to pull the squirming, licking surprise toward her. "He's really ours?" she asked in disbelief.

Although they spoke once or twice about getting a dog, they always decided it would probably be too much work. And the dog would be alone too much.

"Since you're working from home now, I thought it'd be a good time for a new addition to the family," he smiled. "The rescue shelter named him Lincoln, but we can change it to anything you like. They believe he's part Labrador and part German Shephard. He may be a big boy."

"Lincoln is a perfect name. He's perfect. And you're beyond perfect," she said, reaching over her new addition to kiss the man who continued to amaze her.

They shuffled the bags and Lincoln inside and Elizabeth was not at all surprised to learn Jonathan had outfitted the kitchen with all the essentials needed for a new puppy. There was a puppy crate, chewable toys, a retractable leash, and a food dish decorated with black and white paw prints. She insisted on hearing all the details regarding Lincoln's arrival, and as Jonathan brewed her a cup of tea, he proudly explained how he stumbled into the shelter on a whim and came out with a plan to expand their family. When Jonathan first arrived at the shelter, Lincoln appeared a little nervous, but was the most loveable, albeit most anxious, of all his puppy siblings. In fact, the volunteers nicknamed him Nervous Nellie. And that was all Jonathan had to hear. He was in love and Nervous Nellie would be coming home to them.

And when it was time for bed, Jonathan summoned Lincoln to his crate where he was expected to sleep. But when Elizabeth took one look at his sad little face, with his nose peeking out of his crate, she tip-toed over, lifted him out of the crate into her arms, and carried him upstairs to their bed, where he would sleep. As Jonathan followed his wife to their bedroom, he shook his head while he smiled and didn't appear either upset nor surprised.

Elizabeth wasn't sure who needed the added comfort more, her or Nervous Nellie, but the nightly ritual continued, even as Lincoln grew into the 60-pound dog who hogged her pillow and stole the covers.

Twenty-Three
2017

D ressed and ready to go much earlier than necessary, Meghan was one of the first attendees to arrive. The New England Literacy Symposium in Portsmouth, New Hampshire was just thirty-five minutes from home and the traffic was light. The mostly empty conference room at the hotel was expansive and based on the number of empty chairs and the welcome table full of name tags, more than a hundred participants were expected. She registered, chose a name tag, and was suddenly grateful for both a common first and last name. It would be doubtful Elizabeth Bennet would even notice her, let alone allow an incredibly common name, such as Meghan Murphy, to ring a familiar bell from her distant past. It was possible she hadn't even thought about Jack Murphy in over twenty years. It had likely been even longer since she had seen him.

Meghan's stomach turned as she poured a cup of steaming coffee into a non-descript white hotel mug chosen from a table adorned with an equally plain white table cloth. Elizabeth Bennett was only one of the speakers during the day-long event and wasn't scheduled to speak until after lunch. She would have to pick a good seat, settle in, and try to be patient.

People began to enter the conference room and chat quietly among themselves. She carefully scanned faces for anyone who resembled Elizabeth, understanding that book jackets and author websites, often held outdated pictures. No one mulling about the room looked even remotely like the pictures she committed to memory. Meghan realized she would likely have to wait until after lunch, when Elizabeth Bennett was introduced.

As the presentations began, she refocused her attention and found herself taking copious notes to keep herself completely engaged. At first. Unfortunately, the first speaker's voice was monotonous, and her presentation dry and boring. Suddenly, Meghan began to doodle in the margins of her notebook as her mind drifted. Her doodles began as a series of wavy lines, bubbles, and shaded ovals. Her favorite pen would glide over the page as her imagination slowly took her to the land of make-believe, much like when she was a child. But rather than her childlike daydreams taking her to amusement parks and faraway lands of rainbows, faeries, and enchanted libraries, she had visualized her impending meeting with Elizabeth Bennett. There in her narrow seat, at the end of the 4th row, Meghan created a vivid scenario where Elizabeth thanked her for helping her re-connect to Jack and credited their very encounter, in this hotel in New Hampshire, for bringing her back to her true love. In this fantasy, Elizabeth would later decide to write novels from the crooked seaside cottage in Kennebunkport, and while sitting nearby, Jack Murphy would paint with contentment and a full heart. Soul mates together, once again. Just the way it was supposed to be, Meghan thought to herself.

The silly little fact that Elizabeth was married and living in Virginia with said husband, mattered little in her delusionary, make-believe world.

Staring into the distance, Meghan was knocked back to reality when she realized people were beginning to file out of her row and step over her purse and her body, since she was not exiting for lunch as quickly as they were. Did the speaker announce the lunch break? What did she miss? She had to shake herself back to the present moment.

Too nervous to eat, Meghan chose a small coffee shop just outside the hotel, ordered a hazelnut coffee with a shot of espresso and a blueberry scone she planned to pick at, hoping the lunch break would pass quickly. There was just one tiny table open in the back corner of the shop by a large, sunny window. She squeezed her way past numerous strangers and plopped down for what she hoped would be a swift break. Elizabeth Bennett would be speaking right after lunch and Meghan was eager to find her way back to her seat and experience the reality of being so close to the woman her father loved, and possibly planned a future with, before he knew he was a father. A woman who likely loved him back and was devastated to learn their plans were doomed. All before they knew Mella was keeping a life-changing secret.

While picking at the crumbs of a dry scone and waiting for her scorching hot coffee to cool, she heard a young voice just a few tables away say with delight in her voice, "Miss Bennett, would you mind signing my book?"

And suddenly, without warning, there she was. Just two miniscule, crowded, tables away sat Elizabeth Bennett with a friend or colleague. Her back was to Meghan, so she had no choice but to focus her attention on the young girl standing in front of her. She was maybe seventeen, with a wide smile and a pink streak in her dark hair. The young fan held out her copy of *Saving Samuel* and it occurred to her that the quirky girl, dressed in a black plaid romper and who wore oversized black rimmed glasses, looked more like a New York City girl than a New Englander. As Elizabeth returned the signed book to her, Meghan immediately decided she should try and get a closer look, so she nervously rose from her seat, grabbed her belongings, and walked by the table where a woman, once in love with her father, sat. Elizabeth's blonde hair was longer and curlier than in her pictures, but Meghan was still unable to see more than a bit of her profile. But then, what she did see took her breath away.

On Elizabeth's right wrist she wore a number of silver bangled bracelets that slid up and down her arm as she moved with grace and sipped her latte. When she lifted the cup to her mouth, her beautiful silver bracelets slid down her arm just far enough to reveal a tattoo. A single bird in flight sat permanently on the inside of her right wrist. Meghan felt the room spin and the need to immediately remove herself from the crowd as the overwhelming confusion that sat firmly upon her chest, made it hard to breathe.

In one gulp, Meghan took in the cool outside air and sat down on a stone wall, unable to will her legs to take her a step further. How in the name of all that was holy, was it even possible that she had a vivid dream of that same tattoo?

How was it even remotely possible that the dream involved her following Elizabeth in a park and calling her name? And what was a seagull, Meghan's seagull, doing on *her* wrist?

Meghan forced herself back into the conference room to stake her claim to a seat that would allow her the perfect vantage point to watch Elizabeth's every move and mannerism, hoping to hang on her every word. She had not yet decided if she would be able to muster the courage necessary to stay after the event to meet the writers and potentially insert herself into the life of this mystery woman. Even if only for a moment.

Elizabeth Bennet was, in fact, the warm, but reserved author of two books. Her presentation on the brainstorming and outlining process for writers of both fiction and non-fiction was not overwhelmingly thrilling, but helpful. She noticed people jotting down ideas and nodding in agreement throughout her presentation. She smiled often and told a few stories that reflected the trials and tribulations of her own writing process. She was humorous and connected well to the audience of writers in the room. She mentioned nothing of her personal life, her husband, or her hometown. No personal self-disclosure at all. Even the inspiration for her stories reportedly came from her love of history and historical fiction, and her childhood love of literature, not her own experiences or relationships.

Meghan found Elizabeth Bennett to be engaging and kind, but not at all the dynamic, mysterious superstar she made her out to be in her active imagination and fantasies. She wasn't sure what she expected, but she could hear Elliott now, reminding her that reality is often not nearly as enthralling as her wild mind and daydreams. However, there was still the tattoo. Could that tattoo on her wrist be a coincidence? It hardly seemed possible. Meghan's dream was so vivid and lifelike, she reminded herself. At the time of her dream, she was so sure the events were real, she sat up in her bed, felt the warmth of the dream sun on her skin, and was surprised to find no tattoo on the inside of her wrist. That image was as real now as it was then. Interestingly, Meghan had recently wondered if she should get the tattoo from her dream since maybe it was a sign. But what kind of sign?

How could something like this happen?

With that perplexing thought, she felt a gentle vibration coming from her purse. Except, she had turned off her phone before Elizabeth began her presentation. Meghan reached into her purse and took only a moment to locate the source of the tremor. Before she left the house, she slipped her selenite crystal into her bag for added support. Just in case. She took hold of the crystal. Its warmth and small pulses of earthly vibrations were powerful today. She closed her eyes for a moment and silently asked what she should do next. And before she knew it, she was in line, waiting to have a book signed by Elizabeth Bennett, published author and former lover of Jack Murphy. She didn't remember the steps she took to get there but she attributed her absentmindedness to adrenaline. Or nerves.

Before she knew it, she was next in line and although she had been shaking and nervously rehearsing what to say, when she stepped up to meet Elizabeth who was seated at a small table, an unexplained calm came over her and she made confident eye contact before she spoke. Elizabeth looked up at Meghan and smiled, but she also held her stare as if she were trying to place her. It was as if she thought knew her but couldn't put her finger on how. *Oh, if she only knew*, Meghan thought to herself.

Boldly yet calmly, Meghan slid the book toward the welcoming author and abandoned her rehearsed script. The words flowed as if someone else was speaking. She heard her own voice say, "Hi, my name is Meghan Murphy. You once knew my father and I'm sure he'd love a signed copy of your book. His name is Jack. Jack Murphy."

Elizabeth looked at Meghan with surprise and a genuine smile. "I'd be more than happy to sign a book for your dad." She began to set the pen in motion but hesitated and looked at Jack's daughter before she placed her signature on the page. She added thoughtfully, "Please tell your dad I said hello and I hope he's well. It's been a very long time." Of course, she had no way of knowing Jack didn't even know she was there, so Meghan would likely not be able to deliver her message.

Elizabeth signed the book before returning her attention to the woman behind her, and Meghan felt the strange urge to hug her, but luckily there was a table between them, preventing an awkward moment from occurring. "Thank you so much. I really appreciate it. I know my dad will love having a signed copy of your book."

And that was it. Anticlimactic? Maybe. But Meghan quietly celebrated the opportunity to see, hear, and almost touch the mysterious and until now, elusive, Lizzy Bennet. Elizabeth left her with a feeling of calm and a strong sentiment that she and her father shared something very special. Meghan could see why he loved her so. And it warmed her heart and soul to know she was right. At some time, in some place, he was in love.

Meghan left Portsmouth feeling fulfilled by a simple and uneventful exchange. A polite interaction between two people that under any other circumstances would be considered quite ordinary. But for Meghan, it was anything but. She carried the signed book to the car, clutching it close to her chest and waiting until she was safely seated inside the car before opening it to reveal a brief message to her father.

> *Jack,*
> *The magic of missing you lingers*
> *Be well, be happy, and look for the signs*
> *Lizzy*

Her words, scribbled upon the page in pale blue ink, were perfectly shaped, rounded at the edges and filled with intrigue. Meghan wasn't sure what the message meant, but she read it over and over again, reading between the lines as well as analyzing even the words she omitted, such as the word 'love.' She also neglected to try and reconnect with him. When you tell someone to *be well and be happy*, you are pretty much saying *I don't plan on seeing you again*. However, she made it clear, she did still miss him.

Meghan obsessed, like she often did, over every detail of the day in Portsmouth. She exhausted herself as she replayed the moments in the coffee shop, as well as memorized the book signing's words and feelings between her and Elizabeth

Bennett. She took out her journal and wrote the words *magic of missing you* and *look for the signs* over and over again. She doodled and sketched and daydreamed with her crystal by her side. She couldn't help but connect the phrases to the messages she herself had received from Sadie the psychic, from Julia her resident guardian angel, and of course, there were the messages from her dreams. How might they be connected? How was this even possible?

Meghan decided she wanted that tattoo. Maybe it was even more than that. Maybe she *needed* that tattoo. Either way, she felt like the universe had spoken and given her clear signs. She continued to wonder what the tattoo signified, but in her heart, she thought it must simply signify magic. And maybe the magic shared between Lizzy and Jack. She just wasn't sure why she was involved or why the universe had decided to include her in their story.

She couldn't decide if it was a good idea to give her father Lizzy's book with her message. She considered the pros and cons of such a gift, and for sure, she would have some explaining to do. So, she decided to wait.

For the time being, she tucked the book and Lizzy's heartfelt message under her pillow for safekeeping.

Twenty-Four
2001

The second book was almost complete, and the title had changed a dozen times. Nothing felt right. Whereas with *Saving Samuel* the title came quickly and effortlessly, this time, it looked like Elizabeth would have a completed manuscript before a title appeared on page one. She was hoping it came to her in a dream or was shouted from a passing billboard. She was willing to take any sign, any offering. Every day she asked Lincoln for his help. He just stared lovingly at his mom with his big brown eyes, tilted his head to the side, and waited for a treat. No help at all.

As Lincoln grew, he had unknowingly helped Elizabeth through her conflicted feelings about New York city and Jack. Before Lincoln, it was just her and Jonathan and she was always contemplating whether her feelings for her husband were strong enough, always comparing them to thrilling, mysterious, and breathtaking feelings for Jack. A man she couldn't have. But Lincoln made them a family. The kids came home to visit so infrequently, it was nice to share dog walks and bond over all the silly faces Nervous Nellie made and all the tricks he had learned. Jonathan and Elizabeth presided over him like helicopter parents, taking countless pictures of him. Lincoln was a godsend.

Luckily, she hadn't had a single dream and there hadn't been a single sign of Jack Murphy to distract her from domestic bliss with Jonathan and Lincoln. It became clear to her that true love was sometimes safe and quiet, rather than electric and tumultuous. Real love was proven in the unexciting and small ways someone altered your universe. The way they bring you breakfast in bed for no reason, the way they kiss you on the forehead, the way they surprise you with the perfect rescue pup you didn't even know you needed.

"I need a title," she jokingly said to Jonathan over the phone. She pictured him at work, deep in documents piled high in his tiny office, answering her call even though he had twelve other more important things to do.

With the phone wedged between his ear and his shoulder he blurted, "Well, how about *Love You Most,*" referring to their frequent exchanges when one of them said *I love you*, and the other argued, *No, I love you more* and the winner added, *but I love you most*. Although completely in jest, it was completely perfect. She hung up the phone, and frantically typed the words *Love You Most* on the cover of her manuscript; a story about a series of fictional journals and love letters written by a young Anne Brontë, the lesser known and most mysterious Brontë sister.

For a writer, true love is demonstrated when the man in your life quickly and easily hands you your book title after almost a year of banging your literary head against the wall. Once again, Jonathan saved the day and altered her small bookish world in the most endearing way. Was there anything that man couldn't do?

Jonathan suggested celebrating the completion of Elizabeth's second book with a fancy dinner, but she opted for a simpler affair. They agreed to celebrate *Love You Most* by spending Sunday at a country fair, about an hour from their home. The agricultural fairgrounds bought her back to her childhood and she looked forward to watching pig races, riding on the massive carousel, and eating fried dough sprinkled with powdered sugar. The idea of wearing torn and faded jeans, a flannel shirt, and old but perfectly worn boots, made life seem idyllic in a perfectly uncomplicated way.

Sunday was overcast and chilly and bit unseasonably cold for rural Virginia. Parking was a nightmare and they ended up far from the fairgrounds. They looked toward the sky and hoped it wouldn't rain as they locked the car and set out to walk toward the fair. The small-town excitement was building as they got closer to their destination. The town had come alive to host thousands of visitors every fall before returning to its sleepy slumber until it was time to do it again the following year. They could smell the hay, the barn animals, and the dusty earth before even arriving at the gate. It was going to be a perfect day.

The crowds were dense and the sounds of children playing and parents chasing after them reminded Elizabeth of the years she spent at the fair with Ashley and Conner. She told Jonathan how Ashley loved the fast rides the most and Conner refused to leave the animals in their barns. He once sat down in protest in front of the goat's pen and insisted his mother should leave him there and come back for him later. "Sometimes I miss them being small," she said. "It's true what they say when you have little ones. The days are long, but the years are short."

"A truer statement has never been made," Jonathan agreed and grabbed her hand. With a brisk breeze at their backs, they played a few carnival games and bought tickets, so they could ride the carousel and the majestic Ferris wheel. They also agreed to eat their way through the fair and it would be forbidden to discuss calories, fat or sugar content, as well as consider the way they would likely feel tomorrow. This was a day to indulge and celebrate with fried pickles and cotton candy, minus the guilt of adulthood and the five extra pounds they each carried since having married.

On their way to see the animals and the agricultural exhibits, Elizabeth's attention was drawn to a woman seated at an exhibitors table. Her sign read *Palm Readings by Willa Rose,* and she pulled Jonathan playfully in her direction. Her jet-black hair was long and straight, her ears heavily pierced, and her eyes twinkled beneath thick black eyeliner. Her lips were painted a soft lavender color and she smiled slyly as they approached. As they got closer, they noticed her fingers displayed multiple gemstone and silver rings, and her nails were painted black. She looked to be in her fifties but her pale skin was flawless, and she wore the wrinkles around her eyes with pride.

"She certainly looks the part," Jonathan joked.

"Twenty dollars doesn't sound like such a big risk," Elizabeth joked. "Should we do it?"

"Up to you. Not my kind of thing, but you should do it," he added. "It'll be fun, if nothing else," he said with a relaxed smile.

There were two metal folding chairs positioned in front of Willa's table and as soon as Elizabeth slid into one, without warning, she became dizzy and the earth beneath her began to soften. For whatever reason, images of Jack came to her out of nowhere and she immediately regretted the decision to sit down in front of a self-proclaimed seer, with Jonathan watching closely. What was she thinking? A moment of panic set in as she heard Jonathan speak.

"Hey Elizabeth, I'm going to go find a bathroom while you get started. I'll be right back. If you finish up, don't wander. I don't want to lose you," he joked.

Oh, there is a God, she thought to herself.

Willa Rose looked carefully at Elizabeth's unsteady palms, placed her hands atop of hers and closed her eyes. While deep in thought, her eyes and long dark lashes fluttered. "She's more than a little spooky," Elizabeth said to herself and if she didn't feel so off balance, she would think this was all nothing more than a comical hoax. But then her dark eyes opened slowly and looked calmly across the table, intensely at Elizabeth.

"I see paper. A lot of paper, or pages," she said. When Elizabeth didn't respond quickly enough, she repeated, "Does this make sense, paper or pages all around you?"

"I'm a writer," Elizabeth responded hesitantly. "I just finished my second book."

She nodded, confirming her vision and accepting the answer.

"See this line," she asked as she ran her thumb over Elizabeth's palm. "This tells me you're intuitive. You may see, hear, or sense things." She looked at Elizabeth intensely, awaiting a response.

"I don't think so," she said. But Elizabeth wasn't sure she was being honest with her carnival fortune teller, or with herself for that matter.

"Well, it could be something you haven't noticed or developed. But you're intuitive," she insisted flatly.

Elizabeth shrugged her shoulders, "Huh, not really sure." She made a strong, but unconvincing effort to appear un-phased by the information she had just received.

"There's a man. He is handsome, and you are deeply in love with him," she smiled. You are connected on a spiritual level. A soulmate level. In fact, you have been together in past lives and are experiencing one another again in this lifetime."

Elizabeth felt herself beginning to break out in a full sweat and she took off her flannel shirt and tied it around her waist. She looked around searching for Jonathan, but he was nowhere to be found. She silently wished for long lines at the men's room. She stammered, "There is a man, yes," Elizabeth admitted as images of her dreams flooded her mind and she felt lightheaded. *Damn you, Jack. Not here, not today* she wanted to say aloud.

Willa Rose hesitated and added, "His name. It starts with a J?"

Confused, she stuttered, "Umm, well my husband's name is Jonathan. But…" And before she could continue, she was interrupted.

"Yes, Jonathan is your soulmate. But you need to be sure

to take down walls you have built. Allow your relationship to flourish. Let him in," Willa said as she smiled gently and looked deeply into Elizabeth's eyes, like an old friend.

Elizabeth looked around quickly for Jonathan and leaned across the table and decided if she was going to ask about Jack, she better act quickly. Before Jonathan returned. "What about a man from my past? His name is Jack. Also, with a J."

She looked down at her palms and closed her mysteriously soulful eyes once again. Elizabeth's heart raced, and she begged her to call upon her black magic quickly.

"Oh, he's not your soulmate, my dear. You're married to your soulmate. Have you ever heard of a twin flame?" she asked. When she shook her head, no, she continued. "You undoubtedly have a special connection. One that cannot be broken by time, space, or special circumstances. And you burn brightly and simultaneously. You are forever connected, just not always together. You help each other, even when you are not near one another in time or space. But make no mistake about it. You aren't supposed to be with your twin flame."

Willa moved on to tell Elizabeth that she had three kids, when she only had two, and insisted there could be another child in her future, a daughter. Elizabeth was glad she was wrong and was eager to move away from Willa Rose's unsettling gaze. By the time Jonathan returned from the long bathroom lines, they were finished. Elizabeth paid twenty dollars and thanked her for her time. She was still a bit shaken about the twin flame information, but overall relieved. She told her she was married to her soulmate, possibly for the second or third time and she seemed to miss the mark on enough details that Elizabeth could safely tuck the experience away under the "entertainment" category. Still shaken, but determined to push thoughts, images, and feelings of Jack Murphy away like an unwanted visitor, Elizabeth tried to relax.

As the cool breeze began to pick up, the sun hid behind the clouds, and Elizabeth put her shirt back on and leaned into Jonathan for warmth and security. They rode the carousel, the Ferris wheel, and shared heavily buttered popcorn as they walked through the crowded fairgrounds, hand-in-hand. As much as she tried to force images of Jack from her mind, the struggle remained. Despite Elizabeth's efforts, she now felt oddly connected to Jack there at the fair, which made no sense at all. It's not as if they ever visited the country fair together. And there was no way Jack would stumble upon this fair, so far from his home in Maine. She suspected Willa Rose's messages had interfered with her most recent marital bliss and felt annoyed at herself for participating.

While wandering through the arts and crafts tents Elizabeth simply couldn't shake the feeling that Jack was there, nearby. She would feel him or hear his voice and turn around to find nothing. Of course, there was little chance that she would bump into him in Virginia, on a random Sunday, but it wasn't completely impossible either. She fantasized about someday bumping into him and his little girl. Would he be happily putting his daughter on a ride at the country fair while she walked by? Elizabeth tried her best not to look as distracted as she was.

By the time they were ready to leave, Jonathan was exhausted and ready for a hot shower and some warm snuggles with Lincoln. Before they walked back to the car, Elizabeth decided to grab a coffee at a food truck parked near the exit. *Mimi and Pa's Roasters* promised a hot cup of freshly roasted goodness for the long, chilly walk to the car. Jonathan waited just steps away and with only two people in line ahead of her, they were both more than ready to head home. As an older gentleman wearing a name tag adorned with the name Pa, handed Elizabeth a medium French vanilla coffee, she smiled wearily, and thanked him. She noticed he had kind eyes. But before turning toward Jonathan, she caught a glimpse of a napkin sitting on the shiny metal counter. This, however, was not just any other used napkin. It was a napkin embellished with a pen and ink sketch of a country fence, tall grass, and a seagull floating above. She immediately recognized the artist connected to this piece of fairground art. To make matters worse, as she pulled the napkin closer to her, she noticed the message at the very bottom of this small, square napkin. *Missing you Lizzy* were the only words scribbled.

She discretely folded the napkin and placed it in the front pocket of her faded jeans before returning to her husband, medicinal coffee in hand.

Twenty-Five
2017

Packing for Key West was incredibly easy since Meghan and Elliott decided not to eat at a single establishment that would require anything but flip flops, suntan lotion, and sunglasses. They were excited to find the small hidden places where the locals dined, and Elliott was intent on exploring some of the other tiny islands that made up the Florida Keys. They would spend a week in bathing suits, drinking frozen daiquiris by the sea, and lying in hammocks beneath palm trees. Their first vacation as a couple would commence in only a few hours. Already having checked into the flights online, all that was left to do was make their way to the airport. As Meghan placed a final few items in her small suitcase, she grabbed a small framed picture of her mom off the bedside table and studied it. It was a picture of the two of them on Meghan's first day of Kindergarten and Meghan noticed her mother looked young, beautiful, and proud. She looked happy. Not depressed or sad, but like any other proud mom on the first day of school. Mementos like this helped Meghan in the dark moments when she was afraid

Mella, as a young mother, struggled with depression without getting help. Normally, she would call her mom and tell her about her vacation and share details of a boyfriend she would now never have the chance to meet. Her mother was an adventurer and would love hearing about this trip, and that made Meghan sad. For as many years as she had been looking at this picture, she realized she had no memory of who actually took the picture. It could have been her dad. Or, she supposed, it could have been her grandparents. She tossed the frame into her carry on and decided to take her mother with her on her first vacation with Elliott.

She carried her small suitcase downstairs, and as an afterthought, grabbed a few snacks from the pantry to throw in her purse for the flight. The quiet stillness of the house always prompted Meghan to gaze out the kitchen window to appreciate the stunning harbor. The miniature hand-carved seagull who remained perched upon the windowsill reminded her of Elizabeth Bennett, and suddenly and impulsively, she decided to leave her dad a small gift before leaving on vacation. She ran back upstairs, quickly retrieved the signed copy of Elizabeth's *Love You Most* from beneath her mattress and left it on the kitchen table with a note.

> *Dad,*
> *I met Elizabeth Bennett at a writer's conference. She signed this, just for you. See you in a week.*
> *Love you,*
> *Meghan*

While sitting in the airport terminal, an hour ahead of their flight, Elliott turned to Meghan and out of nowhere blurted, "I have something I want to ask you." He seemed nervous and Meghan immediately became worried. "You know, I've been thinking about asking you to umm, to well, move in with me. When we get back from Florida. I know my apartment is small, and I suppose we could look for another apartment, but..." he began to stammer, appearing more and more nervous as he continued.

"Really?" Meghan said with the excitement of a teenager. "Holy cow, this is a huge surprise."

"I know, and you totally should take your time to think about it. I know it's a big step, but honestly, I love having you around and I've come to dread the nights you go back home to stay at your dad's," he added. "And I know you lived with someone once before and it didn't work out, so I completely understand if it's too soon."

She let her book close in her lap, without even holding her place, and took Elliott's hand in hers. With their fingers intertwined, she spoke, "It's true. I lived with William and that ended in disaster and heartbreak. But if that didn't end the way it did, I would have never found you. I'd love to move in with you. Nothing would make me happier," she added. "And your apartment is perfect. We can walk to town and bike to the beach. I love it. And if we're each paying half the rent and expenses, we should even be able to save some money. You know, for all of our many travel expenses."

"Well, it's settled then. You have a roomie," he added with a sly smile and a quick kiss.

Meghan had trouble refocusing her attention back to

her book, so she simply rested her head on Elliott's shoulder and closed her eyes. Not because she was tired, but because she wanted to soak in all the details of the moment of pure and uncomplicated happiness. Happiness she didn't think was possible. She wanted to remember the sounds of the airport, the smell of Elliott's freshly laundered t-shirt, and the tangible excitement she felt over this next step in their relationship. Although she didn't want to rush things and they had plenty of time ahead of them, she couldn't help but think about a real future with Elliott. A little over a year ago, Meghan was crying over William who cheated on her and who always treated her like an afterthought. Now, she was here with Elliott, the cutest, sweetest, and most practical man she had ever met, who was asking her to move in with him. It was almost more joy than her previously shattered heart could hold.

"I wish you could have met my mom," she added after a few minutes of quiet contemplation.

"Me too, Megs."

"She'd have loved you. She was quite a character, my mom. A little wild and carefree, but her heart was always in the right place," Meghan sighed a heavy sigh. "I miss her."

"I know you do," Elliott added while he kissed the top of Meghan's head.

As their plane was announced for boarding, they simultaneously rose from their seats, grabbed their carry-ons, clasped their hands together, and boarded the plane as a young couple with a bright future.

Twenty-Six
2001

The rain was steady, and the wind was howling outside but the conditions inside were stormier and scarier than the elements pelting angrily against the window. Jack's napkin and haunting message sat upon Elizabeth's desk, not far from a steaming cup of strong, black coffee. The oversized mug, a birthday present from Ashley, taunted her with its sunny and encouraging words, *Anything is Possible*. Elizabeth no longer found these unexpected messages from the universe comforting or comical.

He was there. She felt him and sensed his presence at the country fair. She felt him in the cool breeze, in the air around her, and especially when she sat down for the palm reading. She was sure of it. The napkin left behind was all the proof Elizabeth needed. It was haunting and thrilling at the same time. She was left with a nervous energy she couldn't explain. She paced fretfully within the confines of her small home office, the one Jonathan created to make her life easier. An ominous storm was brewing while she stared at an empty computer screen. Generating words on the page for the next book was proving impossible at the moment. Ever since the country fair, she couldn't get her mind off Jack, off New York City, and away from the haunting dreams, so she pulled a legal pad out of the top drawer of her desk to begin drafting a handwritten letter. Whether she sent it or not, it might be good for her to process the confusion and allow the uncontrollable thoughts swirling deep within her tortured soul, to cathartically heal her.

The black ballpoint pen in her hand moved quickly and without hesitation. The words formed effortlessly, flowing as if channeled from another, stronger, more self-assured woman. One who successfully let go of her inhibitions, guilt, and regret.

Dear Jack,

It's hard to know where to begin. Do I begin on the day you left Harborside and made the decision to permanently remove me from your life? Or do I leave that in the past and tell you about the years I have spent seeing, hearing, and feeling signs from you, making it difficult to completely move on with my life? Maybe there is no best place to start.

Mostly I am angry and disappointed. And please understand that Meghan has nothing to do with my anger. Of course, there was that night of your phone call so many years ago. Of course, I was angry. But in time, I came to understand that Mella kept her pregnancy a secret from you. There was nothing you could have done about that. I came to accept that you had a little girl who you would forever love and care for. A beautiful little girl I would never know. But I never came to accept the fact that you left your job, your students, and the person you claimed to love, behind. With almost no notice. And an agreement that asked me to walk away from what we had.

I only wish the anger and disappointment was all you left me with. If that were the case, I could proceed, uninterrupted, with my very nice life. Sure, I would harbor some resentment and wonder why you walked away from a life we could have shared. But breakups happen, and people move on. So why couldn't our story, like others, simply end there?

Instead, I see you vividly in my dreams and feel your presence in ways I don't fully understand. The memories of being with you recently in New York City bring back the anger, but at the same time preoccupy me with compelling feelings of our connectedness that is hard to comprehend or put into words. The weight of your body against mine and the memory of your lips on my neck are more than I can bear. When I am near you, I want nothing more than to throw myself into your arms and let you know it is not too late to repair the foolish years we have spent apart. When it is just the two of us, I'm afraid of what I am capable of. Am I capable of walking away from my safe and loving marriage? Am I capable of disappointing a man who loves me without complication? It would be completely selfish and even reckless of me to do such a thing. I am just afraid that when the years are behind me and my life is about to end, I will regret not fighting harder to be in your life. It will then truly be too late.

Jack, will you meet me? Maybe it will be just one last time. In New York, we talked about the kids, we caught up on a decade of days missed. But we did not talk about us. We did not talk about the possibilities. I need to figure out where *we go next. I simply cannot live with the dreams, with the images, and with the feelings we are sharing this lifetime while living so far apart.*

Although there seems to be a certain magic in missing you, I can't help but wonder if there is an even greater magic in being by your side and in your arms. Can we meet in person, please? I am including a private P.O. Box address, so we can communicate without hurting anyone else.

Missing you–

Lizzy

While deciding whether or not to send the heartfelt and hand-written message to Jack and dangerously begin communicating with a man she used to love, and likely still did, Elizabeth opted for a warm midday bubble bath. Jonathan wouldn't be home for hours and the soothing water might help her decide what to do next. Could soaking in warm water offer her courage or knock some sense into her? She carefully placed a book atop the letter, to hide it from view and glance at the relentless storm outside before drawing her bath.

Soothing lavender bubbles, the soft flickering light of a few scented candles placed upon the bathtub, and the sound of the steady rain drops against the roof left Elizabeth incredibly relaxed but still unable to decide whether or not to send the letter to Jack. Maybe just the act of writing it would release her from some of the guilt and confusion. She hoped. She could always tuck it away and decide to send it at another time. On the other hand, it may be something she *needed* to do. To see Jack one more time. The opportunity to look into his eyes and find out if he had the same feelings and wanted the same things. The bubbles softened and caressed her skin while she closed her eyes, focused on the sounds of the rain, and asked for help.

She imagined Jonathan's kind and trusting face and questioned whether she could hurt him like that. He deserved none of what was happening and was completely unaware his wife was contemplating feelings for a man from her past. A man he didn't even know existed. Shocked and embarrassed at the power of her own deceptions, Elizabeth sank lower beneath the water's surface.

As she slowly dried off and pulled her robe off the hook on the back of the bathroom door, she heard the phone ringing and raced to answer it. A flashback flooded her consciousness and on the way to the phone, recalled that day, so many years ago when she was wrapped in a damp bathrobe and picked up the phone, only to learn that Jack was leaving and the love she thought she found, was suddenly and unexpectedly lost. If she was painfully honest, she never fully recovered from that phone call. This time, though, on the other end of the phone, was Ashley calling from college. Thankfully, her cheerful and happy voice allowed Elizabeth to return to the present moment.

Ashley was excited to tell her mother that she made the Dean's list and was loving her life as a college student. They talked for almost an hour and she didn't seem to mind Elizabeth's questions about friends, the meals on campus, and how her coursework was going. She even revealed she decided to apply for the pre-med program. Before they said goodbye, Elizabeth grabbed a notepad by her bed and made a list of a few things (mostly edibles) that Ashley asked her to send in a care package. Her baby girl was growing up and she was so proud of her. The sound of Ashley's voice reminded her how much she missed having the kids home. Life was simpler when they were the focus of her whole world. As a parent, she had a purpose. Left to her own devices, to care only for herself, she was a floundering mess.

Before rising to get dressed, she stopped to listen carefully to a noise in the hallway. Thinking she heard footsteps just outside the bedroom door, she shouted out fearfully, "Jonathan?" But he wasn't due home for hours. Suddenly, the footsteps ceased and there was no response. She was frozen while trying to decide what to do. But, the bedroom door opened, and there stood Jonathan with a look on his face Elizabeth could only describe as chilling. He glared at her, unable to speak, holding the yellow notepad and her letter to Jack in his hand.

Elizabeth's entire world was about to come crashing down with a vengeance. And she deserved it.

"How could you do this to me, Elizabeth? To us?" he shouted, the muscles in his neck bulging, holding the letter in front of him. "Who the hell is Jack?" he continued, his voice cracked as he willed himself not to cry.

When she was unable to respond quickly enough, he yelled again. "New York? Are you freaking kidding me? I trusted you and you slept with someone at your writer's conference?"

This time she did not hesitate, and her speech was pressured in order to defend herself, "Jonathan, I didn't sleep with Jack, I swear to you. I'm so sorry for all of this, but I swear on my children, I didn't sleep with Jack."

The weight of his legs could no longer support him, and he stumbled to the chair in the corner of their bedroom. The same tartan plaid chair he used when he put his socks and shoes on in the morning before work. The same chair that just this morning represented a sense of marital normalcy they would never experience again. He threw the letter on the floor and dropped his head in his hands. His fingers grabbed his hair and he looked as if he had lost his mind. A long and painful moment passed. She wanted to go to him, to reach out and comfort him, but his demeanor was terrifying. He clearly didn't want her near him. She caused this.

"I decided I wasn't going to even send that letter," Elizabeth added in an act of desperation they both knew came out sounding like a blatant and pathetic lie. The damage could not be repaired. The look of pain and hatred on his face told her everything she needed to know.

"It hardly matters. You're in love with someone else." He shook while he spoke and before the tears could fall from his eyes, he stared a cold and distant glare and stood to face his wife. He took one step toward her but stopped himself. "I'm leaving," he said, sounding defeated; utterly emotionless. His over controlled anger shook her to her core. He slammed the door, the house shook, and he left without his things, without his clothes, without another word.

Twenty-Seven
2017

E lliott and Meghan returned home, tanned, relaxed and ready to enthusiastically begin their next chapter. The cool New England air felt refreshing and invigorating. It smelled like home. They drove home from the Portland airport with the windows down, the radio on, each quietly pleased with themselves for happily and effortlessly surviving their first vacation as a couple. Meghan was relatively sure her dad would be happy to hear she was moving in with Elliott, but a small part of her was worried about him being lonely. She certainly never planned to contribute to his sadness or loneliness. At least they would all be living only a few miles apart. She also reminded herself he had already been living on his own for years. So maybe, solitude was what he was searching for, after all. Another small part of Meghan worried about his reaction to Elizabeth's book she left behind. He must have more than a few questions about how Meghan knew anything about Elizabeth Bennett, let alone how she managed to get a signed book and a personalized message from her. She had some explaining to do.

"Would you mind dropping me at home?" she asked Elliott. "I think I should tell my dad about my moving out and I suspect he'll want to talk about the Elizabeth Bennett book I left behind. That must have been quite a surprise. I think we should probably have some father-daughter time tonight," she rationalized. She still hadn't figured out how to explain what she knew.

Jack had a lasagna cooling on the counter and a loaf of fresh bakery bread ready in case Elliott and Meghan were hungry upon their return. When she walked in the house, she explained Elliott had a lot to take care of after being away from the University for a week and she thought the two of them could have dinner together.

"That lasagna smells delicious," she told her father. "In the Keys we lived on fried seafood and booze for a full week," she shared. "Some home cooked comfort food is just what I need."

Meghan quickly scanned the kitchen and living room for the book, but it was nowhere to be found. She assumed he had tucked it away for safekeeping. Since he was even quieter than usual, she spoke up again. "So, Elliott asked me to move in with him." She waited for his response.

He finally looked up from the counter where he was preparing large servings of lasagna. He turned to face her with his hands full of dinner plates and said, "Wow, that's a big step. What are you going to do?"

"I'm really excited to move in with him, Dad." She paused and noticed his expression soften. She continued, "He's pretty great, as you know."

"Meghan, he's beyond great. He's smart, hardworking,

and as far as I can tell, he treats you very well. I am happy for you. I really am," he added with sincerity. "You have my full blessing. Not that you need it, of course."

"Thanks, Dad. That means a lot to both of us. Really."

They proceeded to chat about moving her belongings into Elliott's apartment and Jack offered his help. Luckily, she traveled light when she moved up to Maine, knowing her grandfather's house was small, so the move into town would be a simple one.

Over empty plates and nothing left to devour except a half of a glass of red wine, Jack finally shared what was obviously weighing on his mind. He took a deep breath before he finally said, "So, please tell me, how on earth did you come to meet Lizzy Bennett?"

There. It was finally out in the open and the air in the room tightened around them. The time had come. She was trying to choose her words carefully, but in her heart, Meghan knew the only way to deal with it was to speak honestly. Too much time had passed, and she kept this little secret long enough. "I met her at the Writer's Symposium in Portsmouth and I asked her to sign the book for you." There was a long silence as her father turned his head out toward the harbor and crossed his arms in front of his chest. He looked as if he were a million miles away. He thought before he spoke.

"How do you know about Lizzy?" he asked curtly.

His tone was just like when she was a teenager and her father took that silent, 'disappointed in you' approach. That was all it took then for her to sing like a bird on the first warm spring day, and apparently not much had changed. She spilled her guts. Meghan explained how she had 'stumbled' upon the photograph and the letter while storing boxes in the attic and after a little bit of investigative research, found a few details about Lizzy and could not help herself from attending the conference where she was speaking. Meghan was able to sensor herself and not share any details about her dreams and strange feelings of connectedness to Kennebunkport and to Lizzy. Some things could be shared later. Maybe.

She thought she would begin with the fact she clearly violated his privacy by reading the letter and Meghan was fully prepared to admit she had no defense. She would beg for forgiveness. But he neglected to comment on the letter or the violation of privacy and explained, "I was dating Lizzy for a year when I found out your mom had you. We were pretty serious. We were living in Virginia and you were in Maine. I didn't have much time to say goodbye to her. As you can imagine it was all quite a whirlwind."

"You were in love?" Meghan asked.

"Yes," he said with that faraway look.

"That must have been incredibly hard. I'm sorry."

Jack came back to life and looked his daughter straight in the eye. "You have absolutely nothing to be sorry for. Nothing."

"No, I just mean, in general I'm sorry you went through all of that," she added.

"I was in love with her. It's true. But nothing compared to my love for you and the massive responsibility I felt to raise you and be sure you always had my full attention. You became my whole life the moment I learned you were part of my world."

"Dad, I love you with all my heart. And I appreciate everything you and Mom did for me. I had a great childhood, and because of it, I have a great life," she sighed, not wanting to hurt his feelings. "But did you really believe I was the only one you could love?"

Twenty-Eight
2001

Ten long, horrendous days had passed since Jonathan stormed out. Aside from mailing the letter to Jack, buying a few groceries, and taking Lincoln out for walks, Elizabeth had not left the house. She changed from one set of pajamas to another, alternating her ensembles with sweat pants, and on special occasions, an oversized sweater. Some days she showered, others she didn't bother. Her headaches had returned, and she was left to deal with them alone, missing Jonathan's attentiveness and tender loving care she so easily took for granted. She was alone by her own doing and was more confused than ever. Additionally, the dreams returned but this time they were back with a vengeance. As nightmares.

In her nightly dreams and daytime naps, Elizabeth was almost always being chased or run down. She found herself terrified, gasping for air, and running from some dark force intent on causing her harm. Sometimes, in the dreams, she called for help, but no one could hear her. Other times, she frantically attempted to dial 911, but either the phone didn't connect, or she couldn't seem to dial correctly. She often woke up in a cold sweat, unable to sleep through the night. She lost 5 pounds in ten days and had no feelings of hunger.

Careful not to let too much sunshine flow through the windows, Elizabeth made sure the blinds and the curtains were drawn during the day and at night. She convinced herself the dark would help control her headaches, but the truth of the matter was, she was unable to face even the slightest hint of the outside world. Shutting it out helped her feel safe. While on walks with Lincoln, she wore her darkest oversized sunglasses, even the gloomiest of days.

Elizabeth checked the post office box regularly for any response from Jack, but each day was met only with suspicious stares from workers, mulling about the post office, becoming used to her peculiar daily visits. At home, Elizabeth's mailbox was filled with bills, junk mail, and legal journals that only served as a reminder of the damage she caused the innocent man she had hurt. Understandably, Jonathan would not return her calls to his cellular phone or to his office. Her messages had gone unanswered for almost two weeks. At some point, they would need to talk and figure out how to proceed. If he wanted a divorce, they were going to have to consider what to do with the townhouse and with Lincoln. The idea of not having Jonathan in her life seemed unbearable. She fell asleep each night, crying into her pillow, and asking aloud "What have I done?"

On the twentieth day, Jack's response finally appeared in her post office box. She rushed out to her car, single envelope in hand, and impatiently tore it open in the front seat, sitting behind the steering wheel, like a crazy person.

She possessed none of the restraint that would be required to sensibly take the letter home and open it in front of the fireplace with a soothing cup of tea. Instead her raw emotions took over like a powerful tidal wave and there she sat, pathetic, lonely, and un-showered at three o'clock in the afternoon. In the crowded parking lot of the post office, a car beeped its horn, hoping her parking space would soon be free but Elizabeth ignored the interruption, unable to move for someone else's convenience. Someone else who had probably showered that day and was happily married. *Move on,* she sarcastically mumbled to the impatient stranger and threw a dismissive wave in his direction. There was no time for distractions.

The first thing she noticed was how long Jack's letter was. His response had obviously been well thought out and his words plentiful. She was encouraged by the mere number and shape of his words and the way they appeared to be strung together so thoughtfully and comprehensively. Finally, his response.

> *Dear Lizzy,*
>
> *I was so surprised to receive your letter but eager to connect to you and read your words that I opened the envelope in my driveway, standing there leaning on my dented and weathered mailbox, unable to wait a moment longer to hear from you. You always had this effect on me and years later, nothing has changed. My heart skips a beat whenever I hear your name, hear a song that reminds me of you, or see something I think you would love, like a sunset, a used bookstore, or a bunch of wildflowers, your favorites. Sometimes, I even feel*

like you are nearby, and I must convince myself my active imagination is responsible.

First, I owe you an apology. I owe you a thousand apologies. In fact, I don't even know where to start. I guess I will start with my leaving. When I left Harborside, I knew no other way. I couldn't imagine dragging you and the kids into my life with Mella and moving your children so far from their father. I felt as if I needed to focus on being a father and being a good one. I doubted I could be a father to Meghan, be a potential stepfather to Ashley and Conner, and be a dedicated partner to you while managing Mella's expectations at the same time. And all of this being over 500 miles apart. I needed to leave, but that did not make leaving any easier. Even though Meghan keeps me busy and fills my life with love, at the same time the years have been lonely, and I have missed you every day since.

Coming to see you in New York may have been a mistake. On one hand, I simply couldn't stay away and so desperately needed to see you. There were things I wanted to tell you. On the other hand, I had no right to barge back into your life. I had no right to stand in that hallway and kiss you. I replay that night in my head every day. I can still smell you, feel your touch, and hear your heart beating against my chest. Sure, in that moment I wanted to convince you to run away with me, start a life with me in Maine, and spend the rest of our days selfishly wrapped up in each other. But I had no right. I made a decision ten years ago that forever changed my life and that decision allowed you to move on, to fall in love, and live the life you deserve. I am afraid all I have done now is confuse you.

Lizzy, I don't think we should meet. Already, we have been dreadfully unfair to your husband. I am afraid of the powerful feelings I have when I am with you and don't trust myself to make logical and sensible decisions about life, love, and all things Lizzy Bennett. Do I love you? Yes. Will I always love you? Of course. Do I wonder if we will connect someday, when we leave this earth, after long and healthy lives? I do.

Lastly, there is something you should know. Every time I see a seagull circling above or swooping down to greet me, I think he might be the same seagull that graced us with his presence that day on the pier. You probably don't even recall that day, or our visitor, but something about him seemed to speak to me. That day, we stood on the pier next to one another, looked out over the Potomac River, and I felt an incredible electricity in the air between us. It was a moment filled with an unexpected magic that has stayed with me all these years.

So, look to the sky, Lizzy. When you see our seagull circling above, know that he is there to remind you of our cosmic connection and our love that knows no boundaries. How lucky are we to have experienced something so special and filled with so much magic? Even if for a short time. I suspect most people go an entire lifetime without experiencing something so extraordinary.

Go on with your life, be amazing, and know that my love for you fills the universe.

All my love,

Jack

The loud banging on the front door was followed by repeated and incessant bell ringing. Elizabeth knew for certain who her visitor was. Charlotte had called on a whim, expecting to catch up with her dear friend and instead her innocent phone call was met with uncontrollable tears, sobs, and her friend's confusing explanation of what had transpired over the last few weeks. Still holding Jack's letter in her hand, Elizabeth did her best to tell her, in summation, how she ruined her marriage, and single handedly found a way to simultaneously alienate the only two men she had ever loved. "Impressive, even by my standards," Elizabeth explained to Charlotte. When they hung up the phone, Elizabeth suspected Charlotte was on her way to save her from herself.

Charlotte took one long look at Elizabeth standing in the doorway, and marched past her, without as much as a hug. From down the hall, Elizabeth heard the shower turn on and Charlotte promptly returned to order her to sit on the sofa.

"You can't do this to yourself. Look at you," she said, a wave of sadness in her voice. "Now, get into that shower, wash your hair, shave your legs, exfoliate. Get yourself clean and moisturized," she expertly ordered.

A confused and emotional Elizabeth did as she was told simply because she didn't possess an ounce of strength to argue with her friend. She wanted to. But couldn't. Plus, she was right. Although Elizabeth's eyes were still sore and puffy from days of crying and a lack of sleep, the shower helped. Wrapped in a towel, she sat on the edge of the bathtub while Charlotte took a blow dryer to her unruly hair. She expertly turned Elizabeth's waves into smooth, straight locks and forced her into applying some light makeup. Elizabeth looked into the mirror and recognized herself for the first time in weeks and was shocked that her outsides could so drastically contradict her insides. She put on jeans and a sweater while Charlotte threw in a load of laundry, consisting of pajamas, sweat pants, and oversized shirts. Elizabeth had only heard rumors about this thing called 'rock bottom,' but she was now a full-fledged member of the club.

"I wrote the letter to Jack but wasn't sure I'd even send it. I obviously never intended for Jonathan to see it," she explained over matching mugs of steaming tea. The cup warmed her shaky hands while she spoke.

"But he did see it. And you did send it. It's all out in the open now, so all you can do is move forward. Try to repair the damage," Charlotte reasoned matter-of-factly. "*If* that is what you want to do."

"I don't know what to do. For weeks, I've been trying to sort out my feelings for Jack and Jonathan and all I can come up with is I love them both in very different ways. I can't even compare them, in fact. It is almost as if I wish I could merge them into one human being, creating the perfect man for me."

"Honey, we don't get to custom order the man of our dreams and choose the characteristics we want and discard the less desirable qualities. It just doesn't work that way. And in this culture, sadly, it isn't socially acceptable to have them both," she laughed.

"I know, I know. But the romance, the lust, and electricity I feel when I'm with Jack seems like a once in a lifetime love.

And the safety, friendship, and love I feel for Jonathan is perfect, except for the images of Jack that contaminated my relationship with my husband."

There was a moment of difficult silence before Charlotte added, "You know, when I came here today, I was determined not to give you my opinion. I told myself I'd be here for you and be your friend, no matter what you decided to do. Because, in the end, I am here for you and I love you. You know that, right?"

Elizabeth nodded silently, her tired eyes fixed on Charlotte, her heart hanging on her every word. In this moment, Charlotte was all Elizabeth had. She was her lifeline and needed to hear her out.

"Intense and romantic feelings aside, what has Jack ever done to prove his love for you? He walked out of your life completely, over ten years ago, when he found out he had a child with another woman. He couldn't muster the strength or the compassion to salvage this relationship or even communicate with you. He could have been a father to the baby and your soulmate. But he opted out, Elizabeth."

The words stung, but she was right. Elizabeth felt her eyes begin to fill with tears, but she held them back, trying to be strong, while she continued.

Charlotte reached out to hold her hand. "He had every chance to get things settled with his child and reach back out to you. Every day for ten years, he had that chance. People make long distance relationships work all the time. Sure, it would have been hard, but not impossible."

In an unexpected and impulsive move to defend him, Elizabeth blurted, "He came to New York to see me."

"You're right. And when you wrote him a letter, telling him that you wanted to explore those feelings and see him again, what did he say?"

Elizabeth started to speak but Charlotte firmly held her hand up before Elizabeth could utter a word and said, "Don't even try to defend him. He told you to have a nice life, right?"

Elizabeth put her head in her hands and let it all sink in. She was right. My God, she was right. Jack may be all those wonderful things to her, but he was also completely absent. Maybe after all these years, it was time for her to admit that what Jack and Elizabeth had was special, but not enough.

"If I'm honest with myself, I never really gave Jonathan a fair chance. Jack was always a third party in our relationship and Jonathan had no idea. I've never been fair to him."

Charlotte looked her friend in the eye and asked the million-dollar question, "Well, then do you love Jonathan? Do you want to be with him?"

She looked squarely at Charlotte and for the first time in weeks, was sure of something. It was a small something and still, a gigantic something. "I love Jonathan," Elizabeth said softly and sincerely. "I am sure." Her gaze moved to their wedding portrait, elegantly framed on its perch above the stone fireplace. "He's the best husband, but all this time I've been sabotaging our relationship. I can't imagine he'll ever forgive me."

"Well, before you win Jonathan back, there's something important left to do," Charlotte said with a wicked smile Elizabeth had come to love. "You need to find a way to close this chapter of your life. You have to shut, no slam, the door on Jack Murphy once and for all."

"I can do that. I'm ready," she replied confidently. "I miss my husband."

"I really think you need to burn Jack's letters or write a message in a bottle that you throw into the sea, but you need to do *something* to permanently celebrate this chapter in your life coming to an end. I think it's important. Maybe then you can then move on and see if Jonathan will forgive you."

"What should I do?" Elizabeth asked, her eyes wide with curiosity.

Charlotte grabbed her lofty designer purse and car keys off the kitchen counter and directed, "I don't know, but I know how to find out. Get your coat. We're going out for drinks to celebrate your new chapter. And large amounts wine will help us think of something."

Before they walked out the door, Elizabeth hugged her best friend and thanked her for being there for her. She knew she couldn't call her mom, her kids, or her coworkers who knew Jonathan. And since Jonathan was always the person she would talk to when she had a problem, she was stuck. Stuck until Charlotte came knocking.

Of course, the bar Charlotte chose was a dimly lit trendy spot with a stone bar-top, and an extensive wine list. As their first drink was delivered by a stunningly handsome, tattooed bartender, Elizabeth reminded Charlotte there was something special about her relationship with Jack, even though it clearly wasn't meant to be. Apparently, she was desperately clinging to her final moments of being connected to a man who she had to admit was all wrong for her. Elizabeth knew Charlotte wasn't Jack's biggest fan, but she needed her, and the universe, to understand that she would always love and appreciate the magic that existed between her and Jack. But she also knew it was time to move on. Time to appreciate it for what it was and fall more wildly and madly in love with the man she married. If he would ever speak to her again.

When the second drink arrived, they joked about holding a ritual of sorts and lighting a bonfire, where Elizabeth would incinerate all letters, notes, and mementos from Jack. They also seriously considered writing Jack a goodbye letter and watching the message in a bottle drift off the shore by Harborside Academy. But they laughed when they realized that The Potomac would likely drift the bottle straight back to shore and someone they knew would find it. They also decided it was too much of a cliché since Nicholas Sparks had already cornered the market on the concept of messages in a bottle. Charlotte and Elizabeth continued to giggle and reminisce, and Elizabeth felt amazing to finally be out of the house and part of the real world once again. By the time they left the bar, Elizabeth admitted she wanted to think of something quickly, because the sooner she did, the sooner the spell would be broken, and she could try and repair her relationship with Jonathan. The sooner she could tell him how sorry she was and that she would do whatever it took to earn his trust and his love back again. She only hoped it wasn't too late.

As they sauntered to the car, they passed a few small shops that caught their attention. It was a beautiful day for window shopping and chatting with a good friend. There was hope and optimism in the air when they were tempted by a small gift shop that sold candles, bath products, and anything one would need to pamper themselves amidst a rough patch in an otherwise lovely life. They resisted the temptation when suddenly a small tattoo parlor came into view and as Elizabeth glanced in the window, something stopped her in her tracks. "Oh my God, Charlotte. I know what I need to do." There in the window, among various tattoo designs, sat an image of the very same tattoo Elizabeth saw in her dream. That vivid dream. She would never forget the day she left New York City and fell into a deep slumber on the train home with Jonathan. That same tattoo in the store window, was the very tattoo both she and Jack shared in the dream. What were the chances?

That tiny tattoo, she decided, would be placed strategically on the inside of her right wrist and would come to symbolize both the mystical and unexplainable magic she shared with Jack, as well as her newfound ability to let go. The tiny bird in flight would also come to stand for acceptance, freedom, and happiness.

It was time to let go.

Twenty-Nine
2017

The alarm was loud, unwelcoming, and jarring. The first days back to work after a vacation were always the hardest. Meghan hastily threw the covers off and realized it was time for work, with Elliott having already left for the University. Their new living arrangement was relatively fabulous. Since the bathroom was tiny, they decided to stagger their morning routines, so each would have some time and space to get ready. Lucky for Meghan, Elliott was a morning person and preferred to get up first for an early start. This allowed him the opportunity to arrive at work before his colleagues and get a jumpstart on his work. Meghan stretched her arms high above her head and grinned when she smelled the small automated coffee maker beginning its day from the kitchen.

Once dressed, she threw on a jean jacket and a cream-colored gauze scarf before pouring her coffee into a travel mug on her way out the door. As she climbed into her car and put the key in the ignition, she noticed a small stone sitting atop the dashboard. Not only was she sure it wasn't there before, once in her hand, she was certain she had never seen it before. The small stone was black with a luxuriously smooth and shiny surface. She held it in her hand and couldn't help but wonder if Julia had stopped by for a visit. She smiled to herself and placed the stone in her jacket pocket for safekeeping. She decided that when she got to work, she would try to research what type of stone it was and the kinds of healing properties it had. Since her miraculous experiences with the selenite stone, she had been wanting another crystal.

Meghan greeted the few coworkers she passed on her way into the office and dropped her oversized bag on her desk. The first thing she did was shoot Elliott a text to make sure he hadn't come across the curious stone in his travels and place it in her car. When she learned he hadn't, she suspected Julia might be wandering around once again. Smiling at the idea, she grabbed hold of her new *gift* in her pocket and reminded herself to learn more about the crystal later. She placed it on her desk. Unfortunately, she had plenty of work to do first.

The day moved at a record pace since Meghan was catching up on emails and a week's worth of work. Her thoughts lazily drifted to Key West and her body warmed with delight, while thinking about her and Elliott's romantic and adventurous week spent exploring. They talked about their future as if they both assumed they would be experiencing it together. They agreed their future plans included more extensive traveling and even more sightseeing in the scenic state they now both called home.

It was a good thing she had a hearty breakfast, because

Meghan's lunch consisted of an iced tea and snack sized bag of popcorn. They still hadn't been grocery shopping since returning from Florida, so they opted for an early dinner in town. While waiting for him at a high-top wooden table at *H.B. Provisions*, Meghan grabbed a cup of coffee and opened her laptop. She learned the mysterious stone was apparently called black tourmaline and it removed and blocked negative energies, which she found odd because if Julia was trying to help her out once again, her energies these days could not be more positive. Apparently, it also managed fears and worries. She hoped Julia didn't know something she didn't.

The wooden screen door to the deli closed with a slam and she looked up to see a tired Elliott. He greeted Meghan with a kiss and she closed the laptop to focus on their dinner. They ordered burgers and talked about the day's events. Sometimes she found it hard to believe this little life was hers. This adorable, storybook town coupled with meeting Elliott, was so much more than she expected. A year ago, she was sad, lonely, and lost. In such a short time she felt like she found her home once again, and the person she hoped to spend the rest of her life with.

They decided to take a walk to the beach before heading home, and as often as she thought about her good fortune, she also thought about losing her mom. She had hoped to visit her in Costa Rica and never did. She wished she had more time with her. Wished she hadn't run out of time.

"So, what do you think about the healing properties of crystals?" Meghan asked Elliott on their brisk walk down Beach Road. "It's kind of a new age trend. I find them fascinating." She waited for Elliott to roll his eyes and dispel the myths of crystals as nonsense. She was sure her practical scientist would have something to say.

"Most of the evidence is anecdotal. I think the power of suggestion can be robust and if people who use crystals for healing or magic, or whatever, believe in their power and see results, then I see no harm. But, if you ask me if I believe a stone has a particular power, I'm not so sure of that. Why do you ask?"

She thought for a moment while keeping pace with his long strides. "I think they're beautiful and I'm intrigued by the properties they're thought to have. I like the idea of positive energies."

"I think that's the perfect reason to enjoy them, then," he said while grabbing her hand in his.

Thirty
2017

"And to think I almost cancelled," Elizabeth thought to herself, riding the elevator to her hotel room. After the writer's seminar, she decided against venturing out on the town and instead opted for room service and Netflix. She really just wanted a brownie sundae for dinner and room service meant there would be no witnesses and no judgement. A week ago, she had some anxiety over speaking at the event, something that frequently happened when she was asked to appear in public. It was humorous really. She chose to become a writer to disappear into herself and reveled in the notion of making a living from her home office, wearing drawstring pajama pants. While this was technically her current reality, and writing could be deliciously isolating, she never considered the fact that she might have to unravel herself from a cocoon of safety and cotton loungewear to promote herself and her books in public. It was her least favorite part of being a writer.

Elizabeth was glad she didn't let anxiety get the best of her, she reflected. If she had cancelled, she never would have met Meghan, even if it was only for a moment. Elizabeth always wondered what Jack's daughter looked like, what she did for a living, and what her relationships with her parents were like. She had done a lot of wondering over the years. She suspected Meghan must be an aspiring author or a writer of some sort since she attended the conference. She calculated her age to be about 25 years old and marveled about the pace at which life had hurried by. She remembered the day she learned Jack had a daughter, like it was yesterday. She recalled the span of emotions that included resentment and anger, then desperately wishing she belonged to her and Jack instead of Mella and Jack. In the end, Elizabeth always hoped Meghan was happy and healthy. And for whatever strange reason, she always felt oddly connected to the beautiful little stranger who unknowingly stole her dreams and happiness like a masked bandit in the middle of the night. That little stranger was no longer little, but a lovely young adult who wondrously appeared with a copy of one of her books. Meghan Murphy was now an adult. Life sure had a way of being bizarre.

In the morning, Elizabeth would hit the road early since it was Conner's 33rd birthday. He and his wife, Emily, had been trying for years to have a baby. Emily was throwing him a little party at their house, and she wanted to be home in plenty of time to make the salad she had promised and to change into something respectable. Emily was a sweet girl and somehow found a way to tame Conner's wild streak. She would be forever grateful to her for that. But Emily's parents had loads of family money, belonged to a country club, and had a summer beach house on Long Beach Island. Elizabeth always felt underdressed and outclassed when around them, so she wanted some time to pull herself together. And a small part of her hoped Conner and Emily would announce tonight that a grandchild was on the way.

Since Ashley was as committed to remaining single as she was to her career as a Psychiatrist at Boston Children's Hospital, she realized Conner and Emily were her best chance at becoming a grandmother anytime in the near future. Ashley was driven, worked too many hours at the hospital, and didn't particularly believe in the 'institution of marriage,' as she called it. Since she kept her dating life relatively quiet, Elizabeth stopped asking and continued to hope she would someday fall in love and change her mind about participating in the archaic institution of marriage. Conner and Emily's wedding was beautiful, but she still yearned to help her daughter choose her wedding dress.

Driving down the turnpike, she wondered how it was possible that she was already 58 years old with adult children? Adult children with their own careers, hobbies, and happy lives with little need for their mother's daily intrusions. She'd been wrestling lately with the idea of accepting her accomplishments and aging gracefully, versus desperately wishing she was 33 again.

She arrived home with plenty of time ahead of Conner's party. His gift and card had been purchased and wrapped weeks ago. She hoped he loved the navy Brooks Brothers blazer she decided to splurge on. Elizabeth would still be able to run to the market for salad supplies and decide on an outfit for the evening. As the garage door lifted, she thought of Lincoln, even though it has been almost two years since he left her. She still missed coming home to his wagging tail and big brown eyes. Sometimes she still ended up in a puddle of tears when she realized he wasn't greeting her at the door. It was unfair that dogs couldn't live as long as their humans, since their absence was almost too much to bear. He was there for her in the best of times and the worst of times. Maybe someday there would be another furry friend in her life, but the time never seemed right.

As she entered the kitchen, and dropped her overnight bag on the floor, she noticed her favorite large teak salad bowl, overfilled with a beautifully prepared salad, sitting on the kitchen counter.

"I thought you could use a hand with the salad. I hope you don't mind, I took the liberty of trying my hand at your cranberry walnut salad," Jonathan greeted her with a kiss and a long embrace.

"You're a life saver," she told him and snuggled comfortably into his embrace. "I missed you. I wish you would have come to Portsmouth with me." His arms surrounded her, and Elizabeth automatically inserted herself into that familiar place against his body; the perfect place that reminded her she was exactly where she needed to be. Her eyes closed in a moment of perfect contentment and gratitude.

"I wanted to, I really did. Work always gets in the way of fun," he admitted.

She reluctantly pulled from his embrace as he held her face in his hands and lovingly kissed her forehead. "I think I may take a quick nap before we head out for Conner's party. Will you wake me about an hour before we have to leave?" Elizabeth asked her husband.

"Of course, I will my love. I'm always so jealous of your ability to nap at any time, in any place. It's such a gift," he laughed.

She slowly climbed the stairs to the bedroom and happily remembered their new bedding and the pricey Egyptian cotton sheets waiting to envelop her. Oh, it was good to be home. Before drifting off to sleep, she considered once again how fortunate she was that Jonathan agreed to give her another chance so many years ago.

———«(0)»———

Sixteen years ago, Elizabeth acted like a fool and almost ruined her life with her amazing husband for a fantasy. For another man who didn't love her enough to find a way to be with her. But the day she tattooed the small seagull on the inside of her right wrist and granted herself the permission to be free of Jack Murphy, her life changed for the better. There may have been some magic involved in the tattoo itself, but more likely than not, the tattoo permanently changed her mindset. It allowed her the permission to honor her short time with Jack, while setting him free and allowing Elizabeth to rediscover the reason she fell in love with Jonathan in the first place. Frequently, she thanked her lucky stars Jonathan allowed her back into his life. The first year or two wasn't easy. It took him a long time to trust her and trust her feelings for him. It took him time to recover from the day he read his wife's words and learned that the woman he married, inconceivably loved another man. But with weekly marriage counseling, some brutally honest conversations, and two romantic weeks in an isolated thatched hut on a beach in Belize, they made a comeback. She discovered a passion with Jonathan she didn't know could exist, and sixteen years later, things couldn't have been better. Sure, she thought of Jack from time to time. She even had a few dreams, although they had almost completely subsided. Life was good. And she would never do anything to compromise her marriage again.

Her restful nap, like they usually did, came easily.

Thirty-One
2017

It was an idyllic summer Sunday in Kennebunkport. The sun bigger and brighter than it ever was in New York City, and the sky far more expansive somehow. Runners, bikers, and sightseers filled the streets, some experiencing the compelling allure of the coastal neighborhood for the first time. As Meghan looked around and absorbed the reality of being back in the place she clearly belonged, she felt fortunate to call such a place home. This was the kind of picturesque place people visit and think, *wow do people really live here?* And Meghan did.

Elliott and Meghan stopped by Jack's to have an early breakfast, and since the beaches and shops in The Port would be crowded, they decided to lounge on his porch and help plant some herbs and vegetables he had picked up at *Frinklepod Farm*, just outside town. Rarely was there a day when the three of them had no plans, so the idea of a lazy Sunday sounded delightful, if not indulgent.

Jack decided to plant in large pots on the porch rather than dig up the earth in the yard, as he would find them easier to water and care for. The colorful ceramic pots stood proudly on the porch, waiting patiently for their embellishments. The pots were a striking and a stark contrast to the weathered shingles of the windswept house by the sea. The plants and bags of potting soil were strewn haphazardly, nearby. While Elliott and Meghan poured the rich soil from the bags and debated which flowers and plants should be combined, Jack cleaned up their breakfast of bacon and eggs and put on a second pot of coffee. Birds chirped gleefully, and neighbors walked down the street and waved from afar. Church had just gotten out and the town was coming to life like it did every Sunday morning in the summer. They chatted, planted, joked, and shared bottomless cups of coffee before Elliott asked Jack what he was going to do for the rest of the day. Meghan's legs swung lazily over the side of the hammock and she took a moment to appreciate the simplicity and joy packed into this mundane moment.

Jack shrugged his shoulders, looking completely relaxed and said, "I think I might spend the day reading Lizzy's book. She signed it for me, and you went through all the trouble, Meggie, so I think today is the perfect day to get lost in a book."

"Ah, and what better than a book written by an old friend?" Meghan smiled coyly as she emphasized the word friend.

Elliott rolled his eyes and grabbed Meghan's hand, partially lifted her from the hammock, "Let's go, Megs. Leave your dad to his well-deserved R & R. The ride from Nashville must have been a long one. Vacations are the best, but you always need a day or two to relax afterward.

Reading and lounging sounds like the perfect Sunday. And you ordered the perfect weather."

As they said goodbye to Jack and hopped in the car, Meghan commented on how perfect the day was turning out to be. As they drove away, Jack contently sat down in the rocking chair on the front porch, Lizzy's book in hand. He waved an effortless goodbye as the kids drove away.

Meghan turned to Elliott as they pulled away from the house, "Do you think he misses her?" she asked wistfully.

"Hard to say, Megs. But I think maybe he does."

Thirty-Two
2017

D usk would soon fall over the small town of Alexandria, Virginia. Warm breezes blew through the charming town as a typical work day came to an end. It felt good to browse the shelves of Brighton's Books on a quiet Thursday evening. When Elizabeth's world felt busy and life became chaotic, she visited, sometimes for hours. Sometimes for inspiration when writer's block inevitably descended upon her desk, which it most recently had. Some people go to church, others go to the beach. She found her peace and divine inspiration in a bookstore. In some ways, this charming bookstore was where it all started. She held her very first book signing here for *Saving Samuel*. Now, years later, as she carefully perused poetry, bestsellers, memoirs, and young adult fiction, she couldn't help but feel a sense of pride over three published books, multiple award winning short stories, and even one high school history textbook on the American Great Depression. Now, standing in this neighborhood bookstore, she was able to celebrate each word placed on every page of every book so beautifully shelved here, from floor to ceiling. Intimately appreciative of the exquisite yet excruciating process each writer endured to bravely offer their words to the universe, for all to see.

It was a quiet evening in the store, with only three or four other customers mulling about. She was facing the shelves, her nose in *Big Magic,* the newest Elizabeth Gilbert book about living your best creative life, thumbing through its pages, when the feeling hit. Completely unexpected, the feeling was almost impossible to describe in words. It was a little like a sudden case of the chills with a shot of a warm, tingly sensation. It was the old, but still familiar feeling of Jack Murphy. Maybe it was the quote she was staring at. Maybe Elizabeth Gilbert's words were the cause. She glanced at Gilbert's words placed so deliberately upon the page. She wrote, "The universe buries strange jewels deep within us all, and then stands back to see if we can find them." Her words *were* eloquent and powerful. They stirred feelings of innovation and inspiration for Elizabeth's next novel, maybe. Or, possibly something in the air that elicited deeply suppressed memories of another lifetime. *Harborside Academy* was only a mile away, she convinced herself, trying to shake off the sensation.

But when she turned around, she understood. At almost sixty years old, his hair was gray, and he wore round rimmed glasses while intently reading a book. Jack Murphy was standing no more than twenty feet away from her, completely unaware of Elizabeth's presence. His rumpled jeans were big on him and his black t-shirt faded. His beat-up pair of converse sneakers could either be considered hip or juvenile; she couldn't decide. He had aged well. As she clutched *Big*

Magic like a security blanket, she stood dumbfounded and had a decision to make. She could quietly and unobtrusively sneak into the adjoining room that housed trinkets and gifts. Or stay and say hello? While standing frozen, trying to decide which path to take, Jack Murphy lifted his head, sensing someone watching him. There was no way out once their eyes met.

Twenty-seven years melted away in an instant as they each generated a warm and welcoming smile. "Fancy meeting you here, Jack."

He snapped his book closed, never taking his eyes from hers. "Lizzy Bennett, wow, what a surprise. How long has it been?" He removed his reading glasses.

"Let's not even try to do the math," she joked.

"Do you still live locally?" Jack asked, taking a few steps closer.

"Not too far from here. My husband and I live just outside of the city." She found herself quickly inserting Jonathan into the awkward equation. A gentle reminder to herself, she supposed.

"I still live in Maine. A slower pace. And quite beautiful."

Jack went on to explain that he was on his way home from a road trip from Nashville where he explored a city on his bucket list and decided to stop off in Virginia for a dose of nostalgia. Apparently, he stumbled into the bookstore for some coffee and to stretch his legs. He admitted to driving by the school for old time's sake and reminisced about his time there. Age had softened them both, physically and emotionally. Elizabeth was less panicked in his presence now, more certain of who she was, and more confident than ever that she and Jack ended up exactly where they were meant to, after all these years. Jack, still handsome, appeared older and maybe a little sadder. His kind wrinkles and salt and pepper hair reminded her just how long ago they had their first cup of coffee together. And how young they once were. They proceeded to catch each other up on the kids, who were now all adults leading their own lives and agreed how quickly the years had passed.

They continued to stand amongst the mahogany shelves, chatting like long lost friends when Jack looked around and asked if they could step outside. He explained he would need to get back on the road but there were a few things he wanted to tell Elizabeth. There was no sense of drama. Instead, it felt to Elizabeth, like a composed and reasonable request.

They found themselves casually sitting on a wooden bench overlooking Main Street. Almost dark, couples walked by hand-in-hand, children tagged along with their busy parents running errands, amidst the typical small-town buzz of a week night. They were not alone, yet invisible to pedestrians, absorbed in the banality of their own Thursday evening. Jack looked at Elizabeth and said, "Thank you for the signed copy of your book. I was floored when Meghan gave it to me and I treasure it. She's something else," he added with a gentle smile.

"You're welcome, Jack. It was wonderful to meet her. So, grown up and beautiful," she said, speaking from the heart.

Looking down at the sidewalk, he muttered, "I want you to know something. Something that at our age, at this time, matters. And it matters to me that you hear what I've kept from you all these years."

"I'm trying to turn over a new leaf and work on myself. Even this road trip was part of an effort to live more honestly, more boldly, and to focus on me," Jack tried to explain. "Now that Meghan is grown, it's obvious to me that I could end up a very sad and lonely old man if I'm not careful." His green eyes, wrinkled at the corners, twinkled with not only a hint of humor but a whisper of melancholy.

"I understand how that feels. It was a big adjustment for me when the kids left home, and I had to focus on myself. It was a scary time," she shared. She left out, however, details of the flashbacks, of missing him so desperately, the dreams, and the headaches. There simply wasn't enough time to share it all, sitting outside of a bookstore on a Thursday night. And what would be the point?

"I promised myself I'd be honest with you about our past, if ever given the opportunity. I know it was a very long time ago and you don't need nor want to hear my sob story. In fact, one of the things that warms my heart about our crazy history, is that you were able to move on and experience true love, even if I wasn't."

Elizabeth tried to understand where he was going but was struggling. She probably looked confused, but he continued. "It never seemed possible to raise our children so many miles apart and…."

She interrupted, like an old friend, trying to tidily sweep their complicated history under an imaginary rug. "It was a lifetime ago. Please, there's no reason to…"

But Jack would not let her finish. "I understand. But I guess for me, it's important for you to know something. I want you to know that I cared. I want you to know that if not for unexpected events, well, things would have been very different."

She stared at him, still confused.

He stood as he went on, "There's something in my car I'd like you to have."

She followed Jack a short distance to his car and he retrieved a small brown bag from his glove compartment. "I've carried this around for over 25 years now. I'd like you to have it."

As he handed her the soft, worn bag, she kept her eyes on his and since she didn't know what to say, and remained silent. Elizabeth tentatively opened the bag to find a small black velvet box. Hesitant to open it, she paused and said, "Are you sure about this? Are you sure this is meant for me?"

He nodded silently and as she opened the box, a delicate gold ring with the tiniest sparking diamond glistened in the orange glow of the now setting Virginia sun. Confused, she looked up at him.

He went on to explain, "This is the ring I bought for you a week before Mella called and I learned about Meghan. Lizzy, I was going to ask you to marry me. It's not an expensive ring, but that isn't the point. I planned to ask you to be my wife. This was your engagement ring. I'm sorry we never got the chance to share the excitement of an engagement and a happy marriage. I'm so very sorry life happened the way it did. But I saved it and now I want you to have it. I need you to have it. Even after all these years."

Elizabeth stared at the ring for a long time because lifting her eyes to his didn't seem possible in the moment. When she finally found the strength to look at him, his eyes glistened with gentle tears. "Jack, this is beautiful. I had no idea. But you're right. Life happens. And in our case, it *happened* many years ago. Time has a funny way of coming full circle, doesn't it?"

As she lifted her hand to wipe a tiny tear from her own eye, Jack reached out to softly take hold of her wrist. He looked bewildered as he stared at the small tattoo of a seagull in flight and said, "I had a dream about this tattoo. In fact, in my dream you had the tattoo, but so did I."

She looked at Jack in shock. "What? I had a dream like that too."

He ignored her shock and continued, "Do you remember New York City?"

"Of course I do," she replied.

He went on. "The next morning, I pulled my car to the side of the road because I was afraid I was going to fall asleep at the wheel. It was all just too much. I hadn't slept all night. I dozed off for a few minutes, and when I did, I had a dream we were sitting by a river and you had this same tattoo on your wrist." He touched her wrist and gently and rubbed his thumb over the symbol that stood for their connection. Their love. "And in the dream, so did I."

Astounded, Elizabeth added with wide eyes, her other hand on her heart, "Oh my God, Jack. I had the exact same dream. On the same day. Probably at almost the same time. I fell asleep on the train ride home from New York. That dream, our dream, is the reason I got this tattoo."

They stood somberly on the sidewalk, frozen in haunting shared emotions and circumstances impossible to believe and difficult to explain.

The sun had set, and a full moon shone in the clear and almost dark sky. Elizabeth couldn't find the courage nor the energy within to fully face the events of the evening. All she was able to do was give Jack a hug and thank him. Thank him for the ring, for sharing part of their story she didn't know existed, and for showing up in her life on this particular Thursday evening. As they said their goodbyes with a warm embrace, she wished him a safe trip back to Maine and knew with complete certainty she had just said goodbye to him for the last time. Something deep down in her old tortured soul told Elizabeth she would never see Jack Murphy again. And then the sadness came. It arrived like a vigorous and angry gust of wind. And it was overpowering.

She drove to the river, parked her car, and sat motionless with both hands on the wheel. With the windows down, she could hear the soothing sounds of the water. The moon provided a warm light that flooded the deepest parts of her heart and soul as she began to cry. It wasn't at all like the other times she had cried over Jack Murphy. She wasn't hysterical. She wasn't even devastated by his leaving. This time it wasn't even heart wrenching to watch him walk away. This was different. This time the regret or massive sorrow typically driving her emotions was absent. Elizabeth was ready to go home to her husband. She knew their story was over and this time the tears stood for an acceptance of what had been, what was, and what would become of their shattered and ugly, dysfunctional fairytale.

Alone in the car, she allowed herself only about a half hour to wallow in the ending of the story. The dramatic conclusion snuck up on her forcefully and without warning.

It was like turning to the last page of a book. A book you were so engrossed in, you couldn't wait to read the last sentence, yet you dreaded the moment you would need to exhale and admit it was over. You were done, and you didn't know what to do with yourself, because you weren't ready to walk away from the imaginary life, created within the pages.

It was exactly like that.

———⋙‹⟨⟩›⋘———

Luckily, life had returned to normal, with Jack's ring safely secured in Elizabeth's safety deposit box. Although she knew she would keep the ring, she decided against keeping it in the house. For one, she didn't want to wrestle with the temptation of touching it, holding it, or gazing at it, as it would surely conjure memories and emotions she was determined to lay to rest. Secondly, she was superstitious and afraid of the negative energy the ring could bring to her home, and she wasn't willing to take any such risk, as mystical and illogical as it sounded. It took many years and a lot of hard work to overcome the curse of longing for and loving Jack Murphy, and Elizabeth wanted to be sure nothing she did would jeopardize her marriage or her happiness. She had learned from her mistakes.

She did, however, carry with her a sense of closure and silent sadness, but also a feeling of contentment as she treasured her fateful book store rendezvous with Jack. They were older and wiser, but their hearts and souls felt the same as they did way back when. It must have been the way it was meant to be. Her mother once told her, *what is supposed to happen, is exactly what will happen.* And she was supposed to marry Jonathan, live happily ever after with the man of her real-life dreams, and say farewell to Jack Murphy on a surprising weeknight in a bookstore, finishing the last chapter, and shutting the book once and for all, before placing it on the shelf.

That is what she told herself, anyway.

Ashley was on her way home from Boston for the weekend and they agreed to spend the time shopping, lunching, and watching a movie. It was rare for her to take time away from the hospital and she loved Boston so much, she rarely left the city. Elizabeth was thrilled she would soon be home to spend some quality mother-daughter time together. As proud as she was of all her accomplishments and was in no way surprised by her fierce independence, she missed her terribly. Just yesterday, she was a spunky little girl who wanted to spend all her time with her. These days it seemed she was checking her mother off her lengthy and important to-do list. But Elizabeth would take what she could get.

When she noticed the cab pull away from the house, Elizabeth ran to greet her daughter on the front porch because she simply couldn't wait for her to ring the doorbell. She carried a pricy, leather overnight bag, monogrammed with her initials, and her position at the hospital had clearly elevated her wardrobe budget. Her shoes were sensible but expensive and her hair and make-up minimal yet cosmopolitan. She was as gorgeous as ever, and still possessed the sharp glean in her eye of the motivated powerhouse she was on the soccer field as a child. Elizabeth was proud to call her hers, but sometimes wondered where she came from.

"Mom, you look fantastic," Ashley said as she hugged her mom. Her enthusiastic embrace reminded Elizabeth of her teenage self and she quickly forgot she was a doctor and a grown woman. In that moment, she was just her Ashley and it felt good to have her home for the weekend.

"My goodness, Ash, it's so good to see you. Phone calls and text messages only take a needy mother so far, you know."

"Hey, you used to come to Boston a lot more than you do now. I have a guest room and you and Jonathan are always welcome," she retorted.

"Yeah, well blame it on old age," she joked. "Plus, you work crazy hours and are always burning the candle at both ends. I get the sense you don't get a lot of leisure time for socializing."

"Well, that's true. But I'm here now, and we shouldn't waste any time at all complaining about how old we are or how hard we work. Let's have some fun this weekend and catch up," she demanded.

The weekend flew by with late night chats over containers of mint chocolate chip ice-cream, Ashley's favorite, and leisurely lunches on the deck. They even saw a movie, complete with buttered popcorn and oversized reclining theater seats. Ashley told funny stories about her busy days at the hospital and it was clear how much she loved her job. Finally, on Sunday afternoon, they strolled through an art gallery, just before Ashley had to catch her plane back to Boston.

As they entered the airport, Elizabeth pulled the car to

the curb, checked her watch, and realized she had plenty of time before Ashley boarded a flight that would whisk her back to her regularly scheduled life. Elizbeth turned to her daughter, grateful for a lovely weekend, but concerned about her work ethic. "Ash, do me a favor. Don't work too hard. So hard that you don't have time to let someone love you."

"Mom, please," a familiar eye roll followed.

"I know, I know, but let me be your mom for a second. And let me give you advice. Even if you don't take it, I'll feel better for giving it."

Ashley took her mother's hand and appeased Elizabeth as she softened and said, "Okay, Mom, advise away. I'm all ears."

All her attention was on Elizabeth and she smiled because she was a captive audience and realized she would soon escape the motherly rant, as her mom continued, "All I want you to know is, as a somewhat old woman who has learned a few lessons along the way, don't take being in love for granted. Don't sell yourself short. You can have an amazing career *and* be in love. It can be pure magic. A magic I don't want you to miss."

Thirty-Three
2017

Meghan couldn't remember the last time she was ill, but as she lay in bed, she was considering calling in sick. She had the days, she might as well use them. Oddly, she didn't feel that bad, but her body and bones disagreed. She didn't have a sore throat nor a fever, no cold symptoms, and no stomach bug. So why did she feel so terrible? Her legs ached and felt heavy as she shuffled to and from the bathroom, as if wading through cement. She felt as if she were wrapped in a weighted blanket and her body couldn't fight through the added burden. Slowly, she found her way back to the waiting bed. Sick day it was.

Elliott leaned over her in the bed, propped by a few pillows. "Are you sure you don't need to see the doctor? I can take you before I head to work," he said, sounding concerned.

"No, I think I might be coming down with something, but it's hard to say. I'll go to the doctor later today if I feel worse. I'll check for a fever, stay hydrated, and try and sleep this off, whatever it is," she promised him. Unfortunately, the words didn't sound very convincing, even to her.

He looked worried but kissed her on the head, pulled the covers up to her chin, and tucked her in for good measure. "Call me or text me and let me know how you're feeling."

Even though it was summer, the weather outside was cloudy and cool and perfectly appropriate for a sick day. At least Meghan wouldn't feel as if she were missing the sunshine on a beautiful day. She sent an email to the station manager using her phone and notified him that she would be taking a sick day. She tried to scroll through her email messages, but her arms ached simply from holding the phone in position. Everything hurt. She tossed the phone on the bed, closed her heavy eyelids, and gave into the overpowering and peculiar lethargy.

Intoxicated by a long, deep sleep, she fumbled for her phone to check the time. It was almost 4:00 p.m. and it appeared she had slept the day away. There were text messages and three missed calls from Elliott. She placed the phone back on the bed, devoid of the energy required to generate a response. He would understand and likely assume she was sleeping off whatever was plaguing her. She forced her body into a seated position and swung her legs over the side of the bed. She felt about the same. No better, but no worse, either. With no other symptoms emerging, she decided a doctor's visit could wait at least another day, figuring she was just fighting some type of virus. There had been a flu going around the office and she had obviously picked something up. Interestingly, the only other concerning symptom she possessed was an unsettling feeling of doom. She felt like something was either terribly wrong or about to *be* devastatingly wrong. As much as she tried to brush the ominous feeling aside, it kept resurfacing, like a dark and looming visitor. She felt an anxious panic, impossible to ignore. Maybe she would try to read a book to distract her mind and body from the misery.

When even reading a book was unsuccessful, Meghan called Elliott to assure him that she was, in fact, alive and just resting. He had a few more hours of work to attend to and would be home later with some chicken soup and crackers from her favorite market. She wasn't hungry until the mention of soup and the sudden realization that she hadn't eaten all day. She made her way into the kitchen, filled a large water bottle, and decided she would give herself a chance at a quick recovery by flushing whatever it was out of her system. She even added a generous slice of lemon and headed back to the bedroom to check her messages. But just as she climbed back into the rumpled bed, the phone rang.

As soon as she heard the phone ring, she knew something was terribly wrong. She didn't know how, she just knew. It was Henry, her father's elderly next-door neighbor. He sounded panicked. "Meghan, can you come over?" he added, "Please come quick. It's your dad."

She replied as she jumped from the bed with the abilities of someone completely healthy. "Yes, I'm on my way. What's wrong, Henry?" she asked, as she pushed her feet into a pair of flip-flops sitting at the end of the bed.

Henry sounded confused and concerned, "I don't know. I noticed him in the yard, sitting out on the bench by the water. He looked slumped over, so I ran to check on him. He says he's feeling lightheaded and I'm worried. He's sweating and short of breath. He keeps talking about someone named Lizzy. Said he needs to get to her."

Lizzy? What did Lizzy have to do with this? Meghan wondered as she ran out to the car. "I'll call 911," she shouted into the phone at Henry.

"I already did. He asked me not to, but I didn't listen to him. He needs to be checked. I'm really worried about him. They should be here any minute."

Of course, Jack tried to refuse help with all the stubbornness Meghan had come to expect. Fortunately, help was on the way. Thank goodness Henry was nearby and noticed something out of the ordinary.

Luckily, living in a small town meant a quick response with the fire station just up the street. They would be there at once. Likely before her. She sped nervously to her father's house praying for him to be okay. Racing through the small town, terrified of the unknown, she had flashbacks of being at her mother's bedside on the day she died, embracing her yet incapable of helping her. Unable to bring her back. Unable to right the wrongs. Flashbacks of the funeral and memories of the months of torment and tears were overwhelming. "Please, God, not Dad. Please let him be okay," she whispered.

She pulled over to let a young police officer in a dark blue cruiser rush by her with his lights and sirens on. She could only assume he was responding to an emergency. Jack's. Her heart pounded as she reminded herself to stay calm and focused. As she pulled down the street, much faster than was safe for the narrow seaside road, she approached a woman walking down the lane, toward her father's house. As Meghan passed her, it only took a moment for her to realize it was Julia walking quickly toward Jack's cottage. With no time to waste, she continued on but was gravely concerned about

Julia's presence. Why was she there? Meghan even guessed she could be hallucinating. Her mind could be playing tricks during a time of stress. She probably just *wanted* Julia to be there, she told herself as she raced past her, unwilling to stop to confirm her presence.

One ambulance, one fire truck, and the passing police officer crowded Jack's small home and neighbors were beginning to pace nearby with looks of concern on their faces. Meghan parked in the driveway and ran toward her dad and the small crowd of helpers already on the scene. They were talking to him as they were helping him onto a stretcher, asking important questions about possible chest or arm pain. He was breathless and clammy but able to answer all of their questions.

Jack spotted his daughter in his periphery as he was being loaded into the ambulance. "Hey Meg. I'm okay. Really. But it's Lizzy. She called me, she's calling me." He was whisked away before he could finish explaining.

Meghan looked worriedly at the paramedic and shrugged her shoulders. His phone was not nearby, and they all wondered what call he was referencing. He wasn't making sense and she was afraid he might be having a heart attack. Or a nervous breakdown. Dear Lord, she begged, please let him be having a nervous breakdown. Apparently, he reported that his chest felt heavy and since he was having trouble breathing, they were going to give him an aspirin and assess him for a heart attack.

Meghan was grateful they let her ride in the ambulance with him to the hospital.

Thirty-Four
2017

A lthough Elizabeth was incredibly happy for her, she secretly wished Charlotte hadn't moved to London. She met a handsome playwright and after six months of a long-distance love affair, he invited her to join him overseas. Admitting she wanted a break from teaching, Charlotte vowed to come back if things didn't work out. That was years ago. Charlotte was now married, living in London, and although she didn't have to work, she had a job in a small upscale boutique that catered to the rich and famous. She and her handsome and eccentric husband did not want children, so they lived a quiet life, dined at only the best restaurants, and traveled the world often. Charlotte had manifested the life she always wanted. And Elizabeth never doubted she would.

It was days like today when Elizabeth wished she could pick up the phone and ask her best friend to come over to share a pizza and a ten dollar bottle of wine. Charlotte's life had changed drastically, and she was happy for her, but Elizabeth missed her terribly. She scribbled on her legal pad as she sat at her desk, hoping for lightening to strike with an idea for her next book. She had exhaustively researched different time periods, natural disasters, famines, and even dabbled in some war history. But nothing had developed into a plausible storyline for the next book. She tapped away at the keyboard, made some lists on her legal pad, and forced herself to daydream. But, nothing.

She walked over to her bookshelf, the one that held her favorites. Books from her childhood, teens, and adulthood she either loved deeply or that had changed her life in some way. She casually ran her hand against their spines, hoping for some sort of cathartic revelation, and wondered how each author found their grand inspiration when they sat down to write a book. She marveled at the mere magnitude of a writer's existence. There were only twenty-six characters in the alphabet, only so many ways those letters could be combined to form sounds, and only so many words in the English language. Yet, there were limitless ways a writer could combine letters, sounds, and words to craft their unique story. A story no one else thought to spawn given the same letters and words to choose from. She was fascinated by the strangest things.

Her hand stopped at an old copy of *Charlotte's Web* by E.B. White. It was the first "chapter" book she remembered devouring one summer. Back then, lazy summer days were filled with quiet moments in the back yard, perfect for reading. There were no cell phones, cable TV, or any other electronics to speak of, competing for her attention. As a young girl, she read while she ate breakfast, while she meandered through the yard, and while she relaxed on a flimsy reclining beach chair on the back patio. That summer alone, she read *Charlotte's Web* three times.

On the bottom shelf, she noticed the new hardcover copy of Elizabeth Gilbert's *Big Magic*, stacked proudly atop a few book sale treasures. She read it in just two days and while other books that impacted her life gave her gentle messages and quiet whispers of encouragement, this book gave her a push. A physical shove in the direction of her own creativity. Whereas some authors provided her subliminal messages and beautiful symbolism, Gilbert took her by the shoulders, looked her in the eye, and shook her. She spoke to her in the way she needed to be spoken to and in no uncertain terms told her to get moving. It was time to start making her own *Big Magic*. But what would that be? She tried painting and found nothing but frustration at her lack of ability. Already being a writer, she felt she needed to try something new and channel her creative efforts differently. But then it hit her. Maybe that stroke of creativity needed to come out in a different form of writing. Historical fiction was based in reality and in the facts and events of a historical period. Maybe being creative meant abandoning what she already knew how to do and forge ahead with her writing by being innovative. Maybe she should write from a mystical, magical, or fantastical perspective. Maybe she should write something she would normally never, in a million years, write. Yes, that was it. It was time to think differently.

Elizabeth stepped out of her office to make a cup of coffee and considered the ramifications of such a decision. Her editor would work with her, but would her publisher? Would anyone want to read something so different from her? When artists veered from their expected path, they were sometimes ridiculed and told to stick to what they knew. Could she handle the criticism and the feelings of failure that could accompany her on this journey? The strong aroma of the coffee filled the kitchen and a feeling of confidence and excitement came over her. This is what she needed. And as Elizabeth clutched her empty mug, waiting for the last drops of caffeine to plunge into the coffee pot, she glanced down at her tattoo. Her tiny symbol of everything right and wrong in her life. Everything that had made her who she was today. That freeing symbol of all things love, magic, and acceptance. She would write a fairytale. A modern-day fairytale. She didn't know how it would begin or how it would end. It might end up a glorious, sunny fairytale or maybe an ugly and dysfunctional fable. But fiction and fantasy would meet on her pages normally filled with facts, times gone by, and characters who came alive out of the reality of the time period. This would be very different.

Hoping to master a new genre and the art of fantasy, Elizabeth aspired to learn how to outline a story based in the realm of enchanted make believe. As any good neurotic would do, she immersed herself in preparations for her next novel. She scoured the library and the internet to find the secrets behind success in this genre. Desperate to be prepared, she read interviews with authors like Neil Gaiman and Alice Hoffman. She wanted to know their ways and understand their thinking, because good thinking was good writing. Days of this repetitive behavior led to weeks of this time-consuming behavior. When clinical levels of frustration set in, she decided to jump to the silly conclusion that a person

THE MAGIC OF MISSING YOU

could over prepare for a task or a role. She was a published author, after all. And since she had likely read thousands of books in this category over her lifetime, she should simply consider the pre-requisites met and deem herself qualified for the job. Learning the hard way, that the over prepared never got to the writing itself, she forced herself to just write. She would worry and obsess about the quality of the writing later. It was counterintuitive, and uncomfortable, but it was time to see if she could do this.

Elizabeth tried to relax, clear her mind, and channel her inner artistic self. Surprisingly, she was able to let her imagination take her places she had never before had access to. She simply chose a setting, crafted a few flawed and quirky characters, and began to deliriously daydream her way through an introductory chapter. She visualized a miniature, charmed and captivating stone cottage she chose for the backdrop of the story. She imagined the overgrown but colorful gardens that surrounded the cottage and described them with enough detail for a reader to immerse themselves in the scene. She hinted at the mysteries or possible magic surrounding the small house and its inhabitants in ways that felt charming, and not at all bizarre. Happy with the five pages she had generated, she decided she needed a break.

Without any particular destination in mind, Elizabeth grabbed a notebook and her favorite pen, and hopped in the car to visit her local coffee shop for more caffeine and some inspiration. It was a cool summer afternoon and the warm cup in her hand was comforting as she walked back to her car. A breeze was picking up since an evening summer storm was expected to blow through the area later. She had plenty of time to find an outdoor spot to drink her coffee and conjure a few plot lines for the new project, before the weather turned.

She chose a small park near her house where runners moved at a constant pace on paved pathways, where people walked their dogs while looking at their smart phones, and a few children kicked a ball around on the grassy area. It was not crowded and she picked a faded, lopsided picnic table, adjacent to the walking path, to park herself and her latte. It was a beautiful summer afternoon, with the breezes moving the leaves and the branches of the many trees like a soothing and dramatic waltz. She found the perfect spot to enjoy a cup of coffee and to let nature encourage her new writing project. She began doodling on her pad and wrote the words *Cottage Breezes Dancing*, wondering if she could choose a title for the new book before she had a legitimate story line. She supposed there were no rules. She liked the phrase and the new approach, working outside her comfort zone; she might go with it.

While sketching, thinking, and absorbing the beauty of the park's surroundings, an elderly couple taking a stroll stopped at Elizabeth's picnic table. "There's a storm coming," the tall gentleman pushing his walker said." They each possessed kind eyes and she immediately envied their leisurely afternoon spent enjoying each other's company.

"I know," she said, pausing to glance upward toward the dancing trees, "the winds just before a storm are beautiful, though. I'll make sure I dash to my car at the first sign of raindrops," she responded with a smile. Elizabeth wished she had more time to spend with the unexpected visitors, intrigued by their mesmerizing souls. The mysterious way they drifted through the park caused her to look about, to see if anyone else was aware of their presence.

"Stay safe," the woman said flatly, as she looked past Elizabeth, making no eye contact. And with that, they continued slowly and methodically to the safety of their car.

As they walked away, she was struck by their odd charm and innocence, but considered the stories of love, children, heartbreak, illness, and maybe even betrayal they might have endured to earn the right to be the loving elderly couple that strolled through the park on a summer afternoon. The man and woman were only in her life for a moment, but in that instant, she decided they would be the characters that would reside in her enchanted, stone cottage filled with magic and intrigue. Yes, they would be her inspiration for an enthralling and dysfunctional fairytale. The universe presented them to her as the winds strengthened and they certainly fit the part.

Although there was no sign of rain, the clouds were moving hastily across the sky and the bright afternoon was suddenly darkening. Elizabeth noticed the other inhabitants of the park, quickly moving toward their cars and ushering their pets and children to safety. She loved summer storms for their drama and exhilaration and this one would be particularly captivating. *Just a few more minutes,* she thought to herself. As branches began to bend and leaves violently forced to the ground, she wanted to take in all the magnificence of the approaching storm.

It was easy to get lost in the moment. She began to visualize that lovely, peculiar couple in her cottage and feverishly began to scribble ideas for a plot. It was as if they were placed in her path for the purpose of divine literary inspiration and she didn't want to leave the park's creative offerings just yet. It was at that exact moment she felt the first light raindrop and noticed a seagull circling above. He was beginning to voice his high-pitched warnings to other birds of the impending storm. She looked down at the tattoo on her wrist and considered maybe he was circling above to warn her, not other birds. She should make a run for it.

During her short sprint to the car, the skies opened up and large, heavy raindrops came down. By the time she closed the car door, the storm had fully arrived, and she was drenched. She looked down at the notebook she had thrown on the passenger's seat and the blue ink was blurred from the raindrops. It would be difficult to decipher her notes later. She had to push her wet hair away from her face and searched the car for a towel or anything she could use to dry off but found nothing. In no hurry to put the car into drive, she looked up through the windshield, at the torrential rains and wondered if she should wait for the storm to pass before heading home.

And it struck her, that charming elderly couple could have been her and Jack. The couple could have seen trying times, but in the end, were happily married, side by side, well into their eighties. Maybe they were separated for years and found their way back to one another. Of course, she was filling in the blanks with creative license.

The elderly couple could certainly be the inspiration for her next book. For that they were perfect. But they left her with a feeling of profound sadness for what could have been. She sighed deeply as the rain pelted her car. "Jack, I miss you," she said quietly, with the rhythm of the rain surrounding her.

Thirty-Five
2017

Jack Murphy woke to the subtle sounds of machines designed to monitor his blood pressure and heart rate. Steady rhythmic beeps filled the impersonal air in the unfamiliar room. Quiet, confident voices spoke in medical jargon and it was not difficult to conclude that he was in a hospital. But he didn't know why. Through an eerie stillness and the cool darkness, he could make out dim lights placed ominously above. His body and mind felt heavy and immoveable as his thoughts drifted quickly to Lizzy. Was she in danger? How is it possible that he was able to feel her panic, her pain, and hear her calling his name when they were many miles and lifetimes apart. He tried desperately to will his eyelids to open but the effort fatigued him as he drifted back to a deep and sedated sleep, imagining the years missed, the vacations not taken, the sights not seen. Now, it was too late. He was too old, and his life decisions had been made. And Lizzy was miles away, in danger. He was sure of it.

Jack tried to move his arms, open his eyes, or to yell out

to someone, anyone nearby who might be able to help. But it was of no use. Trapped in his own body during a time of helplessness, Jack regretted his life's decisions. The decisions that left him alone in a sterile room, unable to help her and unable to help himself. It was too late.

The bright orbs of light hovering above were intrusive and made it difficult for Jack to keep his eyes open. Tremendous fatigue overtook him, and he was forced to succumb to whatever it was that was happening to his body and mind. Just as he was about to give in to the lethargy, he heard his name being gently called. He opened his eyes to find a young nurse standing by his bedside ready to help. He blinked to be sure he wasn't dreaming, and in an instant her image became clear. Her hand was resting on his wrist, checking his pulse and her white uniform stood in stark contrast to her auburn hair and kind green eyes. "Mr. Murphy, I am here to get you ready for your procedure. Go ahead and close your eyes. We will take good care of you," she promised softly. As she reached for the stethoscope strewn around her neck, Jack noticed a small pin on her uniform. He closed his eyes, trusting her words and reassured by the small seagull pinned to her chest.

"Miss Murphy?" A young doctor approached Meghan in the waiting room of the brightly lit and barren Emergency Room. Her nervous pacing interrupted, and it occurred to her he didn't look old enough to vote, let alone old enough to be giving life-saving medical advice. However, she clung to his every word since he was the only qualified human in a white lab coat ready to give her an update on her dad.

"Yes, Doctor. How is he doing? Can I see him?" she asked, hands on her hips, meeting his serious gaze. He stood only about an inch taller than her own 5'4" frame but possessed a strong sense of authority. He was a force to be reckoned with, she guessed, and his persona helped her understand that her father's life was in capable hands.

"Your dad has had a heart attack," he said with little emotion, but absolute certainty. "He's headed to the Cath Lab now to see how extensive the blockage is and that will determine the treatment. We'll be moving quickly to open the blockages, possibly with a stent. We'll know more once we get inside and see exactly what's going on."

"Is he going to be okay?" she asked with despair and worry. A heart attack. She really thought it was possible he got a phone call from Lizzy and maybe he was having a panic attack. She hadn't let herself consider the worst. She wasn't prepared to face the possibility of a heart attack.

"He was lucky to get to the hospital so quickly. We'll know more soon."

The doctor gave details about the procedure. It was hard work to absorb and retain the information considering her anxiety levels, but she did her best while her mind raced, and her own heart ached within her chest. She thought she should be writing it all down, but instead was trying to commit his words to memory. About 5 minutes after the doctor shook her hand in an unspoken agreement to save her father, Elliott arrived with a cup of tea and settled in to wait with Meghan. It was an excruciating wait filled with periods of silence, worry, and some whispered conversation between them.

"Do you think my dad spoke with Lizzy and the stress caused a heart attack? Could she have told him something that caused this? Why would he mention her before getting into the ambulance?" The questions were unanswerable, of course, but she posed them anyway.

Elliott look perplexed as he started straight ahead and said, "I don't really know, Megs. I wish I could explain it. I doubt a phone call would cause a heart attack unless he was already walking around with a blockage, which is very possible. He was lucky to get to the hospital and fortunate Henry was watching and decided to check on him."

"Small towns and good neighbors are the best, aren't they," she said gratefully. Meghan stood and resumed the repetitive pacing. "He's going to be okay, right?" she asked Elliott. Knowing that Elliott couldn't give her the guarantee she wanted, she looked to the floor, continued to pace, and tried her best to endure the long wait.

<hr/>

Sure enough, Jack had two partially blocked arteries and since the procedure was a success and he was recovering nicely, he was able to come home to rest. With a new heart-healthy diet and careful attention to his cardiac health, he was expected to make a full recovery and lead a full life, despite having had a heart attack in his own backyard at the age of fifty-nine. It was impossible for Meghan to comprehend the idea of losing him suddenly, the way she lost her mother, not so long ago. It shook her to her core to realize how close she just came to losing him. If it wasn't for the quick thinking of Henry and the first responders who came to his aid so rapidly and expertly, she might be parentless. Grateful didn't begin to describe it.

"Meghan, there's something I need your help with," Jack said while reading a book, snuggled into his favorite chair overlooking the harbor.

"Of course. What do you need?" she responded, expecting him to request a special meal or maybe some laundry to be done before she headed home for the evening.

"I need you to help me find Lizzy. I'd like to call her, but I don't have her number and I certainly don't have a current address for her. I'm concerned about her and will feel better if I could just check in and know that she's okay."

She thought before she spoke, because Meghan wasn't sure if he remembered muttering her name the day of his heart attack. She still hadn't determined whether or not Lizzy called, or if they spoke on the phone, upsetting him on that day. Not wanting to upset him further, she proceeded carefully. "You did mention talking to Lizzy when you were getting into the ambulance." Meghan let her comment sit in the air between them as she waited for him to elaborate. She didn't want to push.

"I was sitting on the bench in the yard. By the harbor. Lizzy's book was in my hand because I had just finished the final chapter. It was the oddest thing, because out of nowhere, I heard her voice. I was sure I heard her calling my name. She sounded panicked. She was in danger. That's when I began to feel my chest tighten. I was dizzy and couldn't stand up. Something overcame me. I suspect now those were signs of the heart attack. And it's possible hearing Lizzy's voice was some sort of strange reaction in that moment." His voice trailed off.

"And you're worried and just want to check in with her?" Meghan added.

"Yes, I'd feel a lot better. If you could help by finding a number or an email, anything at all. I'd really appreciate it. It's been bothering me for days."

"You really loved her, Dad. Didn't you?" she asked as she sat down beside him.

"I really did. And although I made some mistakes, I suspect both our lives ended up just the way they were supposed to. Years ago, when I learned she was married and had her first book published, I was so happy for her. All I ever wanted was for her to be happy. Now, I just want to be sure everything is okay."

"When I get home, I'll do a little research. I'm sure we can find a mailing address, or a phone number and you can send her a message. I'm sure everything is fine, and it wouldn't surprise me if your senses were playing tricks on you considering you were in the middle of a heart attack. Please, don't worry."

"I'll try. But I'm not so sure everything is okay," he said as he gazed blankly toward the harbor. Before Meghan left her father, they both felt a chill enter the room, a powerful sensation difficult to ignore. She glanced over her shoulder at her father, who felt her gaze, but continued to stare out the window, enveloped in sadness and regret.

Thirty-Six
2017

Fighting back the ambush of tears, Elizabeth decided to put the car in drive and force the frustrating onslaught of Jack Murphy from her consciousness. Sometimes reminders of him came out of nowhere and this appeared to be one of those inconvenient and fateful times. Feelings of grave disappointment washed over her for allowing this lifetime obsession with what could have been, cloud what was positive, healthy, and happy in her life. However, she continued to willingly and quietly carry Jack with her like a private, weathered journal, so expertly hidden beneath the floorboards of her person, that no one else had access to the story.

The rain, refusing to give up made the trek home slow and dangerous. The windshield wipers worked overtime for naught, as they raced rapidly across the windshield. The ferocious storm came fast and hard. It was impossible to see beyond the steering wheel, and Elizabeth considered pulling over, but it was difficult to find the right place. Better to proceed slowly home, she decided. Thankfully, the traffic light, swinging wildly in the wind in front of her, turned red and she was relieved to have a few moments to rest from the constant acute and painful attention required to drive in this threatening weather. She was longing for a warm bath and a cup of tea. Soon enough.

While anxiously waiting for the light to turn, unexpected flashbacks of time spent with Jack played like a vibrant motion picture in her mind. Their awkward first meeting in the teacher's room, the crowded coffee house, dancing in the art room, opening presents under the Christmas tree, even their desperately passionate and forbidden kiss in a hotel in New York City. Memories and fantasies so incredibly vivid and powerful it felt as though she left her body to experience them. They included images, emotions, and scents in an attack on her spirit. It was if they all happened yesterday rather than a lifetime ago. She chuckled softly at the thought of possibly turning the events of Jack and Lizzy into a book one day. What a story it would be, she thought to herself as the light turned green amidst the intensifying storm.

Proceeding carefully on her route, the wind and rain continued to wreak havoc on driving conditions and that is when it happened. Just as she was considering the notion of writing their story. That idea itself might have caused what happened next. Or maybe, what happened next was simply destiny and supposed to happen on that particular day. It's hard to imagine one ever knows their world is about to change, in the very moment leading up to misfortune.

An enormous and deafening bang caused Elizabeth's hands to leave the wheel, her head to be thrown violently backward, and although it was hard to understand exactly what was happening, she knew without a doubt something terribly serious had just happened.

The best way to describe the event that changed everything was that Elizabeth watched what was happening to herself, from outside the vehicle. Although the pain was intense, and she was unable to will any part of her body to move, she was calm and oddly composed as she realized she could feel the fierce wind and constant rain on her skin. She called Jack's name. No, she screamed Jack's name. Over and over again, until she no longer had the strength. She wasn't sure where he was or what she expected him to do, but during that critical moment, she assumed he could hear her screams. And assumed he would know she was in trouble. It never occurred to her to call for anyone else in that moment. The moment, amidst a raging storm, that changed everything.

⟶◉⟵

Her name was Julia and although Elizabeth was sure she had met her before, she could not place her. Julia hugged her visitor tightly and welcomed her like a dear old friend. She handed her a beautiful bouquet of wild flowers, tied with an elegant lace ribbon. Elizabeth had never seen flowers so beautiful with such intense colors. They were so perfect, they were almost dream like. She ran her hand over the marvelous blooms to feel the textures of the stunning flowers and held them to her nose to take in their magnificent fragrance.

Elizabeth didn't question where she was simply because

she felt like she belonged. The perfectly magical place she stumbled upon might be a dream, she considered, and if that were the case, she was in no hurry to wake. In the distance, there was a whimsical white picket fence, flowering trees swaying in the gentle breeze and an overwhelming feeling of peace and calm in this extraordinary place. Julia took Elizabeth's hand in hers as they walked carefree through a sunlit filled garden to a waiting blanket, laid out perfectly for a midday picnic. She noticed a jug of iced-tea with sliced lemons floating lazily, cheese and crackers, fresh fruit, and cookies made of perfectly spun sugar. Yes, wonderfully dream like.

"Lizzy, I'm here to explain some things to you. Some things you may have figured out, some others you may not have understood. Being a person is at times hard. Being in love is sometimes complicated. You have loved many people in your lifetime, in many different ways. All of these people you have loved, all of the relationships you have had, are all equally important and equally powerful. Some have been more challenging than others, and in those cases, you were sent signs. You were sent little pieces of 'magic' for lack of a better word," her face lit up as she smiled, trying to explain the unexplainable. "Your seagull, for instance. She was there for you from the time you were born. She watched you grow, followed your journey, and at times tried to give you signs. But she was always nearby, ready to help." Her blue eyes danced as she spoke.

Stunned and shaking her head, Elizabeth said, "Really, wow. I wish I'd realized that. I wish I'd paid more attention. And I always thought that seagull was a male."

Julia laughed with the aid of her entire body, "You'd be surprised to learn how many important male figures are actually female. The world's power is often represented in a male form, but that power, along with intrigue, and wonder, is more often female."

Elizabeth's dream state answered all the questions she had about life, love, mistakes, and accomplishments. She learned that sharing dreams and feelings with Jack Murphy was simply part of their captivating journey, and although at times they each refused to accept the signs, they were there. And they were real. She learned that illness, error, and heartache were simply human experiences. As humans we do our best and are not evaluated harshly. We love who we love, when we love them, how we love them, without condition. And we are not judged. Ever.

Julia described Elizabeth's life as an amazing and glorious journey. And as she spoke, everything became crystal clear, just like this peculiar dream.

Thirty-Seven
2017

With Elliott fast asleep, Meghan thought she would do a little light investigating with a well-deserved cup of green tea. With Jack safely home from the hospital and recovering nicely, she rationalized that reading Lizzy's book and learning that Lizzy met his daughter had likely been weighing on her always serious and sometimes solemn father. Memories of their past had been flooding his heart and overwhelming his soul. If he were walking around with a clogged artery, the stress and worry could have contributed to the heart attack. Thinking back on her childhood, she considered how serious her father always was. He quietly kept everything inside, and it didn't concern her much until now. Everyone considered Jack Murphy to be strong and sensitive, the silent type, or simply reserved. Now she believed he may have actually tormented himself by keeping everything in and hiding his feelings from everyone, especially himself. In Meghan's mind, he spent a lifetime keeping secrets that didn't need to be protected. She felt for her father and hoped he would someday find someone special to share his time with. Because the thought of him being alone for the rest of his life was too much for her to bear.

As the cursor on her computer pulsated rhythmically in the small apartment flooded with the peaceful illumination of a full moon, Meghan stood to look out the window, pushing the curtain out of the way. With her mug of tea in hand, the moon bathing her in its radiance, she suddenly remembered another one of her grandfather's stories. And with the blink of an eye she was thirteen. As a teenager, Meghan enjoyed sleeping over at her grandparent's house, eating grandmother's soups, stews, and homemade breads, and taking walks with her grandfather on a full and satisfied stomach. On this particular night of her childhood, the moon was full, and darkness had just fallen on the village of Cape Porpoise.

"The moon energizes us, gives us a new start, over and over again. So, it's the perfect time for making wishes. What do you think, Meggie? Let's make some wishes."

Meghan recalled carefully choosing rocks to toss into the still harbor with her grandfather by her side, beneath the beams of the moon. She could recall with perfect clarity the sensation of the smooth rocks in the hand of her younger self. They laughed and made a few silly wishes. They wished that grandma was making a freshly baked dessert while they worked up another appetite. They wished for a clear and calm day to take the canoe out the next day. But Meghan also recalled one of her silent wishes. Meghan held a perfectly round and shiny stone in her hand and felt its cool vibrations. She lofted the distinctive stone as far as she could manage while she wished her wish. At thirteen years old,

Meghan wished for the guardian angel of Cape Porpoise, the full moon, and all of the universe, to bring her father a wife. Someone he could love, so he would be less lonely. Her heart and soul wished beneath magical moonbeams that made her believe anything possible.

Back in Elliott's apartment, looking up at the familiar moonbeams from an adult and rational perspective, she realized what a juvenile wish that was, but she wasn't sure her wish would be much different now. Especially after her father's heart attack. No one should be alone.

Sitting back in front of her computer, Meghan took a big sip of tea and finally began her search. It took her less than a minute on the internet to find the information she was looking for. She simply typed the words *Elizabeth Bennett Alexandria Virginia,* hit the enter key, and there it was. It took only an instant. An earth-shattering headline staring back at her while her computer screen illuminated her dark and eerily silent living room. She was unable to move, unable to read further.

> *Elizabeth Bennett, Virginia author, educator, and mother dies at the age of 61.*

She squeezed her eyes shut, wishing it weren't true. Meghan found herself crying for a woman she didn't even know. She stood up to pace about her small apartment, before returning to the article. Unable to sit, she leaned over her chair and peered at the unbelievable details revealed in a short article in the *Alexandria Times.*

Elizabeth Bennett was killed in an accident during a violent storm, when a tree came crashing down on her car. She was pronounced dead at the scene.

The article went on to list her family members. Her husband Jonathan, her daughter Ashley living in Boston, and her son Conner, living with his wife in D.C. She was also survived by her mother, Beatrice Bennett. The obituary listed her accomplishments as an educator and a writer and her countless contributions to her community. Meghan wasn't only sad, she was devastated. And it wasn't lost on her that there was no mention of Jack Murphy in the words on the screen blurred by her tears. Absolutely no hint at their love or their connection in the article. According to the world at large, Jack Murphy didn't matter. Their love didn't exist, and it apparently wasn't worth a mention in the highlights of Elizabeth Bennett's life. But Meghan knew better.

It shocked her further to learn that her father likely did hear her screams, after all. Somehow, in some unexplainable way, he knew she was in danger. He felt her pain and her panic. In the same ways Meghan was unable to explain her visits from Julia, her dreams, and her mystical connection to the little town of Kennebunkport, she was unable to rationalize how it was even possible that Jack Murphy heard Lizzy's terrifying screams. He felt her danger, in his body and in his heart. And at that very same moment he had a heart attack. Unbelievably, the dates lined up.

Meghan woke Elliott to tell him the news and they decided to call Jack's cardiologist in the morning before giving him the news of Lizzy's death. They wanted to be sure he was strong and healthy enough to learn this shocking news. Although Elliott was able to drift back to sleep, Meghan was not as fortunate. She tossed and turned, dreading the news she would have to deliver.

The next day, the doctor advised Meghan that her father's heart was strong, and he would be okay, physically that was, to hear the devastating news.

They told Jack together, and Elliott and Meghan stayed with him for hours, to be sure he was okay. He cried quietly and uttered very few words. "I knew. I knew she was gone." He said, although he didn't want to admit it to himself, deep within his heart he knew Lizzy was gone. He finally explained in better detail that he felt differently after his heart attack, not just emotionally, but physically, and although he couldn't completely explain it, he knew something was very wrong. He also believed his heart attack was a direct result of her accident and since they were able to confirm that the events of both coincided, they all agreed to accept the impossible.

Meghan Murphy had met Lizzy Bennett only once, in a brief and uneventful encounter, but her mysterious connection to her through her father, remained. It was unexplainable, unimaginable, and a little magical. Meghan finally got that tiny tattoo she first dreamt about when arriving back home in Kennebunkport. That mysterious bird in flight. It stood for a magic she would never completely comprehend. It stood as the promise to believe in love, and the commitment to live her life with an open heart and an open mind.

Thirty-Eight
2017

C harlotte wept uncontrollably in her London apartment, looking out over the Chelsea neighborhood she called home, when the news of Elizabeth's accident finally reached her. Jonathan's call was unexpected, and at the first sound of his voice, she knew something was dreadfully wrong. The call was brief, because Charlotte was simply at a loss for words and their respective tears made communicating clearly almost impossible. Jonathan promised to send her a small package Elizabeth had left behind with her name on it. He was sure it was a gift she meant to send, since it was addressed to Charlotte in London. Sadly, she never had the chance to send it, he explained. Jonathan, composed but shattered, likely still in shock, thanked Charlotte for her friendship with his loving wife, and reminded Charlotte how important she was to Elizabeth. She promised Jonathan to see him at the funeral and said she would be making travel plans as soon as they hung up the phone. Her heart exploded into a million pieces when she pictured grown up versions of Ashley and Conner, learning of their mother's sudden and unexpected death. Life was unfair.

The scenes of their friendship played over and over in Charlotte's mind as she wished with every fiber of her being that she would awaken from a bad dream. Elizabeth was always the responsible one. Always did the right thing. She raised two amazing kids who would now live the rest of their adult lives without their mother. She had a master's degree, published multiple books, and fought for Jonathan, the man of her dreams when the road was bumpy and uncertain. If anyone was going to die young, it was going to be her, Charlotte thought. Reckless and selfish. It should have been her, she insisted, through impossible grief.

On the flight to the states, she wrote a short eulogy for her best friend. She wasn't expecting to read it at the service, but it helped her nonetheless, and felt like something she was compelled to do. She wanted Elizabeth and the world to know how much she meant to her. She typed on her I-pad, her husband reclined by her side, unable to sleep on the eight-hour first class fight to the Washington Dulles Airport.

The day of the funeral was a perfectly clear, sunny, and warmly optimistic day in Alexandria, Virginia. Charlotte pictured soaking rains and wind on the day of her friend's funeral when she played out the tragic scenario in her mind. But apparently, Elizabeth had other plans. Always the perfectionist, Elizabeth Bennett planned the perfect day for her own funeral. She wrote her own glorious ending, she thought to herself. The church was overflowing with guests, some Charlotte remembered from *Harborside*, but most unknown to her. Family, friends and colleagues of Elizabeth's, Jonathan's, Ashley's, and Conner's, she surmised. The church was nothing short of majestic, sunlight beaming through stained glass, and mahogany pews shined to perfection, handsomely supporting grieving visitors.

Ashley, strong and confident, voice shaking at times, stood in front of hundreds, looking and sounding strikingly like her mother, and spoke of Elizabeth's accomplishments, but mostly of the loving wife, friend, and mother she was. Gone far too young but leaving behind a legacy for them all to learn from and remember fondly. Ashley ended with a quote from Ralph Waldo Emmerson, "It is the secret of the world that all things subsist and do not die but retire a little from sight and afterwards return again." As her composure began to wane, she added through a fallen tear, "Today we will leave here, missing Elizabeth Bennett. But her loving spirit is strong, and we will carry her with us in our hearts and deep within our souls, forever."

Loving messages from a proud daughter ended as the choir sung *Amazing Grace* and church guests emptied out onto the sidewalk and gathered in front of the church.

Between tears and loving embraces, stories of Elizabeth's friendship, passion, and talents were told in small groups as they filtered outside onto the sidewalk after the funeral. Charlotte was sure to hand a printed copy of her eulogy to Ashley, so she would know her mother was an amazing woman who greatly impacted her life with her friendship. Ashley hugged her tightly and thanked her for coming such a long distance.

As Charlotte and her husband approached their car, she looked up to meet the eyes of a man she suspected might be there but was still stunned to see. An older, thinner version of the art teacher she remembered stood in front of her. It was easy to forget they all had aged almost thirty-years since their time at *Harborside*; it all seemed like yesterday. In her memories, they were all frozen in time. There he stood, Jack Murphy, the man who broke her friend's heart, standing motionless with a young dark-haired woman by his side. They exchanged greetings and made the proper introductions. The beautiful woman with him was not his young girlfriend like Charlotte suspected, but his daughter. Shockingly, Meghan, the baby, was no longer a baby but a full-fledged adult attending the funeral of her father's old friend, Charlotte guessed. Meghan was a dark-haired beauty and it struck her how little she looked like her father. She must look like her mother, Mella, who Charlotte noted appeared to be absent on that day, unaware that Jack had also endured the loss of the mother of his only child.

Without hesitation, Charlotte pulled a large envelope from her black Hermes bag and handed it to Jack. "Elizabeth sent this to me, but it's meant for Meghan. The letter inside explains everything."

Meghan put a hand to her heart and asked, "It's for me? But we only met once."

Charlotte, surprised at the revelation, realized how many moments of Elizabeth's life she missed while being in London. Elizabeth never mentioned meeting Meghan, and it broke her heart a little that her best friend didn't share how she came to meet the baby girl that stole her fairytale, so many years ago. "Elizabeth asked me to make sure this made its way to you," Charlotte said with a tenderness that surprised even her.

Charlotte and her husband ducked into a waiting black town car, their driver whisking them away since the burial was to be private and only immediate family members were invited. Jack and Meghan walked somberly toward a small park adjacent to the church. They chose a bench beneath a beautiful cherry tree and the colors of the park, the warm breeze, and the towering white steeple of the church in the background set the stage for a mysterious gift, sent to Meghan from a woman she hardly knew.

Jack took one look inside the envelope, his shoulders fell, and he knew exactly what Lizzy had sent his daughter. Once again, his eyes filled with tears, as he handed the envelope over without as much as a word. Meghan reached her hand in the oversized envelope and removed a handwritten letter neatly folded in half, and a small, black velvet box, aged from time. Only because she felt like it was the right thing to do, sitting in front of her father, she read the note first.

Dear Meghan,

Before you were born, your father and I loved each other very much. In the span of a lifetime, we were together a very short time. Only about a year. But our time together was meaningful, loving, and very special. We had planned a life together and were very much in love. By now, you may know that the universe had far better plans for Jack Murphy, because just before we said goodbye to one another he learned of his greatest gift, his baby girl. Your father never faltered in his love and devotion to you.

As adults, we often forget what life was like before we had children. But our past makes us who we are and creates a foundation for who we are meant to be. Your father bought this ring a lifetime ago. And though it was originally meant for me, I know now that it symbolizes all the love and light in his heart as a hopeful young man.

I wanted you to have this, hold it dear, and know that it carries with it love, magic, and blessings as you become an adult and live the life you were meant to live. My hope is that you find everyday magic in everything you do.

Love and blessings-
Elizabeth Bennett

Meghan opened the black velvet box and removed the delicate gold ring that sparkled in the midday sun beneath the most beautifully flowered cherry tree, celebrating Elizabeth Bennett's life with vibrant pink blossoms and messages of hope and contentment. "Dad, I don't know what to say. This is beautiful. And so incredible that she wanted me to have it."

Jack pulled Meghan into a strong embrace, wiped the tears from his eyes, and finally summoned the courage to look at his daughter. "She was incredible, Megs. Carry it with you always, baby girl."

THE END

CPSIA information can be obtained
at www.ICGtesting.com
Printed in the USA
BVHW071838201121
622059BV00003B/13

9 781977 232823